IT'S DARK IN HERE

.

IT'S DARK IN HERE

TWENTY-ONE WEIRD TALES AND ONE POEM
ABOUT SQUIRRELS

FRANK ORETO

It's Dark In Here: Twenty-One Weird Tales and One Poem About Squirrels is published by Dragon's Roost Press.

This anthology is © 2025 Frank Oreto and Dragon's Roost Press.

Artwork by Luke Spooner.

Printed in the United States of America

Ingram ISBN: 978-1-956824-72-8

Print ISBN: 978-1-956824-73-5

Digital ISBN: 978-1-956824-74-2

Dragon's Roost Press

2470 Hunter Rd.

Brighton, MI 48114

thedragonsroost.biz

No AI was used in the creation of this book.

PUBLICATION HISTORY

All God's Creatures Got Reasons - *Gehenna & Hinnom* (28 Feb 2018), *The Years Best Hardcore Horror* (2019), *Tales to Terrrify* Ep.474 (2022), *NoSleep Podcast* S18E16 (2022)

God, Bingo, and Pierogi – *Pick Your Poison* Owl Hollow (2017)

The Care and Feeding of Household Gods – *Beyond the Veil*, Flame Tree Press (2021)

The Worms that Crawl Up from Under the Leaves and Eat You…Through Your Butt!! — *Unnerving Magazine* (Oct 2021)

God Damn You to Hell, John Glenn! — *Novus Monstrum*, Dragon's Roost Press (2023)

Regulars – *Pseudopod* 4 Sept 2009

Overnight Home Companion – *PseudoPod 818: Flash on the Borderlands LXII* 15 July 2022

Decoration – *Who Knocks Magazine* (2018), *Tales To Terrify* Episode 562, *Dragon Gems Fall* 13 October 2023

Live from the End of the World – *Pseudodpod* 778 (08 October 2021)

The Great Should Have Been — *The Overcast* podcast (08 October 2017)

The Hand You're Dealt – *Pseudopod* (28 May 2010), *NoSleep Podcast* S16E10

Phase II - *Tales to Terrify* Episode 538, *NoSleep Podcast* E8S14

Survival Is An Act of Selfishness – *Fear the Future* Corpus Press (2021), *Tales to Terrify* Episode 599

The Worms Turn – *In Darkness, Delight: Creatures of the Night*, Corpus Press (2019) , *Tales to Terrify* Episode 610

A Song from the Dark – *NoSleep Podcast* S21E02

All others original to this volume.

These stories are dedicated to my mom, Josephine Oreto and to my dearest friend, Jack Daves.

My mom let me read anything I wanted as a kid, as long as I understood, she'd be reading it too. She never once told me my choices

were bad or silly. She just read the stories and occasionally said, "Jason, that was weird."

Jack Daves taught me to see the world through his own very special lens. A lens that showed me every inch of this earth is steeped in magic and mystery.

I wish the two of them were still around to read these stories.

I hope Jack would tell me my writing captured some of that magic he

showed me. And I'm positive Mom would read the last page, close the

book, and say "Jason, that was weird."

CONTENTS

Foreword	xi
Introduction	xv
All God's Creatures Got Reasons	1
God, Bingo, and Pierogi	15
The Care and Feeding of Household Gods	19
The Worms that Crawl Up from Under the Leaves and Eat You…Through Your Butt!!	39
God Damn You To Hell, John Glenn!	51
Regulars	69
Overnight Home Companion	85
Decoration	87
Live from the End of the World	105
The Squirrels Look Angry Today	123
The Great Should Have Been	125
The Hand You're Dealt	137
Phase II	157
Survival Is An Act of Selfishness	173
The Worms Turn	181
Ample Free Parking	197
Agnes Mulvaney's Best Christmas Ever	211
God is a Wheel	223
A Song from the Dark	235
The Meaning of Halloween	249
A Dance of Hoof and Horn	255
The Once and Future King	269
About the Author	287
Dragon's Roost Press	289

FOREWORD

I like writing intros to stuff I love (especially considering my selectiveness is legendary-verging-upon-monstrous). But this one is different. Frank is one of my oldest, dearest friends. We've been writing stories together, for each other, and *at* each other… into the double digits of years. Heck, we even edited a couple-a wonderful anthologies together for *Triangulation.*

The writing you're about to discover here (in the dark) has the narrative warmth and invention of the old guard—Charles Beaumont, Ray Bradbury, Richard Matheson, Flannery O'Connor—and the audacity of Joe Lansdale, Gene Wolfe, Joe Hill, China Miéville.

If you're thinking being too close makes me an unreliable witness, well, I understand, but when you've been in the trenches together for as long as we have, honesty is more than a kindness: being clear-eyed is a survival skill. When one of us drifts off the path, the other is expected to give a swift, sharp poke. Like brothers. But I ain't his mom and he ain't mine—there's been plenty I've hated and plenty I've taken him to task for in the process of reading and critiquing pretty much every story he's ever penned.

So listen. This is no mundane ride you're strapping in for. Don't expect the luxury of being able to flip forward to see what's next —at least not before the curtain falls on the tale you're in. Frank is a spellcaster, and a good story is like a spell and like a dream, enfolding you and taking the routines and sameness of your real life away for as long as it lasts. The best ones (and I'm not lying when I say I think you'll find a few in here) actually make your real life just a little bit easier to go back to.

You know that story you read last year that blew your mind, but you forgot to write down the author's name? That wild podcast you listened to with the monster that's still clawing around in your brain? And weren't you just telling your friend about that story in the best anthology you read last year, by old what's-his-name?

I've watched people slowly get on board with Oreto and his work. "Oh, the baby eating story guy!" The blank stares when I mention his name are slowly filtering away and the dopamine punch of the memory of what he's done to us, where he's taken us—into the mine field of possibility and impossibility—is coming to dominate. And that is right and fitting.

"Oh, he's the guy who wrote the…" Yeah, the story about the massive, blood-thirsty sea monkey changed by its journey into space, that would get negative attention from the estate of a certain famous astronaut if it weren't so good. Or the baby-eating story, "All God's Children Got Reasons," with characters so sympathetic you get implicated in the unthinkable. Purveyor of worlds' ends, strange states, and the boundaries of everything that can be considered human. He's that kind of writer, sitting you down in his parlor without a word—scent of whiskey in the air, twinkle in his eye—and taking you somewhere strange, somewhere you've had the good sense never to imagine.

Oh, but wait. I'm saying too much. You came here for surprises. Lucky you: impossible things are about to happen to you.

—Bram Stoker Award–nominated short-story author and editor

Douglas Gwilym

Pittsburgh, 8 Sept 2025

INTRODUCTION

The bowling alley smells of stale beer, and the ghosts of a thousand cigarettes smoked down to the filter. Men in matching shirts roll balls. They're middle-aged, with receding hairlines and beer bellies. But their arms are wiry with factory floor muscle, and their laughter sounds mean and at someone else's expense.

You try to ignore them. You're on a mission. And it has nothing to do with strikes and spares. At the counter, a bald man in a stained white tank top sprays disinfectant into a line of red, green, and pink bowling shoes. He speaks without looking up. "It's league night."

"What?"

"League night. No non-league play until after 10pm."

"I'm not here to bowl." You lean in, lowering your voice even though there's no one within earshot. "I'm here for the other thing."

"The other thing?" The question somehow doesn't sound like a question.

What if you're wrong? What If the rumors are just that?

The bald man finally looks up. He has dark flint-chip eyes. "Maybe you should leave. Or maybe I should put on a pair of size twelves and kick your ass up and down a few lanes."

You think he could do it. He isn't a big guy, but thick bands of scar tissues cover his knuckles. Need gives you courage.

"I want the stories."

"Fuck off." The man's voice is loud. Some of the league men turn and stare.

You don't fuck off. You do nothing. Just wait.

The bald man disinfects a few more shoes. Finally, he sighs. "Okay. Fine. Do it then."

You blink. Feel a trickle of sweat run down the small of your back. "How do I…"

"Jesus Christ. What did you think was going to happen here? You'd put on your footy pajamas, and I'd maybe tuck you in. They're not those kinds of stories. These are the ones that lodge in your brain and stay there. If that's what you want, then you got to pull the trigger yourself."

Your mouth is dry. You know he's right. But you're afraid to say it. Afraid to admit your need. "Just tell me what I have to do"

"It's easy," he says and gives you a slow smile full of tombstone gray teeth. "Just turn the page."

ALL GOD'S CREATURES GOT REASONS

THE HEAVYSET MAN in the red tank top did not look like a monster. He squatted in front of the stroller and waved at the child inside. The young mother, a pretty woman in a green blouse, smiled with pride.

Across the street, Lonnie Phelps took in the scene from where he sat in front of Java Jive. "Mighty nice kid you got there, ma'am," he said, filling in the unheard dialogue. The kid did look cute, from what Lonnie could see—little sailor hat peeking from the stroller. *Probably only a bit older than my Ryan.*

Lonnie sipped his coffee. When he looked back up, Tank Top was holding the baby. He had a big grin on his face, but the mother wasn't smiling anymore. She put her hands out to take the child back, but Tank Top ignored her.

"What the hell?" asked Lonnie.

The mom put a hand on Tank Top's forearm, her mouth moving fast.

Give back the baby. Lonnie willed the action from where he sat.

But his thoughts were no more effective than the mother's words.

Tank Top winked at the woman. It was that slow kind of wink where you get your whole face involved—a get-a-load-of-me sort of wink. Lonnie could feel the teasing contempt. Then the man opened his mouth wider than should have been possible and shoved the crying baby's entire head inside.

The mother screamed and grabbed at the baby's flailing legs, but the man in the tank top whirled away. One heavy arm lashed out at the woman while the other shoved the child further into his mouth. His lips and jaws stretched wider to accommodate the narrow shoulders.

Lonnie ran across the street. Scene details popped in his mind like flashbulbs: a stroller turned on its side, a bottle of formula rolling toward the traffic.

The baby-eater now lay on the sidewalk in a fetal position, protecting his meal from the horrified onlookers. A single leg protruded from the man's mouth, a tiny blue sock hanging half off the foot.

Lonnie reached the sidewalk with no idea how he could help. He pushed through the growing crowd. The mother clawed bloody gouges in the baby eater's face. A bike messenger kicked the man, yelling, "Stop it, dude," each time his worn Timberland connected.

As Lonnie got close, the baby-eater rolled and scrambled back from the crowd on bleeding elbows until he had pressed himself against the wall of Pizza Sola. Between his wide yellowed teeth poked five pink toes—all that remained of the child. Tank Top pushed them into his mouth. His hand disappeared up to his forearm, tamping down his obscene meal. Lonnie could hear the wet, rhythmic sound of the man swallowing.

Lonnie grabbed the man beneath the armpits and hauled him to his feet. "You sick bastard," he yelled. He launched his knee upward into the man's gut, hoping somehow to make him throw the child back up. *Where were the police, an ambulance? Could they cut the kid out?*

The man lurched forward, wrapping Lonnie in a bear hug. He shoved his drool-slick cheek against Lonnie's. "Forget it, man, I finished," he said. "What the hell's wrong with you?"

"Me?" Lonnie bellowed, pulling away.

The baby eater let go and shoved Lonnie with both hands. Lonnie stumbled backward straight into the mother in the green blouse.

"Watch it," she said.

Lonnie froze. The woman wasn't screaming anymore. She just looked annoyed. "Your baby," said Lonnie. "I'm so sorry."

"What baby?" the woman raised her hands, palms out, toward Lonnie. Her voice placating now and a little nervous. "I think you must have me confused with someone else. I'm going to go now."

"Wait. The baby. That guy—."

A tall man stepped between Lonnie and the woman who didn't seem to remember that her baby had just been eaten.

"Dude, hey. Back off," the tall man said. It was the bike messenger, the one who had kicked the baby-eater. He put a hand on Lonnie's shoulder. "You been drinking, dude?" The mother took the opportunity to hurry away.

Lonnie looked around in a slow circle. The stroller wasn't on the street anymore. The crowd was gone. He spotted the baby eater leaning against the wall, staring at him. His face still glistened with a pink sheen of blood and saliva. Fear lit up the man's face, and he looked away.

"Did you see the baby?" Lonnie asked the bike messenger.

The messenger shrugged. "No, dude. I think you need to sit down. Did you lose your kid?"

Lonnie shook his head. "No. I'm all right." He was not. Lonnie walked to a nearby bus shelter and sat. *What just happened?*

He looked back through the shelter's glass enclosure. The baby eater was gone. Lonnie's heart slammed in his chest. Adrenaline still pumped through his system, making his stomach queasy. People walked by, taking in the spring air. No weeping mother, no police cars.

Jesus Christ, he thought, *did I beat the hell out of some guy for no reason?* Lonnie leaned forward, elbows on his knees, and took a deep breath.

He should call Janet. *Hey, Honey, I'm hallucinating people swallowing babies.* Yeah, right. Sure, he was under a lot of stress. They both were. That's why she had insisted he take some time for himself this afternoon. So what? All new parents are stressed, but they don't all have waking nightmares. *Unless something else was wrong.* Lonnie leaned back with his eyes closed and imagined a future full of CAT scans and Thorazine.

I'll sit here for a few more minutes, get my shit together, and then call. Janet would say go to the emergency room. Lonnie wondered if they'd let him leave.

Someone sat down beside him. "You remember me?" The voice had the slightly high nasal accent of the true Pittsburgh native. Lonnie looked to his left and saw the balding, sweaty face of the baby eater smiling back at him.

"Shit!" Lonnie sprang to his feet, fists clenched. His breath came in painful bursts. He wanted to hit the guy, wanted to run, wanted to know if the man sitting on the bench was even real.

"Aw, dammit," said the man in the tank top. "You remember all right." He rubbed a stubby-fingered hand over his mouth. A mouth that was wide, but nowhere near the obscenely gaping maw Lonnie remembered.

"It's okay," the baby eater said.

"I saw you eat that kid." Lonnie gave the accusation in a stage whisper. Aware of the people walking by.

"No, no. I know that's what it looked like, but—" the man waved a hand in dismissal. "It was more like, um, a magic trick. An illusion. You get me?"

Lonnie didn't reply, too upset to answer.

"I'm Doug Kozlowski." The man held out a large meaty hand. Lonnie did not shake it. Kozlowski shrugged. "Yeah, I get it. Hey, I bet you could use a drink. Why don't you let me buy you one?"

Lonnie only stared at the man.

"Come on, kid. I know how you feel. A minute ago, you thought you were ready for a rubber-roomed Hilton, right? You're not crazy. This is good news."

That got through to Lonnie. He had been thinking right along those lines. Something tight in his chest loosened a little, and his clenched fists opened. "You're saying it was some sort of joke?"

"That's right, something like that. We'll go have a couple of drinks. I'll explain things. Life goes on." Kozlowski pulled his barrel-chested bulk upright and walked down Carson Street.

FRANK ORETO

Lonnie didn't want a drink but he sure as hell needed answers. So, he followed.

Irene's Bar and Grill was an old-fashioned place. Lots of dark wood and only two beers on tap. Kozlowski pointed to a booth with high wooden dividers for privacy and hooks for your hat. Lonnie slid in.

Kozlowski went to the bar and ordered. He came back with a bottle of beer and a tumbler of whiskey filled almost to the top. He set the glass in front of Lonnie." I got you a triple."

Lonnie picked up the glass considering it. "No," he finally said. "You tell me what the hell just happened."

"Okay. Here it is. You know how I said it was like a magic trick, me eating that baby?"

Lonnie nodded.

"It's a little more complicated than that. Uh… You know, you really should have that drink."

Lonnie set the glass down.

"Suit yourself. The thing is…" Kozlowski paused, an embarrassed smile on his lips. "I did eat the kid. You think you saw me choke down that baby because that's exactly what happened. At least you're not crazy."

"You said it was a joke. They were actors, weren't they? I'm probably already on YouTube's sickest home videos, right?"

"You saw me do it. Did it look like a special effect to you?"

Lonnie's head began to throb in a slow painful rhythm. He squeezed his eyes shut. *Maybe I'm still in the bus enclosure talking to myself,* he thought. *Hell, maybe I'm strapped down in some mental hospital already.*

6

He lifted the whiskey and took a deep swallow. The amber fluid burned down his throat realistically enough. "But where did the fucking stroller go? Why did no one remember what you did except me?"

"That's where the magic trick comes in. 'Cept not so much the trick part. You see, when I eat a kid, I eat 'em all. I'm not talking about the meaty parts. I eat everything. Like cosmic-shit everything. His first smile, the nine months he spent giving his mama heartburn. I even eat the Friday night his mom and pop put Marvin Gaye on the stereo and got it on. You getting me?"

"No," said Lonnie. "You're crazy."

"What's with you and crazy? Give it a chance why don't you? I ate a baby on a city sidewalk in broad daylight. No one is looking for me. The mom doesn't even remember having a kid. Why? Because she never did. No stroller? She never bought one. I ate that kid right out of the world. No one's going to come after me because no one knows it happened."

"I think you're screwing with me," said Lonnie, sounding as unsure as he felt. "Unless I'm just nuts."

"Fine," said Kozlowski. "Go with the crazy theory if it keeps you from pounding on me again." He looked at Lonnie for a long moment and then gave an embarrassed half shrug. "You know, this is kind of nice."

"What's nice?" asked Lonnie.

"I never get to talk about it with anybody. The whole kid-eating thing. Well, once, but that didn't really count. I got a theory, you know?"

Lonnie took another drink. *I should call Janet or just go straight to the hospital.* But, he did not want to let go of being sane. Not even if it meant this was real. "You have a theory about what?

Why you eat babies?" He tried to speak calmly, but his voice broke.

"Sort of. It's more why God wants me to do it."

"You're blaming God?"

"Sure, people blame God for all kinds of shit. Seriously, though, why the hell else would I eat little kids? All God's creatures got a reason. You think a buzzard just loves the taste of all that dead stuff? No. He eats it because it's his whatchyacallit—his nature. God's own flying garbage can. You see? The buzzard though, he got no brain to speak of. So he never asks, 'what am I doing eating this crap? I'd rather have steak and a nice potato.' Me, I wonder. So, I got this theory. "

"I don't believe in God," said Lonnie. The whiskey was taking effect, softening the edges of his vision.

"After what you just saw, I'd think you'd have a bit more of an open mind."

Lonnie did not have a ready answer for that.

"Anyway, here's my theory—Hitler." Koslowski held his hands out in a see-what-I-mean gesture.

"Hitler?" Lonnie shook his head. "I don't think I'm following."

Koslowski sighed. "Hitler," he said again. "Okay, you know how Hitler is like the worst guy ever, right? All those sci-fi writers always have people going back in time to kill him, but just making things worse. With me so far?"

"Yeah," mumbled Lonnie. "Hitler, bad dude."

"So these kids I eat, they must be worse. God gives me a hankering for babies that would be the next Hitlers. And I eat them."

"So, why didn't God have somebody eat the real baby Hitler?" asked Lonnie.

"Fair point. I got to assume, being a lowly functionary, I am not privy to the big plan. Because if there ain't no reason, that means I'm some sort of monster. And a man can't live like that."

"You are a monster," said Lonnie. "I can't explain that other stuff. The baby never existing afterward shit, but you took a laughing little baby—."

"Baby Hitler."

"A baby," Lonnie repeated. "And you ate him. You are a monster. Maybe God's monster if it makes you feel better, but still a piece-of-shit-baby-killing monster."

Koslowski shook his head. "You know, I met this guy once. Like me. I mean, he did what I do."

"Another of God's Monsters?" Lonnie asked.

"Yeah. But, he was a little like you too. He didn't think there was a reason. I saw him eat this kid. A little girl, maybe six-years-old, pigtails and all. Fat little thing. Took for-freaking-ever. I talked to him afterward, like we're talking now. He'd tried to kill himself a few dozen times. Knives, nooses, bullets. He thought he was a monster and couldn't live with it. Even when he realized all that self-inflicted pain wasn't doing the job, he never stopped trying. It's bad enough to have to eat babies. No way I wanted to be like him. The poor bastard begged me to do it."

"Wait a second," Lonnie said, the whiskey thickening his words a little. "What'd he beg?"

"He told me I was his replacement. That's why I could remember him eating the little girl."

Lonnie's eyes widened. He straightened from his half-drunk

slouch with enough violence to almost upend Kozlowski's beer bottle.

"He said I had to eat him. Then he could be done. I'm telling you, the sap was crying with relief at the idea."

"No fucking way am I your replacement," hissed Lonnie. "I got a kid of my own, for God's sake."

"Hey, I concur," said Kozlowski. "You can only take this fate thing so far, right? The problem is, you saw what I did, and you remember me. I'm pretty sure that means you're next in line for the job."

"I'm not eating you," said Lonnie.

Kozlowski nodded. "Damn right. I thought we'd try something different." He lifted the beer bottle as he spoke and slammed it against Lonnie's head.

Lonnie fell out of the booth onto the floor. He touched the side of his head and pulled away a blood-smeared hand.

Kozlowski knelt over Lonnie. His distended mouth looked like the open end of a mop bucket. It gave his voice a deep, hollow tone. "Relax kid, in a little while it'll be like you never existed."

The bartender screamed.

Lonnie scuttled backward as the tooth-lined maw descended toward him.

"Hold still," boomed Kozlowski. He reached down, scrabbling for Lonnie's collar.

Lonnie didn't know if he was crazy, dreaming, or maybe in line to become God's monster, but he knew he did not want to be eaten by Doug Kozlowski. So, Lonnie opened his mouth and lunged.

Something expanded in his skull. Bones snapped and jittered. It hurt like hell for a second and then felt good, like a satisfying crack of the knuckles. Kozlowski's arm was wedged in Lonnie's throat almost to the elbow. The two men looked at each other for a long moment and then Lonnie bit down hard. Flesh tore, and bones snapped until Lonnie's teeth came together with a click and he swallowed.

Kozlowski's hate-filled bellow of pain joined the bartender's screams. "You don't even want the god-damned job, you stupid sonuvabitch!" Blood spouted from his sheared off forearm.

Lonnie pulled himself to his feet. Strength poured into him from some unknown source.

Kozlowski turned, spraying blood in an arc. He tried to run, but Lonnie had him by the tank top straps.

"What I want is for you not to be here anymore," Lonnie said. Then he swallowed Kozlowski's head down to the neck and began to chew.

It took the better part of an hour. Lonnie ate with a compulsive efficiency, never pausing. As if once he had made the decision, he'd gone on cannibalistic autopilot.

The police came. Lonnie heard the sirens, felt the ineffective blows of nightsticks raining down on his back and head. He was sure someone shot him. But it all seemed distant somehow, and he never stopped eating.

Finally, he finished. Lonnie took a deep breath and spat blood on the barroom floor. He stood and gazed down at himself, surprised he didn't look like a python that just ate a cow. A man stumbled into him slipping on the pool of blood that covered the floor. It was a cop. He didn't even look at Lonnie. Instead, he motioned to the woman tending bar. "You got to clean up this spill. Someone's going to kill themselves."

The bartender looked from her book to the floor and sighed. "I'll get a mop."

As Lonnie watched, the blood grew pale—just spilled beer now. He stood at the bar catching his breath. There was no blood on his clothes, no gash in the side of his head where Kozlowski's beer bottle had shattered. The bartender smiled at him and asked if he wanted a drink. Lonnie ordered a shot of whiskey, a single this time. He drank it slow and tried to think.

Maybe if Lonnie had really been crazy, he could have pretended it never happened. No Kozlowski, no baby from before. He'd just had some sort of incident, a psychotic break. But Lonnie knew with cold certainty he was not crazy. He was God's monster.

He paid for the drink and walked out onto Carson Street. The sun sat lower in the sky, but it was still a beautiful day. An older woman, Grandma no doubt, moved toward Lonnie on the bustling sidewalk pushing a double stroller. Twins burbled away happily in the seats. Lonnie closed his eyes. *Please no, please no, please no.* When he opened them again, the woman had passed him and was halfway down the block. *I didn't try to eat them,* he thought. *But what if they were just good kids, future Ghandis? No,* he thought, *I can beat this thing. I'll resist it. Or go somewhere with hardly any people. An island maybe. It'd be a hard sell to Janet, but they would make it work.*

Lonnie's phone began to buzz in his pocket. He pulled it out. Janet's name flashed on the screen along with a picture of a boy in blue footie pajamas. Lonnie looked at his six-month-old son, and a spasm went through his body. He had always been filled with love and pride when he saw Ryan, but now there was another feeling, stronger than both.

Hunger.

Lonnie put the phone back in his pocket without answering. He looked down Tenth Street at the line of skyscrapers rising from the golden triangle. He thought of the man Kozlowski had replaced—the one who could not accept being a monster. That man had tried to stop himself. "Knives, guns, nooses," Kozlowski had said. Maybe the guy just hadn't tried hard enough. Lonnie didn't remember Kozlowski mentioning tall buildings in the litany of the man's attempts. He began to walk. The PPG Tower looked to be about forty stories high. It would do for a start.

GOD, BINGO, AND PIEROGI

JANICE OPENED the ornately carved doors of St. Barnabus and slipped inside the cool quiet sanctuary. She glanced up at the enormous face of Jesus staring down at her from over the pulpit but didn't stop to pray. She was not here to worship. She was here because of her grandmother. Or baba if you'd grown up in Pittsburgh's South Side like Janice had. This church had been part of Baba's trinity—God, Bingo, and Pierogi.

God and bingo Janice had come along for. The call and response of the liturgy always calmed her, made Janice believe for a moment there was a plan for the world, and her life was a part of it. And bingo could actually be fun. Not so much the game itself, but the stories Baba and the others told over cigarettes and ham barbecue. Stories they would never repeat in the house of God. The pierogi making, Janice had stayed away from.

Baba had chided her, especially when things turned bad with Rob. She firmly believed good cooking made a good marriage. "Come make pierogi with us," she would say, reading the worried look on Janice's face. "You feed your man, show him respect, and if that don't work so well, you feed him again."

But the pierogi ladies scared Janice. They gathered every Wednesday, making hundreds of the potato and cheese filled dumplings to sell for the church. As a child, she would peek in the large basement kitchen, watching them at their work. They'd seemed too much like the crones from her fairy tales. Speaking words Janice didn't understand and cackling with laughter. They seemed even more crone-like now—all wrinkles and sagging flesh as Janice entered the Church kitchen.

Condolences in both English and Polish washed over her as the women approached. "We loved your baba so much. She will be missed." They didn't ask why Janice hadn't been at the funeral. Quick glances at her closed right eye and swollen lip advertised the answer.

"Baba said Zofia should teach me to make pierogi," Janet said after the initial wave of conversation died away. "For my husband."

The women said nothing for a long moment. Only exchanged thoughtful glances as if years of cooking together made speech unnecessary. Finally, Ava, a round-faced woman as wide as she was tall, nodded and took Janice's hands in her own.

"Of course. Your baba knew best."

The crones led her to a long, steel table at the rear of the room. Zofia, the oldest of them, stood alone, eyes white with cataracts, pressing dough into paper-thin circles. The women left Janice there and went back to their own mixing and shaping.

Janice stood in silence, watching Zofia's rapid, dexterous movements. The woman's skin didn't sag like the others. Instead, it wrapped around her thin bones mummy tight. Fine wrinkles lined that skin like spidery letters in a language Janice couldn't decipher. Pregnant seconds ticked by. *Was the old woman deaf as she was blind?* Janice wondered. *Does she even know I'm here?*

Without warning, Zofia's flour-dusted hands rose. Her long, thin fingers probed Janice, somehow locating each spot where Rob had hit her. With each touch, the old woman's face grew darker. Zofia spoke in Polish. Janice only understood bits and pieces of the words. However, she knew what was required. Watch. Listen. Do what I do.

So, Zofia taught Janice to make pierogi. Shaping dough, mixing the potato, onion, and cheese. Much of the process, Janice was familiar with. She'd watched Baba perform the same steps a thousand times in her tiny kitchen on Pious Street.

But there were differences. A way of holding your left hand, three fingers splayed, two curled, as your right hand drew symbols in the scattered flour. And the words. Harsh and jagged, completely unlike the Polish Janice grew up hearing. Words that made Janice's mouth tingle as if she'd eaten hot peppers and, once spoken, fled her mind completely.

Janice felt dizzy. The dough burned her hands and odd colors flowed over the filling. She saw Rob's face. His anger. She remembered the love she'd felt for him, once so huge and all consuming. How his rage transformed those feelings to fear and despair as miraculously as God's love transformed communion wine into blood. "He's going to kill me one day, Baba." So, Baba had told her what she needed to do.

Janice wept, mourning the loss of her Baba, of her marriage. The hot tears flowed down her cheeks, adding themselves to the flour, eggs, and oil. Janice blinked away the tears to find Zofia's blind eyes upon her.

Rough hands found hers, stopping their motion. Janice blinked again. Her mind tingled like a sleeping limb regaining circulation. A plate stacked with half-moon shaped pierogi lay on the table before her.

Zofia spoke for the first time in English. "Not for you."

As Janice walked from the church, the special pierogi covered with a napkin, she heard her Baba as clearly as if the dead woman walked beside her: "You feed your man; show him respect. And if it work out not so well, you feed him again."

A week later, there was another funeral. This one Janice did attend.

THE CARE AND FEEDING OF HOUSEHOLD GODS

PAUL STARTED the day's third load of laundry and shoved the detergent back on the shelf. He paused, struck by something familiar in the plastic jug's shape. *Easter Island.* Those mysterious stone idols in *Ripley's Believe It or Not* he'd gaped at as a kid. The handle formed the nose. The slope of the jug provided the long cheekbones. *Needs eyes. Did the Easter Island heads have eyes?* Paul listened for the kids. No crying, only the sounds of the *PAW Patrol* on TV, solving problems with the power of friendship.

Paul dug through the shit-we-always-need drawer and found a red Sharpie. He took down the jug and started drawing. Two wide triangular eyes, the red circles of the irises slightly too close together. Slashes for the cheekbones. Finally, a thin line of a mouth, the ends sinking into a judgemental frown. Back on the shelf, the jug gazed down, cold and unsympathetic.

Not Easter Island, Paul decided, *better.* "Behold, Washor, god of all laundry."

"Daddy, Sam smells funny," said Jack from the living room.

"Okay, Jack. Thanks for the update."

"Her pants are brown."

"No, they aren't, they're blue." *Aw shit.* "I'm coming, Jack." He turned to go but stopped short. Had to show Washor the proper respect. "Oh, great Washor, I beseech you, by the power of your holy phosphates: Make my whites whiter and my colors bright. And do what you can about the poop stains."

With two kids under five, Paul didn't get a lot of downtime. Lunch, snacks, park for a playdate, feed Hamilton the hamster, attempt naps, find escaped Hamilton the hamster. And of course, the constant diaper changes and ever more laundry. The day blurred.

"What's that, Daddy?" Jack gestured to Washor, glaring down at them as they pulled clothes from the dryer.

"Oh, just a little arts and crafts project Daddy did. Like Him?"

"He looks mean."

"Nah, but he does take laundry very seriously." Paul shook out a tiny onesie. "No poop stains. All praise to Washor." He looked down at Jack, expecting a grin. The boy found poop hilarious. Instead, Jack's face scrunched in distaste as he stared at the laundry god. *Everybody's an art critic.* "Go check on Samantha, buddy. Make sure she hasn't escaped the playpen. Don't wake her if she's asleep."

"Okay." The boy tiptoed off, pleased with his stealth mission.

Paul pulled more outfits from the dryer. Damn if the whites weren't a bit whiter. He reached up to give Washor a congratulatory fist bump then thought better of it, settling for a solemn amen.

Rebecca got home around seven. Her arrival was always the worst part of Paul's day. Alone with the kids, he didn't have time to notice his shortcomings. When Rebecca walked through the door, he saw everything through her eyes. Clothes on the sofa. Crumbs on the floor. She rarely complained. Instead, she'd walk in after ten hours of work and start folding blankies.

They'd made a deal, Rebecca worked fifty hours a week at the university, and Paul quit his sous chef job and took care of the house and kids. She brought home the bacon. He cooked it up in a pan. He wasn't holding up his end, and that failure made him miserable. Rebecca gave Paul a kiss and a smile, showing nothing but love and exhaustion. *It's me. I'm projecting my disappointment in myself on the woman I love.* But self-awareness made him no less miserable.

"I'm going to pour some wine," said Rebecca. She draped a dishcloth over her shoulder and took Samantha from him. "You look like you could use some too." Jack grabbed her free hand and sang, "Mommy, Mommy, Mommy."

"I'll pour the wine. You dispense hugs," said Paul.

"What's for dinner?"

"Dammit." Paul set down the wine and pulled open the oven. "Slightly burnt roast vegetables… with some eggs I haven't started yet. Hey, didn't I used to cook at a fancy restaurant?"

Ten minutes later, they sat at the table, cajoling and cleaning the kids by turn. Jack refused the singed veggies, while Sam threw everything she could reach onto the floor.

"Daddy made a mean art and craft," said Jack around a mouthful of egg and ketchup.

"Your Mom was talking, Jack."

"No, I always go on about work. Let's hear about the arts and crafts."

Paul told Rebecca about the detergent jug's transformation into the god of laundry. "It's silly. But having Washor up there—I don't know—it kind of helps."

Rebecca nodded as she tried to spoon egg into Sam's firmly closed mouth. "A lot of cultures had little gods to help them around the house. The big-league deities were always busy with wars and such."

"Yeah, but back then people believed in the things."

"People believe a prayer to St. Anthony helps them find their keys. Your arts and crafts probably work the same way. The laundry runs smoother because a tiny bit of you believes the great god Sudzy is in charge. Takes the pressure off you."

"Washor."

"What?"

"He's called Washor."

"You suck at names."

"But, I'm not crazy?"

"Oh, totally nuts," said Rebecca. "You worship a bottle of soap. Whatever works though, right?"

"Yeah. Whatever works."

The next day, Paul expanded the pantheon.

"Jackie boy, fetch me the Elmer's glue and a sheet of your finest construction paper." Paul raided the dry goods. Macaroni outlined the face, broken spaghetti for hair. Dried limas for eyes.

"I like this one better, Daddy."

"He does seem more laid back. I think it's the candy corn teeth. Inspired choice."

"Thanks. What's his name?"

Paul taped the new deity on the refrigerator, looking over the magnetic poetry tiles for inspiration. "Hot Pot, god of food and cooking."

As the days went on, Paul made more deities. A playdough head with a dust bunny beard became Vah-Coom, God of Clean Floors. An old circular saw blade, plastic googly eyes held on with caulk, became Handee Lord of Small Repairs. He even dug out the bride and groom cake topper from Rebecca's keepsake box, proclaiming them 'Get-It-On,' gods of fun and absolutely no fertility. His southern Baptist mother wouldn't have approved, God rest her soul, but Paul thought his pantheon was kind of fun. And even though making the gods took time out of his day, their creation didn't put him any more behind than usual. In fact, things were going pretty smoothly.

Not, of course, because of my handicraft pantheon. No. The kids were getting older. Even a few weeks made a big difference in what Jack could do to help and what Sam didn't do to cause problems. *I could just be finding my groove.* But maybe the gods did help. Not in a miraculous way, but like Rebecca said, they took a little pressure off. Instead of ripping the kitchen apart looking for the potato peeler, Paul took a deep breath and asked Hot Pot. The pause let him calm down and find what he needed. *Power of prayer, Mom. You'd be proud if it weren't for my choice of gods.*

Something damp and multilegged squished beneath Paul's bare foot as he stepped into the laundry closet. "Ewww, Jesus," he said then reconsidered. "Washor." Paul peeled away the crushed silverfish, holding it up to the detergent god. "Oh, great and powerful Washor, I offer up unto you this life as a good and proper sacrifice." He thought of laying the insect corpse on the shelf but dropped it into the garbage instead.

Guilt nibbled at him. The result of a childhood full of Sunday sermons. Maybe he should throw out the long-empty detergent jug. But wouldn't destroying the jug be as superstitious as making the idol in the first place? He loaded the dirty clothes and left, eyes lowered to avoid stepping on more bugs, not so he wouldn't have to look at the laundry god's disapproving face.

The socks matched.

Paul scanned the floor for strays. Nothing. How many times had he folded a load of laundry and all the socks matched? Never? The rest of the clothes lay folded neatly on the coffee table. Onesies that had seen a hundred washings gleamed white. He set Sam in her exer-saucer and went to the laundry closet. "You're listening, aren't you?"

The detergent jug god did not answer.

"No, I'm just crazy." *But all the socks freakin' matched. Okay, so test the theory.* Cold weather had brought the first ant invasion of fall. Paul put out traps, but there were always a few left to mop up. "There we go." A tiny line of ants marched along the wall behind the kitchen sink. He wiped a damp paper towel across their path. A dozen or more stuck, tiny legs kicking. Paul held the ant studded towel before the face of his kitchen god. "I offer up these tiny souls to you, Hot Pot."

Paul plucked ants from the paper and crushed them. When the last ant was smashed, he felt a bit lightheaded. *What am I doing? What if the sacrifices work?* He wadded up the paper towel and tossed it toward the garbage pail on the opposite wall, dead center. "Praise Hot Pot."

Paul moved Sam's exer-saucer into the kitchen, where he could see her. "Jack!"

The thud of footsteps announced the boy's arrival.

"Hey, buddy. Is Hamilton in his cage?"

Jack reddened. "I put him back."

Paul gave his son a stern look, but was too excited to be upset. "Guess what I'm making for dinner tonight?"

"Eggs?"

Paul shook his head.

"Soup… or butter noodles."

"Yeah, those are the usual options, but not tonight. You know Daddy used to be a pretty fancy cook. I'm thinking I'll make pork lo mein."

Jack looked dubious.

"Don't worry. Lo mein is like Chinese spaghetti. You're going to help." Paul cast a glance at Hot Pot hanging on the fridge. *So are you.* "First, we line up everything we need. Chefs call that *mise en place*." Paul opened the cabinet, immediately spotting oyster sauce, sesame oil, and kecap manis even though he hadn't used those ingredients in months. *Oh yeah, Hot Pot. That's how we do it.*

Dinner was ready to plate as Rebecca walked in the door. Sam sat in her highchair with a fresh bib, while Jack carefully carried in cups of water. "Can you grab the plates, sweetie?" Paul asked.

Rebecca gave him a kiss and grabbed the plates.

"The pretty ones. Pretty plates for pretty food." He piled noodles onto the good plates and in a plastic bowl for Sam. Then snipped some green onion and cilantro onto his and Rebecca's.

"Let's eat."

Rebecca dragged her last forkful of pork through the glistening sauce. "This is so tender."

"Yeah. I soaked the meat in water and baking soda before marinating. The baking soda breaks the meat down just enough, so you don't have to worry about overcooking."

Rebecca smiled at him.

"What?"

"You're talking about food the way you used to. I think you're finally hitting your stride."

Paul thought about pinching ants to reddish dust between his fingers. "Maybe you're right."

Occasionally, Paul killed a fly or a maybe a moth, but his offerings were mostly ants. As long as he didn't put out more traps, there seemed to be a never-ending supply of the little bastards. And be it psychology or divine intervention the tiny sacrifices worked. Accomplishing his daily tasks went from a rugby scrum to ballet.

He found time to write out a schedule and actually stuck to it. Playtime, cleaning, lunch, naps. There was even a slot for the mailman's arrival at 2:30. Dirt clung to the broom as Paul swept. Kitchen utensils lay in the first place he looked. He folded a fitted sheet! An age of miracles indeed. Jack whined, and Sam pooped as much as always, but everything ran a bit smoother. So, praise the gods and screw the ants.

Then came the souffle.

Paul had just put the kids down for naps when Rebecca called.

"Hey, babe. Everything okay?" he asked.

"First off, you can say no."

"What's going on, Beck?"

"I invited Frank Stivers and his husband to dinner."

"Here?"

"Yes."

"Tonight?"

"I know it's short notice. But you've been keeping the house so well, and you've made all those fancy meals."

"So, you want me to get the house presentable, take care of the kids, and make dinner for your boss and his husband." Paul glanced at the oven clock. "And all by seven?"

"I kind of mentioned those cheese souffles you used to whip up. I told Frank they were the reason I married you. Frank's a big foodie. He and his husband have eaten dinner at Al Burgess's house twice. Al keeps giving me smug looks."

"He's the guy you're up against for the promotion, right?"

"Yeah. I know I shouldn't have invited them, but…" She let the words trail.

Paul's mind raced. Did he have enough eggs? Or any gruyere at all? He looked at the dishes in the sink. Heard the whomp-whomp of laundry that would need to be dried and folded. "Okay, babe."

"You're sure?"

"Yeah. I'll make the house look perfect and cook an impromptu gourmet meal before seven."

"Oh God, I'm sorry. This is crazy."

"No, I can do it. Nobody gives my wife smug looks."

"I'm not the worst wife in the history of wifedom?"

Paul laughed. "Nowhere near. I think I have chicken thighs in the freezer. I can do a braise, maybe something Moroccan. There's a lot of French influence in Moroccan cuisine so the soufflé will work."

"I love when you talk all pompous about food, baby. Seriously. Thank you, thank you, thank you."

"You're welcome. Now, I got to go. Lots to do."

"All right. See you tonight. I'll get wine."

Panic set in. When would he clean the bathroom? Sure, he'd kept the house minimally neat and functioning, but a dinner party for Rebecca's boss? With a promotion on the line? That was a whole other level.

"All right, Hot Pot." Paul pulled open the cabinet. The soufflé dish wasn't there. "Shit." He looked up at the face of his kitchen god. Was there an emptiness where before he'd felt a connection? What the hell did that even mean? He was afraid to open the refrigerator and see what food was on hand.

"I'll check the bathroom. Maybe it's not as messy as I think." Paul ran for the steps, cursing as he stepped on scattered Legos. Upstairs, the bathroom was terrible. *I can't do this. All the ants in the world aren't enough.* A dark thought drifted into his mind and latched on with claws. *A proper sacrifice.* He crossed to the kid's room. *Just to check on them.* Jack lay sprawled asleep on his race car bed. Sam sat up in her crib and stared at her father. Paul froze. Sometimes if he didn't react... sure enough, Sam blinked once then twice and laid back down. Paul waited until her breathing leveled. *Okay, I checked on them.* But he didn't leave. Instead, he crossed the room to the plexiglass box housing Jack's pet hamster.

Ants weren't going to cut it. *What are you thinking? Your so-called gods are just psychological crutches like Rebecca said. They have no real power.* He took a deep breath and walked out of the kid's room. In his hands, he cradled Hamilton.

Paul did not know hamsters could scream.

Hamilton didn't make a sound until laid on the plastic cutting board, then he let loose a wavering howl. Paul imagined Jack coming into the kitchen. His bleary eyes filled with confusion, then fear. *What are you doing with Hamilton, Daddy?*

He grabbed a thick cotton dishtowel and pressed it over the hamster. *Take your kid's hamster back upstairs.* "No. I have to make braised Moroccan chicken and a cheese soufflés." Paul stood poised on a knife-edge of indecision. Then Hamilton gave a muscular jerk, almost rolling off the cutting board. Without thinking—not true, he was thinking, thinking about soufflés and promotions and a good and proper sacrifice—Paul brought his fist down in a sharp, hard arc. He heard the snap of small bones, but the noise was distant, nothing to do with him. He brought his fist down again and again until the thing beneath the dish towel stopped moving. Then the hamster was gone, dish towel and all. On the porch in an old Amazon delivery box.

Paul found himself back in the kitchen, on his knees, denying what he'd done so hard the act almost went away for a few seconds. Then he staggered to his feet and vomited. It was okay; he needed to clean the sink anyway.

He got started. Changing diapers, dusting. Eggs and gruyere right where he needed them. Paul couldn't remember ever even buying the saffron he sprinkled in the braising sauce. He cleaned the bathroom with no worries about the chicken burning. His gods owed him that much. Footsteps sounded on the porch. Paul looked at the time.

2:30, mailman!

Poor broken Hamilton lay on the porch in his cardboard coffin, looking for all the world like a package to be delivered. Paul ran downstairs, past Jack on the couch and Sam in her playpen. "Just bills?" he asked, swinging the door open.

The postman handed him some circulars and paid no attention at all to the box. "Something smells mighty good in there." He was right. Dinner was good. In fact, dinner was perfect.

Rebecca's boss, Frank, turned out to be a broad-faced, gregarious man built like an NFL lineman. His husband was even larger and sported a Brian Blessed sized beard. They laughed loudly and possessed appetites to match their size. If Paul hadn't been so busy hating himself, he would have liked them. Still, he laughed when the room called for laughter and gave heavy-handed pours of the expensive wine Rebecca picked up. Frank raved about the food, asking questions about ingredients and techniques.

Well, you start by turning the oven to 300 and sacrificing the family pet. Aloud, Paul spoke about pan-browning the thighs and how the even heat of the stove was so important. By the end of the evening, Rebecca beamed. She walked the men to the door, promising to have them over again soon.

"Oh, no, our place next time," they insisted.

She waved the men into the distance then turned to Paul. "In Al Burgess's smug face," she shouted and threw her arms around her husband. "I should have never asked, but you did it. The house looks like you rented Martha Stewart. And the food... I thought Frank was going to start singing when he tasted your soufflé. Thank you so much. I'm going to be so grateful to you tonight if the kids don't wake up." She paused. "What's wrong?"

Tears streamed down Paul's face. The dam had finally burst. Guilt and self-disgust poured out. "I killed Hamilton." The confession gave Paul no relief because of the lies that followed. He had not accidentally stepped on the hamster after Jack let Hamilton out of his cage for the hundredth time. But that was the story he told Rebecca. The story he'd repeat despite his son's tearful denials. Until, by the time they buried the box in the backyard, Jack would believe he'd been at fault after all.

I have to lie, Paul told himself. *Because sacrificing my son's hamster to a jug of detergent is not an acceptable fucking story.*

Rebecca hugged him even harder. "Jack didn't notice him missing?"

"No. He never pays Hamilton much attention. Except when he decides the thing needs to roam free." Hamilton's last muffled screech echoed like an accusation in Paul's head.

"We can tell him in the morning." Rebecca took Paul's face in her hands. "It wasn't your fault, babe. There's nothing you could have done."

But there was something he could do now. Paul extricated himself from Rebecca's embrace. On the mantle sat Vah-Coom, the cleaning god. Paul snatched the head from its perch, crumbling the dried Play-Doh.

"What are you doing?"

"Just getting rid of some stuff. The whole household gods thing feels a little weird. I'm the one who cleaned the house. I made dinner. They don't get to share the credit. You go on to bed. I'll be up in a few minutes."

"Okay. Does the whole Hamilton tragedy mean my gratitude should be expressed some other time?"

"Yeah, I think so. But I'm expecting you to be just as grateful tomorrow night." He tried to sound upbeat and failed. That was okay. His lies explained his mood. In the kitchen, he pulled Hot Pot from the fridge.

Later, after Rebecca slept, Paul even took the wedding topper from the bedroom and returned it to the keepsake box. The rest of his pantheon went one by one into the trash after being wadded, torn, or otherwise desecrated.

Only one more god to go. Paul opened the doors to the laundry closet. Washor sat on his shelf, seeming as permanent and immovable as one of the giant stone idols it resembled. Paul threw the empty jug to the floor and brought the heel of his dress shoe down onto its center. Pressure shot the lid across the tiles along with a last splash of blue soap. "Die, you fucker," Paul whispered. He took the crushed jug to the kitchen counter. A pair of heavy shears jutted from the knife block. Paul shoved one of the blades through Washor's sloping cheek and cut. His hands shook with fatigue as minutes later he dropped the twenty some odd pieces of plastic jug into the garbage. The bag of gods went into the big metal can on the side of the house. Paul slammed the lid on to the can with a satisfying clang.

They buried Hamilton the next day. A tearful Jack officiated. Jack told Paul he forgave him and asked for a turtle because turtles had shells and wouldn't squish so easy. Jack's mixture of abject grief and easy acceptance brought Rebecca and Paul to tears, though for different reasons.

Over the next few months, Paul tried to put his brush with madness behind him. He was okay with the clothes not being as clean, and he went back to making eggs for dinner three days a week. When Jack's fifth birthday party came, Paul only flinched a little as the boy opened the box with his new pet turtle inside. Rebecca got her promotion, and a bit more money came in. Maybe they'd buy one of those robot vacuums. Life without gods wasn't so bad.

———

"You okay?" Paul asked as Rebecca pushed food around her

plate. He'd tried making Lo Mein again. Not as good as when Hot Pot helped, but okay. "Your stomach still bothering you?"

Rebecca had come down with a bug a few weeks before. Low-grade annoyance mostly, but she'd not been able to shake the nausea. They even got a home pregnancy test. Negative, thank God.

"I'm okay, hon. Just a lot of stress at work." Rebecca didn't look at him when she answered.

"Is there something you're not telling me?"

"Secrets are bad," said Jack with all the wisdom of his five years. "Sharing is caring."

Rebecca shot Paul a look, and he backed off. "Hey buddy, leave your mother be. She had a long day." After dinner, he asked again.

"I went to the doctor. I didn't want to worry you."

Paul suddenly felt balanced on a high, thin rope. "Okay, now I'm really worried. What did the doctor say?"

"They found a growth in my abdomen. Probably nothing. The body's a weird thing."

Paul fell off the tight rope. Images of cancer wards filled his mind.

"I'm going back tomorrow for a biopsy. Let's not worry until there's something to worry about. Please?"

"I'm coming with you."

"No, you got the kids to watch. The procedure's just a little outpatient thing. I'll go in on my lunch hour."

"Are you nuts? Take the day off."

"No. If I stay at work, I'll be distracted, not bouncing off the walls waiting for the doctor to call."

"You're sure?"

"Yeah. If the biopsy is more involved than I thought, I'll call."

"So, I'm supposed to act like everything's fine?"

"Yes. Now, let's go give those kids some ice cream."

Paul didn't remember falling asleep that night, only opening his eyes to see his mother, kneeling at the end of the bedroom before the altar of the First Southern Baptist church. The wooden cross of Paul's youth had been replaced by a plastic detergent jug with a Sharpied-on face.

"Pray with me, son," said his mother as she turned from the altar, her voice a dry rasp. "You've fallen away from God and been punished. But everything can still turn out all right if you pray with me."

Paul shook his head. "I don't even go to church anymore."

His mother crawled onto the bed and up to where Paul lay. Her body brushed against the sheets with a sound like the rustling of dead leaves. She took his hand, her mouth moving in a whispered exhortation. "It works, Paulie. The power of prayer." Her blackened tongue brushed cracked lips. Breath puffed out, carrion foul. "All you need is a good and proper sacrifice."

Paul shoved blindly outward. His hands burst through a body as fragile as ash. He rolled from the bed, heart pounding, eyes searching the empty bedroom. The sight of Rebecca, asleep on her side, kept the scream in Paul's throat tamped down. He laid back beside her and waited for the sun to rise.

Morning finally came with all the requisite tasks of feeding and dressing the kids. Paul stood last in line for hugs as Rebecca headed for work.

"I'll call you after the biopsy," she said.

Paul nodded and gave her a kiss. "Thanks, it's all going to be fine." He watched the Dodge pull out of the driveway, hoping the words weren't a lie.

He played with the kids all morning. No getting distracted by clothes to wash or rooms to clean. Soaking up all the love and laughter he could. After lunch, Paul checked Sam's diaper and set her in the playpen with a few toys to toss around. "Yo, Jack," he yelled. His son ran into the room.

Paul knelt beside the boy. "Do you think you could hang out here with your sister and maybe watch *Monsters Inc.?*"

"No," said Jack "*Monsters University.*"

"Okay, deal. Daddy's got some work to do."

Jack was already putting the Blu-ray in the machine.

While the kids amused themselves, Paul recreated his gods. Recreated was the wrong word. *You can't kill a god by wadding up a piece of construction paper or slicing and dicing a plastic bottle. I only destroyed their images before.* The gods remained, devising a punishment for their wayward disciple. A punishment not on him but on the woman he loved. Paul felt his household gods all around him. Waiting for new vessels to fill.

First Hot pot, Then Vah-Coom, and Handee. Sam followed Paul with her eyes as he placed the new-forged deities around the living room, forming a circle gazing inward. Jack never looked up from the television.

"You know I love you, right Jack?"

Jack nodded. "I love you too, Daddy."

Paul stepped in front of the TV, squatting down, so he and Jack were eye to eye. "I want you to know, sometimes people do bad things for really good reasons. Does that make sense?"

Jack pursed his lips. "I guess so."

"It's okay, you watch your show." Paul stood back up. The kid was five, of course he didn't understand. *He never will, and neither will Rebecca, but she'll be alive and healthy.*

Paul's phone buzzed. The text read:

> Heading into the biopsy. Nervous.
>
> Everything's going to be all right.

Paul typed. A partial truth. He went to the laundry closet and got the new jug of detergent. This one was red, but the color didn't matter one bit. *Hell, I probably don't even have to draw the eyes and mouth.* He could already feel power coming off the thing. Paul drew the face anyway.

He held the new Washor in the crook of one arm like a child. With his other hand, he took his 12-inch chef's knife from its plastic blade protector. Paul carried them both into the living room where the rest of the Pantheon waited. He set the knife and god on the couch. From her playpen, Sam watched him with sleepy eyes. Paul gave her a wink. "Jack, I need you to go upstairs to your room for a little while."

Jack didn't answer until Paul picked up the remote and turned off the television.

"Dad!"

Paul crossed the room and picked Jack up, hugging him. "Upstairs to your room."

"But it's almost over."

Paul sat his son down on the bottom step. "Room, now. And no coming down until I call."

Jack looked over Paul's shoulder. "Your arts and crafts are back."

"Yeah, for a little while."

Jack turned and marched up the stairs.

Paul checked the time. 2:15. Sam lay on her back now, small chest rising and falling. Paul wanted to hug his daughter to him. But he didn't. Better she stayed asleep, easier. He sat for a few minutes, Washor on the couch beside him. Rebecca's biopsy was probably over. He hoped she wasn't too worried. The results would turn out fine. He would see to that.

"Power of prayer, Mom. Like you said. All I need is faith and a good and proper sacrifice." Paul picked up the knife and went to the playpen. He brushed Sam's tiny pink cheek with his fingertips. Then he straightened and walked from where his daughter still slept to the front door. The time was 2:30. Paul tightened his grip on the chef's knife. The mailman should arrive any minute.

THE WORMS THAT CRAWL UP FROM UNDER THE LEAVES AND EAT YOU... THROUGH YOUR BUTT!!

BILL LOOKED up from the latest issue of *House of Mystery* to find his little brother staring at him.

"Come on, Bill." Frankie had his boots on already and a stocking cap pulled down over his bowl haircut. "The leaf pile was your plan."

Bill thought about saying he'd changed his mind just to watch Frankie's head explode. But the plan *was* his, and a good one at that. "Okay, I'll get ready. You gather supplies."

Frankie ran from the room and down the stairs. Bill had his sneakers and a pullover on by the time Frankie clumped back in, face stricken.

"Mom says we have to clean our room."

They stared out over the junkyard landscape of Star Wars figures, Lincoln Logs, and discarded clothing.

"Closet," Bill said.

Sliding open the closet door, the boys formed a bucket brigade, tossing stray belongings inside until all that was left were their comic books, which they carefully bagged and slid in neat stacks under the beds.

Frankie's face still looked pained. "She's gonna check the closet."

"Trust me," Bill said with all the wisdom of his thirteen years. "Mom'll barely check the room. She doesn't want to know."

They ran down the stairs to find their mom sitting at the kitchen table, scissoring coupons from a stack of magazines.

"Where are you off to in such a hurry?" She scanned the issue of *Women's Day* open on the table. "Oooh, fifty cents off Crest."

Bill opened his mouth to speak, but Frankie was way ahead of him.

"The empty lot over on Dell avenue. We're gonna rake up the biggest leaf pile in the history of ever. It'll be awesome!"

Mom's normal, easy smile faded.

Bill breathed out an annoyed sigh. They couldn't just tell mom their plans. These things took finesse. "We're good Samaritans," he said. "Nobody else is going to rake up those leaves."

"But no one even lives there." Mom crossed her arms. Never a good sign. "No. I don't think so. That yard is probably full of broken glass. Maybe even drug needles."

"Drug needles, Mom?" Bill asked. "Really?"

"Maybe. Why don't you rake leaves for someone who'll appreciate it, like Mr. Powers?"

"Mom," Frankie stretched the word into multiple syllables. "Bill says Mr. Powers buries kids in his basement."

Bill winced

"He does no such thing. Mr. Powers is a very nice old man who used to deliver our mail."

"But Bill said—"

"He was only trying to scare you. Weren't you?"

"Yes, Mom," Bill admitted.

Frankie scowled at Bill for a moment, but was obviously too excited to stay upset. "We're taking the rest of my Halloween candy for fuel. Raking takes lots of energy."

"You'll take sandwiches and apples," their mom said, evidently forgetting about drug needles for the time being. "And gloves. Otherwise, you'll come home with blisters." She leaned close to Bill. "You know your brother believes everything you say, so no more scary stories."

"But he likes them."

"He likes them until the sun goes down, then he wants to sleep in my bed."

At the counter, Frankie pressed peanut-butter-smeared slices of bread together. He looked over his shoulder at his big brother, crossed his eyes and stuck out his tongue. Bill smiled at the little turd-monkey in spite of himself. "Okay, Mom, no scary stories."

"Fine, then. You two go make the world's biggest leaf pile. And you can take *some* of your brother's candy." She hugged her boys then turned and pulled apples from the refrigerator. "But you better come running home when I call. Your empty lot is only a couple of blocks away. Don't pretend you can't hear me yelling."

"The whole tri-state area can hear when you yell, Mom."

"So, you have no excuses."

Rakes over their shoulders, lunches packed, and wearing coats they would pull off as soon as they got out of sight, the boys marched down the sidewalk. Minutes later, they reached their destination, an empty double lot blanketed with orange and red leaves from the big oaks that flanked it. The only man-made structures were a rust-streaked but sturdy set of monkey bars and a few low cement outcroppings jutting from the ground like ancient ruins.

They threw their coats on the grass to form a makeshift picnic blanket. On top, they laid out their lunches, four cans of pop, and a blue plastic bag filled with all the Nerds, Blow-Pops, and fun-sized chocolate bars they had been allowed to make off with.

"Where do we start?" Frankie asked. The plan was to rake all the leaves into a pile beneath the monkey bars. Once no leaf was left behind, they'd climb to the top and make death-defying leaps until time to go home.

"Right here's good," Bill said, dragging his rake across the ground and sending a shower of red and gold into the air. "Watch out for needles."

Frankie dug in with his own rake, grunting with the effort. "Why would there be needles anyway?"

Sorry mom, but he's literally asking for it,

"Oh, I didn't want to scare you, but back before you were born, there was a mental hospital on this lot. Turned out the doctors were experimenting on the patients."

Frankie kicked a few stray leaves in the right direction. "What *kind* of experiments?"

"They gave the patients shots that were supposed to cure them, but only made them crazier and hungry for human flesh. No one noticed until kids in the neighborhood started disappearing."

Frankie launched a rake full of leaves at his brother. "You're full of green baby poop."

"Mom and some of the other parents found out what was going on. So, one night, they barricaded all the doors and burned the hospital to the ground with the doctors and their flesh-eating patients inside. Nothing left but the needles the doctors used. So, watch out, because if you stick yourself with one…" Bill let the words hang in the air.

"Green baby poop," Frankie shouted.

"Ouch." Bill pulled one foot up and hopped toward Frankie. "I think I stepped on a needle. I'm hungry for little brother."

Frankie brandished his rake then suddenly threw it to the ground. His face clouded with disgust. "Eww!"

"What is it?" Bill asked, hoping there weren't really any needles.

"Worms."

Bill kicked at the wet leaves clumped on the end of his brother's rake. He spotted two thin white worms, each no longer than his pinky. "Oh, come on, Frankie. They're nothing."

"I don't like worms."

"There's only two. Those leaves were just wet. Rake off the dry leaves and leave the wet ones behind. No problem."

Frankie still looked leery, so Bill changed the subject.

"I'm going to put my gloves back on. Mom was right about the blisters. Hey, you want a drink?"

Frankie nodded. They each had a Coke and a Blow-Pop for energy then got back to work, the tiny worms forgotten. Later, they stopped for sandwiches and more pop. Despite the cold, sweat soaked Bill's hoodie and his palms hurt even through the gloves. His plan turned out to be a lot more work than he expected. Especially with the occasional leaf fight setting them back.

Frankie was enthusiastic, though. "It's gonna be huge," he said, eying the respectable pile of leaves they'd already deposited beneath the monkey bars.

"Yeah." Bill agreed. He looked over the still only half-raked lot. "Maybe we should jump now."

Frankie took a last bite of sandwich and stood. "When do you think Mom will call us?"

"If she doesn't look in our closet, probably not until dinner."

Frankie whooped and dug into a two-foot drift with his rake. "Plenty of time. When people see our leaf pile, we'll be legends."

Bill gulped down the last bites of his own sandwich and grabbed his rake. Who didn't want to be a legend?

The talking and horseplay died down to a minimum as the brothers carved out swaths in the carpet of leaves. The pile under the monkey bars grew to five feet, then six. Finally, Bill stood in front of a pile of leaves nearly seven feet tall. He turned and looked back at the landscape of dead grass, hardly a leaf in sight.

Frankie jogged over with a fistful of candy. "We did it," he piled candy into Bill's hand. They each unwrapped a Snickers and solemnly tapped them together. "To the legend of Bill and Frankie. World's most heroic leaf jumpers."

The monkey bars were a beast, the institutional kind you find on old playgrounds, solid metal and way taller than the ones at the elementary school. Bill thought the lot had once been a daycare, but he hadn't told Frankie. There was nothing scary about a daycare. He climbed the monkey bar ladder and pulled himself up until he sat on the very top.

Frankie huffed and puffed after him. "Don't you jump," he called. "I'm first. You'll squish all the leaves down with your giant butt."

Bill had to haul his brother up onto the top bars by brute force. Finally, both boys were in position, sitting in the center of the monkey bars. Their feet dangled over what had to be, absolutely, with no doubt, the largest leaf pile in the world. The sun sat low in the sky. Bill wondered what time it was?

"Maybe you *should* go first," said Frankie.

Bill shot his brother a sidelong look. "What about my big butt squishing the leaves?"

Frankie shrugged then flinched and adjusted his grip on the bars.

"You're scared? All those hours raking leaves, and now you're too chicken to jump?"

"Am not," Frankie said, but his voice quavered.

"I thought we were going to be legends. Now what? The legend of Bill and his loser little brother who was too scared to jump?"

"I'm going to jump."

"Yeah? Who's stopping you? Mom's going to start calling soon."

They sat there. Bill looking at Frankie. Frankie staring down into the pile of leaves.

Frankie rocked back and forth a little. He pulled one hand off the monkey bars but kept it close, like a gunfighter about to draw. His eyes narrowed as he leaned forward, shifting his weight.

"Whoa!" Bill clapped a hand against Frankie's chest.

His brother's eyes flew open, and he grabbed the bars again. "What! What is it?"

Bill kept his hand on his brother as if he feared Frankie would launch himself outward at any moment. "It's too late. We waited too long."

Frankie pursed his lips. "No, we didn't. It's not anywhere near dark yet."

"I'm not talking about Mom calling us for dinner. I'm talking about the worms."

Frankie looked around. "What about them? You said they were too tiny to worry about."

"Of course, they were tiny. Those leaves weren't deep enough to attract the real monsters. But a pile this deep…? Oh, man. If we'd gone ahead and jumped right away, things would have been fine. Now, they've had time to crawl up into the leaves. The big ones are man-eaters, Frankie. If you jump, the worms are going to get you. And the worst thing is they always eat people the same way. Through their butt."

"You are so full of baby poop!"

"I'm trying to save your life, Frankie."

"Why aren't people being eaten all the time then? It would be in the news."

"The worms don't come to places where people live. Too much noise. All the mowers running, and cars pulling into driveways. It scares them off. These worms are only found in jungles, forests, and empty lots like this one."

"Baby poop."

"Why would I lie?"

"Why did you say there were crazy zombie needles everywhere or that Mr. Powers killed kids? Because you're mean, and I hate you. And you just smiled!"

"What? No, I didn't." Bill straightened his lips with an effort.

"I saw you. You smiled. Because you're a big mean butthole who thinks he's so funny. But a butthole can't be funny. It can only fart and make baby poop."

"I'm telling you—" The rest of Bill's sentence remained unsaid.

Frankie jumped. He plunged through the air, the middle finger of his right hand jutting up defiantly as he disappeared into the giant mound of leaves.

Bill whooped with laughter. "You did it, you little fart eater!" he yelled, waiting for his brother to crawl out the side before he took his own turn. He kept waiting. The leaves buckled and settled. Bill heard Frankie laughing. The sound came again. Loud and long, even muffled by the leaves. It didn't sound like laughter this time. This time, it sounded like Frankie was screaming. The leaf pile shook. Another wail rose up from inside and was that a word at the very end? "Bill" or maybe, "Help."

Bill shook his head. "I'm not falling for it, Frankie. You better get out of there before I cannonball right on top of you. Look out below!" he yelled, but he didn't move, and neither did the leaf pile. Well, maybe it did, a little. Was that pale white flash Frankie's arm? But hadn't he been wearing long sleeves? The sun lay behind the houses now, the long shadows making it harder to see.

A sick feeling rose up in Bill's gut, and not from the candy and pop. "There's no such thing as worms that eat you through your butt," he shouted. "I made it up, okay? You're right. I'm a big farting butthole. Now, come on out." Why didn't he come out? It had to be hot and itchy in there, hard to breathe. No way Frankie could stay in there much longer.

But he did.

People walked by. Adults casting suspicious glances at the boy in the empty lot. Bill wanted to say something to them. Ask for help. But he couldn't. Right now, this was only Frankie playing a joke. If grownups came and dug through the leaves, Bill would know. Maybe they'd pull out his little brother, laughing and shooting Bill the bird. But maybe there would be nobody inside at all, only a hole at the bottom of the pile, its edges smeared with blood and worm slime.

I'm going to scream now, Bill thought. It would be a very loud scream, and then wouldn't the adults come running? But the scream never came. Bill only sat and waited for Frankie's joke to end.

It really was getting dark. Bill could barely see his and Frankie's coats lying in the corner of the lot. The streetlights would come on soon. Streetlights meant dinner time and mom standing on the sidewalk outside the house, her dress smelling like the meatloaf she'd cooked, calling out in that loud carrying voice of hers. Calling Bill to come home and bring his little brother with him.

Bill stared down at the leaves. No longer individual bits of red, gold, and brown, only a hulking, hungry darkness. "All right Frankie, you win. You fooled me," he said. "But we need to go home now. So, I'm gonna jump. Because it's time to stop joking around." Tears cut warm channels down Bill's cold cheeks. "I'm sorry I scared you. I should have jumped first. So, here I come. Pretty soon we'll both be laughing. Because you were laughing, Frankie, not screaming. And this was a *great day*, just like we planned. And I love you."

Bill let himself rock forward, hands out as if trying to hug someone he couldn't quite reach. He fell. The cold night air gave way to the rasp of dry leaves against his face and a heavy warm pressure like being buried alive. Something moved nearby, rustling through the leaves, wrapping around Bill's ankle. *Good one Frankie. You got me.* The leaves buckled. They shook. Then came a noise like a young boy's laughter or maybe a high, muffled scream.

Afterward, the leaves lay deathly still. Shadows lengthened until the streetlights flicked on with an electronic buzz. A few blocks away, the loud, clear voice of a woman rang through the night, calling for her boys to come home.

GOD DAMN YOU TO HELL, JOHN GLENN!

STEVIE BURST through the front door like an eight-year-old ball of lightning. "Mom, mom, wait 'til you hear! Wait 'til you hear!"

Suzanne looked from the stack of ungraded trigonometry tests to the Cheshire Cat wall clock. Two-thirty. Gerald had promised 5 p.m. She put down her red pen and tried to force all annoyance from her face.

"I saw a launch. A real live Appollo rocket launch. Dad and me got up at four goddamn a.m."

Suzanne took her boy in her arms. "That's not appropriate language."

Stevie's face clouded for a moment. "It's okay between us men. Dad said so."

"Well, don't say it around us moms. How was the rocket?"

"SOOO loud!" Stevie let loose his best rocket roar.

"Oh, my gosh. Sooo loud!"

"And I met an astronaut."

"I bet you did." Stevie's father, Gerald, liked astronauts. He liked to go out to bars with them and hit on the women they drew like flies. Astronauts were one reason Gerald was Suzanne's ex-husband.

"And you know what, Mom? You know what?"

Gerald pushed through the front door. In his arms, he carried Stevie's overnight bag along with a large glass box.

"The Astronaut gave me space monkeys. I gotta clear a spot. I'm clearing the spot, Dad!" Stevie wiggled out of his mother's embrace and raced to his room, leaving the two adults staring at each other.

"Hey Suzie. I just said hi to Harry and Eugenia next door. You know, I actually kind of miss them."

"You said you'd keep Stevie until goddamn five o'clock."

"Oh, come on, Suze. There's no need to—"

"Don't worry, it's okay to talk that way between us men. Stevie said so."

"The launch *was* pretty damned early. But he was so excited."

"*You're* pretty damned early. I plan my work around the times we agree on."

"I know. I'm sorry. I have to get back to the cape. There's a press junket thing."

"Sure, I get it. Dinner, drinks, the grind never ceases."

"Dad, I cleared the spot. Where are you?!" Stevie's excitement verged on hysteria.

"Duty calls."

"Wait a second, is that an aquarium? You can't just bring pets—" But Gerald was already past her and stepping into Stevie's room.

Gerald worked for NASA in media relations. A job you rarely associate with the space program. But it *was* a job that let you give the son you only saw one weekend a month every official NASA themed hat, t-shirt, toy, and now… space monkeys?

I earn a masters in mathematics and teach tenth grade trig. He barely scrapes a BS in communications and works for the space program. "The world is a stupid place."

And now, if I go in that bedroom and say, "Stevie, you can't just have a new pet without asking," I am the giant monster bitch versus his superhero, rocket-launching, astronaut-befriending dad.

Voices came from Stevie's room. "We can fill it up in the bathtub."

"Okay, monster bitch it is," she muttered. Suzanne was waiting when father and son came back into Stevie's room carrying the half-filled aquarium. "Wait. No one asked me if you could have an aquarium in your room."

"Dad said it was okay." Stevie said, as if this settled things.

"Your dad doesn't live here anymore." Her words were like a slap. Stevie's excitement evaporated, replaced with barely held back tears.

Monster bitch.

Suzanne kneeled, so she was face-to-face with her son. "Sweetheart, I need to talk to Daddy alone for a few minutes. Go in the kitchen and have some Tang, okay?" Of course, Stevie looked to his father.

"Do what your mother says, son."

The boy sniffled and walked out of the room. "But… space monkeys," he said in a sad, barely audible voice.

Suzanne turned on her husband. "You can't make decisions like this without talking to me first."

Gerald put the aquarium on top of the chest of drawers Stevie had cleared off, then sat down on his son's bed. He patted a spot beside him.

Suzanne didn't move.

"Fine, I know you don't like me getting him things."

"Oh, screw you, Gerald." Suzanne hissed the words in a stage whisper she hoped didn't carry to the kitchen. "That is so unfair." She gestured around the room. A poster of the Apollo moon landing crew hung on the wall. Signed by all three crew members. In the corner by the closet, a four-foot-tall Apollo 6 replica stood poised for takeoff. "Yes, I don't appreciate always being the Grinch to your Santa Claus, but pets are different. Are you planning to drop off a surprise pony next time?"

Gerald spread his palms in a calming gesture that made Suzanne want to kick him in his khaki-covered shin. "I get you. I've been trying to cut down on the presents. You know, let spending time with Stevie *be* the present. That's why we went to the launch. Even got a look into ground control."

Suzanne felt the anger fade a bit. Maybe Gerald had listened a little over their last half dozen arguments.

"This whole space monkey thing wasn't my fault. It was John. You know, John Glenn."

Suzanne knew John. She'd met him a few times in the last days of her marriage. "So, John was the astronaut Stevie met?"

"Yeah. It's really not a big deal. They'll all be dead in a month… Jeez, I'm not explaining this well. You ever heard of sea monkeys?"

Suzanne shook her head.

"Wait, a second." Gerald grabbed a *Fantastic Four* comic from a stack on Stevie's nightstand and flipped through the pages. "Here." He held up a full-page advertisement showing a family of pink cartoon fish people complete with webbed hands and stubby antenna. Above them the ad proclaimed "Enter the Wonderful World of Amazing Live Sea-Monkeys, Own a Bowl Full of Happiness."

"I think I need a little more explanation."

"This is what John gave him. They're brine shrimp. So small you can barely see them even when they're full grown. You pour the brine shrimp eggs in some water along with a little food and in a couple of days, you got your sea monkeys swimming around. Feed them once a week and they last for a couple of months."

"Stevie called them space monkeys."

"Well, yeah. The eggs are good for experiments. So, they took some on a few Apollo flights. Let them get frizzled by cosmic rays to see what happened."

"They aren't radioactive or anything?"

"No, nothing like that. The scientists hatched a bunch of them when they got back to earth. They turned out just regular old brine shrimp, maybe an extra set of legs or two. So, John got permission to give a few batches of the unhatched eggs to kids. Calls them space monkeys, because he's John. What was I supposed to do?"

Suzanne sat down on the bed next to her ex-husband. "I know you have a hard time saying no. They last a couple of months, that's it?"

"If you're lucky. Once they're gone, you can throw out the aquarium. Better yet, get the kid a goldfish."

Suzanne looked at the aquarium sitting on the dresser. She tried not to imagine a badly thrown baseball crashing through the glass and water cascading over Stevie's clothes. "All right. He did get them from a real live astronaut. Let's give boyo the good news."

They made a deal. The space monkeys were Stevie and Gerald's project. If Stevie had an issue that didn't involve a waterfall in his room, he called his dad. "If I have to deal with your space monkeys, they go to your dad's on his next weekend."

And for the most part, Stevie's word was his bond. Once, he complained he couldn't find his space monkey food. But quickly followed up with, "Don't worry, mom. I'll take care of it." There was also a tense thirty minutes when Stevie ran back and forth from his room to their backyard carrying a large plastic cup.

Suzanne took a peek in his room. No broken glass or soaked carpet. She went back to folding clothes and threw out a casual. "Everything okay, Champ?" on Stevie's next lap. "You watching out for alligators?" There was a small stream just past their lawn that turned the backyard swampy on the rare occasions it rained. "Watch out for 'gators" was a family joke.

This time, Stevie didn't crack a smile. He just frowned into the cup for a moment. "There's not really any alligators outside. Right, Mom?"

"No sweetie. Not enough water."

"Okay, then everything's fine."

By the time Gerald's weekend came around again, Suzanne had to admit the space monkeys weren't a problem after all. She'd arranged for Gerald to pick Stevie up from Hank's Dog Shoppe, Stevie's favorite watering hole. The eight-year-old had already polished off a chili dog and was half-way through his strawberry milk shake.

"Don't eat too much. You might get sick in your dad's convertible." Suzanne reconsidered. "Eat as much as you like." It was nice to be the one spoiling Stevie for a change.

The boy took a deep slurp of milkshake and sighed with satisfaction. "Mom, can you do me a favor? It's about Rudy, my space monkey. I know you don't want to take care of him, but I'll be at Dad's and…."

"You've done a great job with them. Wait. There's only one?"

"Yeah, but he's doing really good."

They must be dying off even quicker than Gerald said. Suzanne almost felt guilty. Maybe she would get Stevie that goldfish. "What do you need?"

"He's fed and everything, but could you just check on him? Make sure he's okay?"

"Of course, sweetheart."

"And I won't have to take him to Dad's for that?"

"No, I'm happy to do it."

With Stevie safely on his way to the Cape, Suzanne took her time driving home. Her neighbor Harry was out watering his grass next door. When Suzanne pulled in, he waved her over.

"So, is this Stevie's weekend with Gerald?" Harry was in his late forties and had a penchant for beachcomber style straw hats and keeping his ever-present Hawaiian shirts unbuttoned down to his pot belly. Despite his fashion sense, Harry was a good neighbor, always ready to lend a hand or loan out a tool or two.

"Yep. Got the place to myself." *Just me and Rudy, the lone space monkey.*

"Well, we're having a few friends over later, if you get bored and want something to do. Eugenia's always saying we should have you over for a drink."

"Sweet of you to offer, Harry. I think I'll probably just bask in the solitude tonight, but If I change my mind, I'll give you a call."

"I'll tell Eugenia you're a firm maybe," said Harry and gave her an exaggerated wink.

Two hours later, Suzanne still didn't feel like partying with her neighbors. But she decided a drink was a fine idea and maybe some Chinese delivery. She opened a bottle of chardonnay when the food arrived. *White wine goes with fried rice, right?*

She woke up snug in her bed with dim memories of corking the half-empty chard and putting the leftover Chinese food in the fridge. *You sure know how to party.* Thoughts of coffee and some aspirin were enough to get her out of bed. *Oh, and don't forget your space-monkey sitting. Better take a peek in Stevie's room.*

The carpet outside Stevie's half-open door squelched under Suzanne's bare feet. *Oh no.* And things had been going so well. Sure enough, the side panel of the aquarium was shattered, and water covered both the dresser and floor. *What the hell could have happened? Stevie's at the cape. And a few glasses of wine do not send me into an aquarium-smashing frenzy.*

She didn't see a brine shrimp flopping on the carpet. Gerald said they were tiny. Well, time for towels and a pair of shoes. Suzanne didn't feel like bleeding this morning.

A crash sounded in the kitchen. "Oh, what now?" Could an animal have gotten in? A cat maybe. "Watch out for 'gators." But the family joke didn't sound so funny just now. "A cat," she said in her no-nonsense teacher's voice. "Or maybe a possum."

It wasn't a possum or even an alligator. The door to the refrigerator hung open. The thing inside was about three feet long. Sickly green horizontal bands covered the length of the creature. The bands looked hard, like tortoise shell polished to a glimmering sheen. At least a dozen legs poked out from the thing's sides. Each limb looked meaty and muscular and ended in three long talon-tipped digits.

Oh Jesus. The house was locked up, windows closed, nothing that big could have gotten inside. Suzanne thought she knew what broke the aquarium.

"There's only one," Stevie had said, "but he's doing really well."

Rudy, her son's last remaining space monkey, pulled its—what? head section?—from the plastic drawer, the smell of leftover fried rice and Oscar Mayer bologna filled the room. Two long antennae—arms? mandibles?—locked onto a half-full gallon of milk and pulled the jug to the thing's head. The space monkey made a sound like Stevie finishing off his strawberry milkshake. The jug imploded.

Rudy's body gave a full-length shudder and grew, broadening and lengthening by a good four inches. A blue ooze flowed out from between the bands of shell. The ooze coated the freshly-grown flesh, hardening into new layers of protection.

Suzanne took a cautious step back, angling for the front door. She held her breath, but the space monkey somehow sensed her. Rudy's head section rotated on its body. A long, segmented tube, extended tentatively in Suzanne's direction. The lip of the tube was red and wet. Black triangular teeth pushed through the red flesh and came together with an almost musical clink.

The space monkey's body spun, its many legs breaking into a galloping scurry toward Suzanne. She turned and ran flat out for the door.

She made it three steps before her foot came down on the Mattel Lunar Lander model Gerald and Stevie had put together three months before. Suzanne cursed and fell hard on her shoulder. The fall saved her life. Rudy was practically airborne when it ran right over her. A few claws tried to gain purchase. They only snagged for a moment on her terry-cloth robe as the creature passed over.

The space monkey rammed the flowered wallpaper with a thud. Its mouth tube brayed a sound that was half bellow, half kazoo. Suzanne let out an involuntary bark of hysterical laughter. She kept seeing the milk jug collapsing in on itself as Rudy sucked out the contents.

Fear gave Suzanne speed and the fortitude to ignore the pain in her shoulder. She rolled to her feet and dashed to the door, slamming it behind her before the space monkey gave chase.

A jolt of panic ripped through her as she realized she hadn't pressed the button on the knob so it would lock when closed. Maybe it wouldn't matter. Could the thing turn a doorknob? As if in answer, the door bulged outward as something strong and pissed off slammed against it.

Suzanne looked around the neighborhood. No one was stirring yet on this quiet Saturday morning. *I have to get to a phone.* Another thud shook the door. Suzanne stopped trying to plan and ran for Harry and Eugenia's sea-foam green bungalow.

Suzanne's front door gave way with a crash. Rudy let out another of its strange kazoo-colored bellows. Suzanne didn't look back. She didn't want to see the black teeth of the space monkey's mouth tube snapping open and closed.

Her hand reached Harry and Eugenia's doorknob. *Not locked. Thank God, it's not locked.* Suzanne pushed inside, then slammed and locked the door. She stared at the white wood, waiting for the thud.

"Well Suzanne, I know Harry invited you to come by, but you really should have called first or at least knocked."

Suzanne turned to her neighbor. "I'm so sorry, we have to call the police—uh…" Suzanne would not have believed it possible, but for the moment she had completely forgotten why she came over.

Eugenia Price, Suzanne's neighbor for the last five years, and vice president of the Caderro County historical society, stood naked in her living room but for a complex arrangement of black leather straps that supported the foot long, bright red phallus protruding at a jaunty angle from about crotch level.

"Now hold on, Suzanne. There is no need to call any police. We're all consenting adults here." Eugenia gestured to a naked man sound asleep on the flower-print sofa. "It's just a lifestyle choice. Nobody's getting hurt."

The door burst inward with a bang and a shower of splintered wood.

The space monkey reared up its top half, mouth tube thrust forward as if tasting the air. Eugenia screamed and ran through a beaded door curtain into the dining room. "Harrrrrry!"

Suzanne spotted a black club on the floor and snatched it up. It wasn't a club, but it was the closest thing to a weapon in the room.

The Space monkey ignored Suzanne and Eugenia. The naked man, now sitting up and blinking dazedly, was not so lucky. Rudy's multiple legs flexed, and he leaped across the room. The man never even screamed. The space monkey's fanged mouth tube plunged into his narrow chest while dozens of legs held him immobile. Blood bubbled from the man's open mouth, then reversed course as the space monkey sucked in its meal.

"Get down, Suzanne." A rapid series of explosions filled the room. Suzanne dove to the floor. Harry and Eugenia stood in the door to the dining room. Harry wore his signature beachcomber straw hat along with a rhinestone studded cod piece and nipple clips. He held a pistol in each hand. Eugenia had a rifle pressed into her shoulder.

Bullets struck the space monkey shell, ricocheting away with shrill whistling sounds.

"Get out, Suze," yelled Harry over the cacophony. "We got this."

Suzanne wasn't too sure about that. The space monkey rocked under the onslaught of bullets, but even where a stray shot got past its shell armor, blue ooze bubbled out of the wound, sealing it.

The crawl toward the front door seemed to take hours. Any moment, Suzanne expected to feel Rudy's mouth tube plunge into her back. Harry and Eugenia were still firing as Suzanne crossed the threshold. *Where did they keep the extra rounds?*

A dry click sounded as Suzanne stood and pulled the door, still hanging by one hinge, as close to closed as she could manage. A few more sporadic shots sounded, and then the house was silent.

Suzanne stood in the cul-de-sac praying that her gun-toting, swinger neighbors had killed Stevie's pet. She didn't even notice the two police cruisers until they'd stopped their engines and one of the policemen yelled to her.

"Ma'am, put down the… um, the object." The man speaking was tall and thin, his face dominated by a bushy mustache. The other officer, shorter, with broad shoulders, stood in the open door of the second cruiser. He had his gun drawn, but he was laughing too hard to point it anywhere.

"Shut up Hawkins," yelled Mustache. "Ma'am, put down the thing in your hand and approach me slowly."

Suzanne dropped the two-foot-long black dildo on to the asphalt. She hadn't even realized she still held it. "Harry and Eugenia." Suzanne pointed to her neighbor's house. "I think they're dead." *No, they killed the monster, they shot it to death, and Eugenia is probably having sex with it now. Please Lord, let that be the way it happened.*

"We had reports of shots being fired." Mustache was talking again. It took a little while for the words to make sense to Suzanne. *I think I'm in shock.*

"Are you hurt, ma'am?"

"No." Suzanne didn't know if she said the word out loud. *I should be the one hurt. Not Harry and Eugenia. It was my monster. I could have stopped it.* She imagined Stevie watching as his space monkey grew. *He would have told me about it. Would have asked me for help.* "Is it supposed to get so big, mommy?" *But I had to make him* take some responsibility *because my ex-husband pissed me off. Now people are dead. What if Stevie had been home?*

Suzanne let loose an involuntary groan.

"Ma'am, I need you to talk to me. Did you call the police?"

Suzanne looked back to mustache cop, then to Harry and Eugenia's door hanging from its single hinge. "Harry had guns, but I don't think it helped."

"Who has guns?"

Suzanne took a deep breath. "Harry, my neighbor." She pointed to the bungalow.

"All right. I want you to go to my cruiser. We're going to take care of this."

Harry and Eugenia's broken front door pushed open almost languidly. As if the creature coming out had nothing to fear.

"What the hell is that?"

Rudy was now the size of a cow, maybe a hippo? *How big is a freaking hippo?* Suzanne shook her head hard. *Get it together, Suze.*

Hawkins, the wide-bodied cop, stood between the two cruisers, his pistol in a two-handed shooter's grip. Bullets struck the enormous space monkey, pinging off in random trajectories.

Suzanne had been here before. She ducked her head and ran.

Mustache cop added more bullets to the party.

Suzanne yelled. "It won't help. Get back in your cars. Drive!"

Maybe it was the bullets bouncing off the space monkey's shell, but mustache cop stopped firing. Suzanne could hear his feet striking the asphalt as he ran after her.

Shots still rang out from the second policeman's gun.

Suzanne reached the cruiser and threw herself into the front seat. She saw mustache cop in mid-stride, reaching out as if Suzanne could somehow pull him to safety. The space monkey's mouth tube burst through the man's chest. Blood and bone sprayed the cruiser's windshield.

Hawkins screamed and kept firing.

Suzanne screamed herself, just to cut through the panic filling her head. It helped. She pulled the cruiser door shut. Keys hung from the ignition. In front of her, the space monkey finished up with mustache cop. Another person who tried to help her, dead.

Suzanne started the cruiser. This had to end. She never wanted to be the monster bitch, but it was time. She shifted into drive and stood on the gas. The cruiser leaped forward with a shriek of tires chewing asphalt. But the only thing to go down beneath its wheels was the dead police officer. Rudy's first leap carried it to the hood of the cruiser. Its second sent it over the car altogether.

Hawkins had replaced his empty pistol with a shotgun. He got one shot off before the space monkey landed in front of him, stretched to its full height, and rammed its mouth tube straight down through the top of the man's skull.

Suzanne watched through the cruiser's rear view as the space monkey grew. "No." She shifted into reverse and punched the gas again.

Maybe the space monkey tried to jump, but the mouth tube was lodged too deep. That didn't matter. What mattered was the sound of shells cracking as the cruiser's rear fender pinned the space monkey against the other police car at twenty miles per hour. Blue goo gouted from the thing's wounds. It poured over the twisted metal of the cruisers, cementing monster and machine into a solid, immovable mass.

Suzanne picked up the shotgun, slick with Hawkins' blood. She'd never fired one, but she figured it out. The first squeeze of the trigger blew Rudy's mouth tube into fragments. Suzanne racked the slide and shoved the shotgun barrel in the crater the first shell had left. She pulled the trigger again and again. Shoving deeper into the space monkey's soft insides with each shot. "God damn you to hell, John Glenn!"

The sixth time Suzanne racked the slide and fired, the space monkey stopped moving. She pulled the shotgun from inside the carcass. Blue ooze stiffened and cracked on her forearms. The pieces fell to the asphalt.

Once she got past her missing front door, the house seemed strangely undisturbed. Suzanne picked up the phone and pressed it to her ear. The number she dialed was not the police. More of them were probably on the way. Instead, Suzanne called a two-bedroom condo in Cape Canaveral.

"Hello, Glenshaw residence." Stevie's high voice articulated each word carefully.

The sound of her son's voice sent a thrill of fierce joy through Suzanne. Stevie was safe in Cape Canaveral with Gerald. *And I killed the goddamned monster.* "Hey Sweetheart. Are you having a good time?" Suzanne's voice only cracked a little, but Stevie noticed.

"You okay, Mom?"

Suzanne wiped tears from her eyes. "Yeah. Mommy just misses you, kiddo."

"I miss you too. Mom. Is Rudy okay?" The silence on the phone stretched as Suzanne thought about her answer. "Mom, I don't mind. I mean, if he's not okay. I don't like him much. He ate up his brothers and sisters."

Suzanne nodded silently. *Of course he did.*

"I saved the ones I could, but he ate most of them."

"What?" An ice-cold void opened in Suzanne's gut.

"Daddy says sometimes fishes do that."

"Honey. What do you mean, you saved them?" She replayed the memory of Stevie running back and forth from his room to the backyard, a large red plastic cup clutched in his small hands.

"I put them in the stream. I was careful, Mom. I didn't get wet or anything. And no 'gators."

Suzanne wondered how many space monkeys Stevie had saved? How many had been outside eating and growing for over a week? "Stevie, guess what? You're going to stay with daddy a few more days." Distant sirens grew nearer. "Tell your dad I'll call him soon."

The phone felt suddenly heavy and awkward in her hand. It took Suzanne three tries to get it on the cradle. She pulled her torn and stained terry-cloth robe tighter, though the day was already heating up. The police would be here soon with more shotguns. While she waited, Suzanne watched the backyard and prayed for alligators.

REGULARS

IT WAS nine p.m. when Jesus Christ tried to get into Drake's Bar and Grill with no ID. Jimmy stood up from wrestling a new keg of Yuengling into position. He spotted Jesus and had to smile. In his thirty years of owning Drake's, Jimmy had seen the local frat kids do a lot of laughable things. But they weren't usually intentional, and more rarely still were they clever. This, he had to admit, was both.

Christ's apostles, all of whom seemed to be members of Phi Delta Theta, argued with Big Pete at the door. Pete, towering a good six inches over the largest Phi Delt, was calmly shaking his head.

Jimmy came from behind the bar and worked his way through the Saturday night Carson Street crowd until he stood within talking distance of Pete and Christ's entourage.

The Fraternity brothers all wore ratty bathrobes with their Greek letters sharpied on them. Jesus's robe bore only the letters J.C., a foot high in bright red ink. Jimmy's smile almost burst into laughter when he saw the large plastic jars some of the brothers carried. Each emblazoned with slogans like "Buy a Round for

Christ" and "Jesus Loves You… and Beer". Damned if some of those jars weren't half full of dollar bills.

Jimmy put his hand on Pete's arm to get his attention, carefully maintaining a serious expression. A look of relief flashed across Pete's face at the sight of his boss. He leaned down to Jimmy's ear and bellowed to overcome the jukebox and those talking over it.

"The guy playing Christ? I read him for a hardcore wino. I think he might be trouble."

Jimmy took another look at Jesus, rendered beatific now by the glow of the neon Iron City and Bud signs filling the windows. Despite his striking resemblance to paintings hanging in Sunday schools across America, this Jesus was a bit ragged around the edges and needed a bath. Jimmy agreed with the wino assessment, but he knew a lot more about drinkers than Pete did. The would-be messiah's eyes burned with a thirst Jimmy recognized. No way these frat kids could afford enough booze to phase the man. Anyway, it would give the crowd a good story to tell their friends over their Sunday-morning hangovers.

He looked up at Pete as if considering for a moment, then gave a short jerk of his head toward the interior of the bar. Pete raised his palms in a "you're the boss" gesture and let the ersatz holy men through.

The bar erupted with laughter, jeers, and requests for absolution as the bathrobed group made their way into the packed interior. As chance would have it, a bachelorette party who had dominated the large round booth in the corner was vacating just in time for Wino Jesus and the Phi Delt apostles to commandeer the seats.

"Divine intervention," Jimmy muttered, and this time he did laugh. He slapped Pete on the back and pointed to the door. The two men made their way outside to the slightly less noisy sidewalk. Jimmy pulled a mentholated Kool from the pack in his shirt pocket and lit up. He had started smoking Kools a few months after the cancer took Helen. A fill-in bartender informed him only 'chicks and black dudes' smoked menthols, but Big Pete understood.

"When I smell those things, I think she's going to come around the corner yelling somebody puked in the crapper," he'd said.

That was Helen: the smell of menthol and White Shoulders perfume, and the voice of a drill sergeant. The Kools tasted pretty foul, but after two years they still brought her back to Jimmy. Besides, it was natural to tear up when you had smoke in your eyes.

"Good crowd, boss," Pete said, but both his and Jimmy's eyes were on the line of people waiting to get into the bar across the street. Since "Nectar" had opened a month ago, with its three dance floors and two-story-tall neon flowers, that long line had become a regular feature of the landscape. "Freakin dance clubs," Pete growled. "Places like that never last."

Jimmy knew Pete was only trying to keep him from worrying. Truth be told, Jimmy wasn't worried. Pete was absolutely right. Nectar wouldn't last.

"Regulars," Jimmy said around a puff of smoke. "That's what it's all about. And that neon nightmare over there won't ever have them." Jimmy closed his eyes and remembered similar words spoken by Helen a thousand years ago. The night Jimmy had asked her to marry him and had gotten more than he bargained for.

"It's all you have to do Jimmy," she had said. "Give them what they want, and they'll keep coming back."

Jimmy pulled his mind back to the present with an effort that got harder with each passing year. "Did I ever tell you about Lou Pamono?"

Pete shook his head.

Jimmy didn't know if he believed that, but he went on with the story. "Lou owned a bar over in Bloomfield. A little hole in the wall called…?" Jimmy paused for a few seconds, looking at Pete expectantly.

"Lou's?" Pete filled in.

"You got it first try, and people think big guys are dumb. Anyway, Lou, he's doing pretty well. So, he decides to open a second location over in Lawrenceville. Something a little bigger, with classier decor. A step up. He sets his brother-in-law up to run the place."

Jimmy paused while Pete checked the IDs on a group of women dressed in nearly identical white-blouse-and-black-miniskirt combos.

"Anyway, the new place goes over gangbusters for a couple of months and then tanks. Things get so bad Lou himself starts pulling shifts to see what the problem is. His brother-in-law is trying all the usual stuff: 10 cent wings, dollar drafts. But all he's really doing is giving away what little money they're making to the cheapskates who eat a few dozen wings and wash them down with water. The brother-in-law doesn't know what to do. Lou though, he'd been in the business for a while. He notices a small group of women down at one end of the bar. They ignore the wings and dollar drafts, and over a couple of hours lay down a good bit of cash on mixed drinks. A couple of nights later, they're back. Maybe a few different faces, but essentially the same group. Lou starts chatting them up. What're their favorite drinks? What kind of music should he put in the juke?

"Hey, Jimmy." The interrupting voice was annoying, cocky and went perfectly with the face of its owner.

Jimmy's own face changed from a raconteur's smile to a look of disappointment and resignation. "Hello, Todd,"

"I was wondering, Jimmy, about—you know what we talked about on the phone?"

Jimmy put a hand on the young man's shoulder. "Go in and get a couple of drinks in you. Don't worry about paying for them. You can help me wrestle in a few kegs later. Then we'll talk."

Todd didn't move. He looked ready to argue, but after a long pause sighed and walked into the bar instead.

Jimmy lit another Kool and stared into space. "Where was I?"

"Lou and the ladies," Pete said.

"Oh yeah. So, a week later the special is five-dollar Long Islands, and the jukebox has got more of a Melissa Etheridge vibe. The week after that, Lou notice's a couple of women dancing together. Not wasting time while their boyfriends get shit-faced—really dancing together. The brother-in-law throws a fit, but Lou's happy as a clam. You get what I'm saying, Pete?"

"You want to open a gay bar?"

"No, smart ass. Lou found his regulars. He found his regulars, gave them what they wanted, and now the man owns a big house in Fox Chapel and spends his winters in Florida like God intended."

"You sure you don't want to open a gay bar?"

Jimmy shook his head in mock resignation. "Regulars," he said again. "I got them, and I know what they want. Jimmy flicked his spent Kool at the neon flowers across the street. "They don't." He turned and walked back into Drake's.

The sight of the crowded bar brought a smile to Jimmy's lips. Sure, it meant good money, but it wasn't just that. A full bar has a beauty to it. That distinctive smell of beer, tobacco, cheap perfume, and pheromones. The ballet of the waitresses weaving through the crowd. Laughter and shouted conversations blending with whatever was pounding out of the jukebox. Jimmy wouldn't know a sonnet if it bit him on the ass, but he recognized the poetry of a place like this.

Jimmy scanned the crowd, reading the faces. He'd gotten good at it over the years. He could tell at a glance which patrons were there to have a good time and which were looking for bed partners. Helen had been the real expert. Jimmy could see basically what a person wanted. But Helen saw deeper. She saw the whys of the desire and the lengths they would go to fulfill them. She'd seen right away that Jimmy was the right man for her, and the right man to keep the family bar going.

Jimmy's eyes found Todd reflected in the mirror behind the bar. There was nothing in that face but a hunger for self-destruction, and a whole lot of 'poor pitiful me.' Jimmy looked from Todd to a beautiful but fragile-looking blonde smoking at the end of the bar. Maybe he could give Todd a push in her direction. Kid wakes up with an attractive woman, might make all the difference in the world. Build up his confidence a little. Give him someone to impress.

Jimmy shook his head. He couldn't afford to think that way. The kid had been spiraling down for the better part of a year. No one-night stand would resurrect him. Jimmy moved behind the bar. He checked the supplies and made a mental note to get a jar of maraschino cherries the next time he pulled a keg from the cave. Tammy, a carrot-topped woman with a Drake's t-shirt knotted at her midriff, asked she could change shifts on Halloween. Jimmy talked to her for a moment, then glad-handed his way down the bar.

"Jimmy," called a short, dark-skinned man in a porkpie hat. His voice had a rich warmth to it, even yelling above the crowd.

"Mr. Portaire," Jimmy called back. "How was the gig at the Jamestown?"

"I ain't gonna tell you. You'll just have to drag your broken-down ass to the next show."

"This place would collapse without me," Jimmy said. "Your next round's on me, by way of apology." Jimmy moved down the bar, greeting those he knew and thanking newcomers for dropping by. Finally, he reached Todd.

"Is that my best Irish whiskey you're drinking?" Jimmy eyed the nearly empty glass in front of the young man. "When you get a free drink, you go all out, don't you?"

Todd threw back the remains of the 16-year-old Bushmills as if he feared Jimmy would snatch the glass away from him. "No worries, Jimmy. I'm going to make you so much money you'll use this stuff for cleaning the shitter."

Jimmy sighed. Todd was an asshole. For a year he'd been coming in, filling Jimmy's ear with self-serving venom. To hear Todd tell it, nobody appreciated him. He'd be a big success, but someone always held him back. That someone seemed to be whoever had the bad judgment to get close to Todd. First, family, then friends, were cast off. Now the only person who listened was the guy tending bar. *That's me,* Jimmy thought to himself. *Therapist to the common man. Last friend to the losers of the world.* Sure, Todd was an asshole, but there were worse things than being an asshole. Jimmy thought about the Bushmills. You couldn't deny the kid had balls.

"That club across the street is killing you," Todd said. "This dive can't compete. Sure, you're busy on Saturday nights, but one busy night won't pay the bills. You need me."

Jimmy had almost felt sorry for the little shit. "You are absolutely right, Todd. I need you."

Todd smiled. "Just give me a place to keep my stash, maybe down with the kegs. I bet once word gets out, we'll be pulling in a couple thousand a night."

"Shut up, Todd, Jimmy said. "We can't talk here."

A scream suddenly rose above the bar noise. Jesus stood on a table, robe flung wide, urinating on the apostles and the few young women who had joined them.

Jimmy looked toward the door to make sure Pete was earning his paycheck. Sure enough, the big man was pushing his way through the frozen crowd.

"I baptize you in the name of the Father! And Me! And the Holy Ghost!" screamed Jesus as he spun like a blasphemous lawn sprinkler around the table.

By the time Pete reached the scene, the waterworks had subsided. Jimmy thought he probably timed it that way. Before Pete could do anything, Jesus snapped to attention and adjusted his robe. He turned to Pete and extended his hand as gracefully as Cinderella waiting for a footman. Pete took the proffered hand and helped Jesus down.

A dripping Phi Delt crawled out from under the table with murder in his eye, but Pete froze him with a glare. All eyes watched as Jesus slowly walked toward the entrance. One hand still clasping Pete's the other extended in benediction to the crowd.

"Head down to the cave," Jimmy growled in Todd's ear. "I'll be down in a few minutes." Jimmy extended the bottle of Bushmills toward Todd. "Take this."

Todd took the bottle and headed for the stairs.

Jimmy walked over to where the apostles were talking loudly about kicking Jesus's ass. He calmed them down. Twenty minutes later, the former Apostles had exchanged their robes for complimentary Drake's T-shirts and were spending what was left in their donation jars.

Jimmy grabbed some rubber gloves and cleaned up Jesus's booth. He could have made someone else do it. But it helped morale if the boss did the shit work sometimes. He hadn't forgotten Todd but was pretty sure everyone else had. If they'd noticed him at all. Jimmy stashed the cleaning supplies behind the bar, checked the cooler, and headed down to the cave. He lit a Kool as he descended the stairs, and his mind followed the smoke back to the beginning.

"So, you want to marry me, Jimmy?" Helen had asked. "Is it me you want, or my bar? I can't tell which you love more."

"Can't I have you both?"

Helen's eyes burned into his, judging him. She smiled and lit a cigarette. "Its hard work Jimmy. Being married *and* running a bar. You have to make sacrifices." Then she led him down these same stone steps and showed him what she meant.

In the present, Jimmy pushed through the heavy metal door at the bottom of the stairs and into the cave. Stacked kegs filled most of one side. Opposite, ran a long row of metal shelving, bulging with institutional-sized containers of drink mixes, garnishes, and cleaning supplies. A narrow path ran between them to where another set of pitted stone steps led up to steel cellar doors. Todd sat on those steps, clutching the bottle of Bushmills.

"I thought you were going to be right behind me. I've been freezing my ass off down here."

"You had the whiskey to keep you warm."

"Are we going to talk now?" Todd stood a bit shakily and pulled a large, unlabelled prescription bottle from inside his ratty trench coat. "I figure on moving mostly party stuff. X, some speed." He rattled the bottle's contents for emphasis. "Nothing to dampen the mood."

Jimmy held out his hands in a catcher's position, and Todd tossed him the bottle. He held it in the light of the compact fluorescents and struggled with the lid. "Freakin' childproof."

"Let me get it," Todd offered. "Shit!"

Blue gel tabs spilled through Jimmy's hands. Todd dove for the floor snatching at them as more poured down like pharmaceutical rain.

"Jesus Christ, Jimmy. These things are expensive!"

Jimmy wasn't listening. This next part had been Helen's job. He'd seen her do it so many times it played tricks on his mind. He reached his age-spotted hand behind the big can of olives, but saw Helen's smooth white fingers come out grasping the syringe. Was he leaning over Todd or was this that first man? The salesman from Ohio Helen had promised a good time?

Todd, engrossed in saving as many of the pills as possible, only looked up as the green plastic sleeve of the syringe fell among them. He tried to jerk away, but Jimmy stood too close.

Jimmy watched the needle slide into flesh—Todd's flesh, the fat neck of the salesman. So many others he'd lost count.

"It's not easy. You have to make sacrifices," Helen said as the needle slid home. She was almost with him now. Here, with the smell of fear, and cigarette smoke, and the needle.

"Give them what they want, and they'll keep coming back." And suddenly she *was* with him. Jimmy was young, in love, and standing over a fat salesman who stank of sweat and arousal, still hoping for his "good time." And as Helen pushed the plunger down, she smiled.

Jimmy saw her smile and a scream had welled up inside him. He shoved that scream somewhere deep and kept it there. Just like Helen knew he would. She had looked into Jimmy's eyes and judged him. She'd known his desires and the lengths he'd go to achieve them. Father Ryan married them two months later, but the real wedding had been that night, with a doomed salesman officiating and a syringe as token.

Jimmy blinked and shook himself. Todd lay unconscious on the stone floor by a keg of Yuengling. *Methohexital works fast,* he thought, and Todd wasn't a big guy.

Jimmy dragged the unconscious man behind the kegs. He stepped back to the shelves scanning them until he found the duct tape. After wrapping Todd's hands, feet, and mouth, he started the cleanup. He groaned as he crawled around on all fours gathering up all the little blue pills, but he couldn't leave the floor covered in X—or whatever Todd said the shit was.

Jimmy shoved the refilled pill bottle and the syringe into one of the pockets of Todd's trench coat. He looked around the room and satisfied, headed back up the stairs. Halfway up, he shook his head and trudged back into the cave. "Almost forgot the damned cherries." A few minutes later he stood at the bar, restocking garnishes and filling pitchers.

The rest of the night was a wash, business-wise. People might laugh about the Jesus incident later. But the son of God urinating on people seemed to have driven out a lot of the patrons. Or maybe it was just the ebb and flow of the crowd. Jimmy didn't care. He was tired and still had a long night ahead of him.

Last call came eventually. Jimmy rang the bell and turned up the fluorescent lights. The last few patrons blinked stupidly at each other and sized up their chances.

The fragile blonde still sat at the end of the bar smoking one last cigarette. Jimmy gave her a smile. He walked over to Pete and took the broom out of his ham-sized fist. "Why don't you offer to walk her home? It's late, and I think you could both use the company."

Pete looked at the blonde then back to Jimmy. "You sure you don't need a hand closing out?"

"Nah, tomorrow's Sunday. I can always finish up in the morning if I need to."

Pete glanced again at the woman. She smiled at him. "Thanks, Jimmy," he said and walked over to the bar.

Alone, at last, Jimmy threw down the towel he'd been half-heartedly wiping the bar with and pulled the heavy black shades down over the windows. His knees still ached from crawling around the floor of the cave. Jimmy wanted to go home to bed. He wanted to cut the duct tape off Todd and dump his doped ass in an alley somewhere. He wanted Helen back.

But running a bar isn't easy, He pulled a cardboard box from beneath the bar and looked at the masks inside. They'd started as burlap sacks with holes punched in them for eyes Over the years, though, Helen had decorated them. Some sequins here, a brightly-colored patch there. Quite a few even had wigs sewn on. Some people might call the things folk art. He added a bottle of Jepson brandy and a heavy tumbler to the box's contents.

Jimmy placed the box beside an industrial-sized garbage can, outside the rear entrance. The back alley was empty, and the night as silent as the city ever got. Jimmy set the tumbler in the center of the alley and filled it halfway to the top with brandy. He touched a lit match to the spirits and stood. Shadows jittered madly on the pitted brick walls. They would be here soon. Jimmy felt the scream he'd swallowed thirty years ago lurch in his gut. He went back in the bar.

Todd couldn't have weighed more than 120 pounds even in his trench coat, but Jimmy had to stop twice to catch his breath as he hauled him up the stairs. Finally, heart pounding, he levered the unconscious form onto the pool table.

"Goddammit, I'm only fifty-five," Jimmy gasped. He took out a tiny Swiss army knife and cut through the duct tape.

Todd moaned a little as the tape peeled from his mouth. Jimmy wasn't worried. After thirty years of this routine, he was practically an anesthesiologist. Todd wouldn't be up for at least another fifteen minutes, and by then it wouldn't matter.

"It's okay, Todd. You just sleep it off."

Todd obediently rolled onto his side and snored. Jimmy lit up a Kool. He heard the rear door opening and looked down at the bar floor. He still wanted to look at them. See how the mask with the red wig and the sequins looked on a real person. But that wasn't the way they wanted it.

Helen had explained. "You keep your eyes down. They see us. They know who we are. Not the other way around. It's a respect thing." So, Jimmy watched the shoes. Wingtips, sneakers, high-heeled pumps. He watched them pass as they gathered around the pool table. A pair of tan and white saddle shoes stopped in front of him. Manicured hands held out a paper bag. Jimmy felt the familiar shapes inside. Thick rubber-banded bundles of fifties. Beneath those, more syringes and another bottle of Methohexital.

The scream clawed at his gut again. Jimmy clamped down on it. The saddle shoes moved on. Jimmy turned and walked toward the stairs. He paused at the top. Voices rose behind him, murmuring, almost singing. Soon, they were joined by a background chorus of soft wet burstings, like thick sauce coming to a boil.

For thirty years, Jimmy's mind had created grotesque images to accompany those sounds, but he had never once looked back. One glance would have replaced his nightmare visions with the truth, and the truth might be worse.

Instead, Jimmy started down the stairs. He lit another cigarette as he went, frantically drawing in the smoke. Trying to get to Helen. As he reached the door, he could hear Todd scream, high and piercing, providing a staccato counterpoint to the murmured song.

Jimmy stepped into the keg cave and slammed the big door behind him. Todd's cry still echoed in his mind. He crossed the room in three strides and picked up the half-empty bottle of Bushmills. The whiskey burned through him.

Jimmy wasn't a good man. He knew that. The money, the bar, Helen. He'd wanted them all and done what it took to get them. But it was Helen most of all. The warm weight of her body beside him, keeping the scream tamped down all those years. Now she was gone, and Jimmy did not want to give those things what they wanted anymore. He opened his mouth, but the scream wouldn't come.

Jimmy sat on the steps and cried. He cried because what little virtue he possessed was, and had always been, eclipsed by a much larger supply of cowardice. He'd go upstairs soon. The bar would be empty. He'd spend a few fruitless minutes looking for some trace of Todd but would find none. The masks would go back in their box. The money and syringes in the office safe. In a few months, he'd choose someone else. Maybe that fragile, lonely blonde. It didn't really matter. He would do it all again.

Jimmy took out a fresh cigarette and lit it from the still glowing butt of the last one. He knew the Kools couldn't really bring Helen back. But if he smoked enough of the damn things, maybe cancer would reunite them in whatever Hell God reserved for people like them. Jimmy gazed through the rising smoke and prayed he wasn't there already.

OVERNIGHT HOME COMPANION

POSITION: Overnight home companion for shut in. Must be able to read. Lack of imagination a plus.

Salary: 250 dollars a night. I've never seen who pays. But the cash is there every morning at sunrise. A brown paper bag in the mailbox, twenties and tens. Good money, right? But I need to explain some things. I don't want you coming in blind like I did.

Pros: No adult diapers to change. In fact, you'll never even see Mrs. Hendricks. I've been doing this for three months and the only reason I know her name is it's written on the letters on the kitchen table. There's an old dirty curtain hanging across the back half of the bedroom. I imagine Mrs. H. behind it, all tucked in beneath her covers. I've never looked though. YOU DON'T LOOK BEHIND THE CURTAIN.

Cons: *Patti Puddleduck's Play Date.* It's a kid's books. Illustrations so cute they're creepy. The book is on the chair when you get there. Cute story. Patti Puddleduck has a picnic, invites all her friends—Betty Blackbird, Reggie Rabbit, Freddie Fishfin. You get the idea. Reading the book is the gig. Seriously. Most of the time what's behind the curtain (Mrs. H. I mean) is quiet. But when you hear a noise you pick up *Patti Puddleduck's Playdate* and you read aloud. Usually the noise will stop right then. But I read it all the way through a couple times just to cover my ass.

When the noise doesn't stop—wet sounds now, dragging sounds —read louder. When the curtain ripples as if in the grip of a cold breeze, you turn your back to the curtain and read louder. When the wind rises and the curtain snaps like a flag in a gale, YOU DO NOT TURN AROUND. You shout out how Reggie Rabbit made carrot cake for the picnic, because of course he did.

And when the wind stops, replaced by a hot breath against the back of your neck, read loudest of all and pray if you know how. When it's completely quiet. No breath. No wind. Not even the rustling noise of an old lady adjusting her blankets. Then you can turn back around.

I thought about quitting. I have enough cash to get a car. Maybe head out west. But during the day, when I sleep, I have dreams. In the dreams, I pull the curtain back. Did you know that's the definition of apocalypse, to pull aside the curtain? I can't quite remember what I see in those dreams, But I wake up crying and reciting lines from *Patti Puddleduck's Playdate*. I only know it's something vast with too many eyes. Eyes that are also mouths.

I don't believe I can quit. But I can't go on either, not without a few nights off. Which is where you come in. The money's good for just staying up late and reading. Like I said, lack of imagination is a plus.

DECORATION

THE BLOODY HEAD squelched as Hank forced it onto the pike. He gave it an appraising look. Gruesome enough, but balance was important too. "Hmm, I wish there was someone to hold this up for me."

Voices erupted from behind him. Hank turned to the gaggle of adolescents staring wide-eyed at his house.

"Okay, so who wants to help?"

Hands shot up. He settled on Freddy, a skinny eleven-year-old, almost skeletal enough to pass for a Halloween decoration himself. Hank handed him the pike and stepped back to the sidewalk. Freddy held the gruesome prop and beamed with pride.

"Oh my God." Freddy's Mother joined the group. She was a pretty woman, with high cheekbones and eyes that sparkled with humor. She'd gotten divorced about the same time as Hank, but seemed to handle it better.

"Hey, Dianne. You okay with your boy helping out?"

She grinned. "Of course. He loves it. But honestly Hank, I don't know how you do it. This stuff gives me the willies."

"That's the idea," Hank said. "Right kids?" The children cheered in affirmation.

Hank looked at the pike. "Could you lean it a little to the left, Freddy? Yeah… right there." He had to admit it was a pretty scary effect.

"You know, you got some competition this year," said Dianne.

"Who, Pete Williams down on Maple? He's mostly into hay bales and happy scarecrows."

"No, a new guy over on Beaumont Street—the house that backs on to the ravine. It's not like what you do. It's hard to describe, but the effect is really spooky."

Within moments, the crowd of children launched an expedition to this exciting new wonder.

Hank took pity on Freddy. He took the pike and shoved it into the earth. "Catch up with your friends."

Dianne watched her son jog down the street. "Whatever happened to loyalty?"

Hank laughed. "Can't blame them for being curious. You got time for a drink? I got a little red wine, or maybe one of my pumpkin beers. If you're in a seasonal mood."

"Thanks, but I need to get dinner ready." She looked back at Hank's home and gave him an encouraging nod. "It looks good —scary, I mean."

Hank took in his handiwork: foam core tombstones, rotting hands thrusting from faux graves. It was good. Fog machines, strobe lights. He even had a flying ghoul that would moan as it swooped back and forth over the trick or treaters. It was going to be a banner year. So why did everything seem a little tawdry?

Because Dianne said he had some competition? "It's only Halloween decorations," he said to himself. But a cold lump filled Hank's stomach. *Maybe I'll take a walk after dinner,* he thought. *Check things out for myself.*

Nine o'clock found Hank on Beaumont Street, a four pack of pumpkin ale in his hand. He recognized the house, a red brick two-story with a tiny front porch. It had a big yard. A rarity for homes this close to Pittsburgh, but the front lawn had always been choked with shrubs and brambles.

The new owner had manicured the dense growth into a fairyland maze. Narrow paths lead off into tunnels of greenery. A pyramid of jack-o'-lanterns blocked the central sidewalk leading to the front door. Trick or treaters would have to take one of the paths.

Hank stepped on to the nearest one. It was dark, and after a few feet, he felt claustrophobic. His head bumped into something hard hanging from a branch. "Dammit," he muttered. This wasn't scary, just dangerous.

"Hello." A voice came from the house. "Is someone there?"

Hank felt guilty, then angry at himself for the feeling. "Hey, sorry to bother you, I was just dropping by to say welcome to the neighborhood."

"Let me find the switch." The voice sounded friendly. "I'm the one who needs to apologize. I didn't make it easy to navigate out there."

Above Hank, a constellation of glass balls—blue, green, yellow—flickered into life. The light was gentle, not so much banishing the darkness as sculpting it, shaping the shadows into something beautiful. The flagstones making up the path were etched with complex patterns. Hank recognized a few shapes he'd seen on heavy metal t-shirts. The rest looked like bizarre geometry diagrams. Tiny jack-o'-lanterns lined the path's edges.

It should have all been too pretty to be frightening, but Hank felt that tingly frisson at the base of his spine. It was the faces staring out at him from the foliage. They were placed perfectly, far enough away so at first you barely noticed. Then, as you concentrated, the horrible details came into focus. Hank reached past dark leaves to touch a hollow-eyed mask made of stiffened cloth. Below and to the left, a stone carving jutted out its rocky tongue in an obscene leer. There were more, each horrible in its own way.

"Over here."

Hank followed the voice. The twisting path finally led back to the old central sidewalk. The glass balls hung like clusters of grapes all around him. More faces peered from the foliage. Hank felt overwhelmed with emotions, the foremost of them being jealousy. This was no cheap thrill. It was an experience.

A thin man in a tweed vest and matching pants stood on the porch, smiling. He had close-clipped blonde hair streaked with gray at the temples and wore round wire-rimmed glasses. He held a mug of tea in one large hand.

Hank swallowed his unkind feelings and attempted a smile of his own. "Wow, this is something." He stepped up on the porch and shook the hand extended to him.

"I'm Elliot Greer," the man said. His grip was firm. Cords of lean muscle standing out on his forearm. "So, you appreciate my little hobby?" He gestured at the display in the yard.

"Oh yeah," Hank said. "I do some Halloween decorating myself. My house is in the paper most years. Maybe you saw my place. It's over on Greenmount?"

"I'm afraid not. I've been so busy moving in and getting all this set up. I haven't had much time to get to know the neighborhood."

"Well, mine's a bit more gruesome. Bloody skulls, zombies. The kids love it. Yours seems almost Christmassy."

Greer stepped from the porch. He stroked the side of a blue globe filled with thin strands of stretched glass. "Actually, these are quite à propos of the season. They're called witch balls. The idea is that evil spirits become so fascinated by their beauty they trap themselves inside. A handy thing to have around Halloween."

Smartass, Hank thought. *Stop it. You barely know the guy.* "Witch balls, huh? Still, a little pretty for my tastes. What I really like are the masks and sculptures. Creepy as hell."

Greer nodded.

"Where'd you get them anyway? I hit all the stores: Target, Wal Mart, Halloween World. You got a source online?"

"Africa."

"What?"

"Most, I acquired in Africa, some from South America, and the Subcontinent. You can still find interesting work in the Mid-East, but a lot's been destroyed in the name of religion.

"Sure," said Hank, nodding. "I guess I won't look for them on eBay then, huh?"

"No, I suppose not," said Greer. "But I'm probably boring you. Once I start going on about my collection…"

No, you're embarrassed for me, thought Hank. He stared down at his shoes and remembered the beer. *I should just take it home, but he probably saw it already.* "Hey, I brought over a welcome gift." Hank held up the four pack. "Pumpkin Ale. It's good stuff."

Greer didn't reach for the gift. He gave Hank a pained smile. "It sounds intriguing, but I'm on a special diet. Rather hideous really, mostly leaves and sticks I'm afraid." He held out the steaming china mug toward Hank. "Believe me, I'd prefer a good ale."

The stuff smelled rank. "Are those ashes floating in there?"

Greer looked sheepish. "Yes. It's burnt joss paper, an Asian thing. My diet is more folkway than medical prescription. When you collect the esoteric, you pick up a few odd beliefs along the way." He lifted the cup to his lips and sipped. "You wouldn't like it."

"I'll stick to beer," said Hank.

"Maybe I could try one in the future?"

Hank took the words as a welcome chance to escape. "Sure. I better get going. More work to do on my place. Halloween is coming fast."

"I'm well aware," said Greer. "I look forward to seeing your... decorations."

Maybe he imagined it, but Hank thought he heard derision in those words. "Hey, before I go, I was wondering, aren't you a little worried?"

"What do you mean?"

"All those kids tramping through your yard, right down the middle of your *collection*. Things might get damaged."

Greer looked thoughtful. His eyes darted from one part of the yard to another. "I believe I have enough."

It was an odd response, Hank thought. "Some of the older kids like to do a little mayhem on purpose. I got four words for you:

full-sized candy bars. None of those baby pretzel bags. You keep the little monsters happy, and you should be okay."

Greer nodded. "Thanks for the advice. Happy Halloween."

"Happy Halloween," said Hank. He walked out the way he'd come. No sooner had he stepped onto the street then Greer's yard went dark again. Hank could still see the witch balls and half hidden faces in his mind's eye. He had to admit Greer's collection was amazing, and that it pissed him off. *I don't get one thing that I can be the best at?* He popped the top on one of the pumpkin ales and took a long sip.

So, who's the bigger asshole? he wondered. *Greer for being so pompous, or me for being jealous?* He turned and walked home. Maybe he'd pick up an extra fog machine tomorrow.

Hank opened the Halloween edition of the *Collier Run Daily* and stared at a photo of Elliot Greer surrounded by glowing witch balls. "No big deal," Hank said to the empty kitchen. "I've been in the paper plenty of times." It was Halloween, Hank's favorite day of the year, and he was determined not to let Greer ruin it for him.

The weather that night was perfect, chilly but not cold, with enough breeze to blow the leaves around. Hank wore a vintage Pittsburgh Pirates uniform. He usually opted for something horrific, but last year Dianne had come over and sat with him on the porch. Hank figured she might have sat a good deal closer if his shirt hadn't been soaked in stage blood.

Jack-o'-lanterns glowed from front porches up and down the street. Hank opened a pumpkin ale, switched on the fog machines, and waited for the monsters. At first, things went great. Ghost and goblins traipsed up the steps, awestruck by

Hank's handiwork. Parents oohed and ahhed like always, but this year there was a difference.

"Wow, you really outdid yourself, Hank."

"Thanks, it's a labor of love."

Then came the kicker. "Did you see that place over on Beaumont?"

Not everyone brought up Greer's amazing decorations. But enough did that Hank turned those mentions into his own sad little drinking game, taking a deep swig of beer every time Greer's collection came up.

The second fog machine had been a bad idea. A thick mist covered the porch steps. A tiny Luke Skywalker slipped and cracked his shin on the cement. His mother—Princess Leia gone to seed—rushed up the stairs and helped the boy up. She glared at Hank, ignoring the chocolate bar in his hand.

"Your house is a menace," she hissed.

"Oh come on, Luke there can't be more than two. You should be holding his hand." Hank regretted the words as soon as he said them. Too much beer, he thought.

"Screw you," Leia said. She picked up the weeping Jedi and stalked down the street. Hank tried to turn off the fog machine but couldn't find the right cord in all the mist. He finally unplugged the whole power strip. The mist cleared, but when he turned the juice back on, neither fog machine would work. Worse yet, the flying ghoul got tangled in its own wires and spent the rest of the night spinning in place, making a noise like a sick sheep. Hank didn't bother unplugging it.

He drank more and blamed Elliott Greer.

Dianne walked over around nine. She looked up at the bleating ghoul. "Are we experiencing some technical difficulties?"

"You could say that. It's not been the best evening."

"At least we have candy," Dianne held out a handful of fun size snickers.

Maybe the night didn't have to end badly, Hank thought. He made room for her on the porch step. An empty beer bottled wobbled beside him. He tried to steady it but misjudged the distance and sent it tumbling down the steps. The bottle shattered with a crash. Hank's lunge almost sent him tumbling after it, but Dianne caught his arm.

"Goddammit, this just isn't my night."

Dianne looked at the collection of empty bottles. "Maybe we should have a little coffee with our candy."

"Or *maybe*, I can drink what I want to on my own porch."

Dianne's warm smile froze.

"Oh Jesus Di, I'm sorry. It's just the fog machines broke down, and that stupid flying ghoul got hung up. The damned thing cost me a hundred bucks."

"So, you got drunk because your toys didn't work. Makes sense."

"Dianne, really. I apologize. I'll make that coffee."

"No. Your porch, your rules. Have another beer. I'm going home."

"Come on. Don't be like that."

Dianne walked down the stairs, stepping carefully over the broken glass. "Happy Halloween, Hank."

Hank watched her go. She was right. He was acting like a baby. "I think I'll get that coffee." He stood up and walked to the door. As he turned the knob, laughter rent the night and an egg burst against the wall inches from his head.

Hank flung himself inside and pulled his home-security baseball bat out of the umbrella stand. He rushed back on to the porch, scanning the streets for attackers. A block away, dark laughing shapes disappeared between two houses.

Hank shook his head. What the hell was he going to do, send some teenager to the hospital for throwing an egg? Besides, there'd been at least four shapes, and they hadn't looked small. Like he'd told Greer, the bigger kids could get up to some real mayhem on Halloween. Hank let that thought linger for a minute.

Maybe one more beer after all and a walk. Probably should take the bat along. Never can tell what you might run into.

Beaumont street was dark. It was after eleven, and most folks had blown out their pumpkins and gone to bed. Only the Greer residence still glowed with the light of witch balls and jack-o'-lanterns.

I wouldn't have bought that second fog machine if it hadn't been for Greer. Wouldn't have drunk so much either. I'd be sitting with Dianne right now. Hank knew it was all bullshit, but alcohol and jealousy were more than a match for his common sense.

He looked up and down the street. He'd changed into dark sweats, hoping to look like just another teenager to anyone gazing out their window. He held the bat close to his leg and stepped onto the nearest path. Even through his drunken anger, he still couldn't deny Greer's collection was amazing. The realization only pissed him off more.

He brought the bat up to his shoulder and swung. If he'd had a plan at all, it had been to smash a couple of the, no doubt expensive, witch balls and run. Go home and let the thought of Greer sweeping up bits of his precious collection tomorrow lull him to sleep. Something changed as Hank shattered his first target. Colored glass rained down, and Hank's heart filled with a fierce joy.

"Pretentious little shit," he grunted, as he swung the bat in short, vicious arcs. He wasn't running away. The plan was forgotten. Hank pushed forward, stomping jack-o'-lanterns to orange pulp, kicking over sculptures Greer had *acquired* on the god-damned subcontinent. It wasn't about the decorations anymore. It was about the divorce. His wife living with that banker in Harrisburg. It was about being two months late on the mortgage. It was every failure and indignity Hank had ever suffered in a life full of them. He knew it wasn't Greer's fault and didn't care. He had a target now, and he couldn't stop if he wanted.

Someone shouted. Arms like cables locked themselves around Hank's neck. He tried to swing the bat, but his arms didn't want to work anymore. Hank felt himself lifted and thrown. He landed hard on wood. Blood rushed to his brain. The first thing he saw was Elliot Greer, his back turned, staring up at a blue-green ball of glass. Hank didn't see any others. *Did I smash them all? Jesus.*

The second thing Hank noticed was the pistol in Greer's hand.

Greer turned. His face red with rage. He didn't raise the gun.

"Who sent you?"

Hank stared up at the man. Not understanding the question and afraid whatever he said would be wrong.

"Xiǎnshì zìjǐ, datgelu eich hunan, Arată-te?" Greer moved closer, shouting more indecipherable questions at Hank with each step.

"Please, I don't understand," Hank said. "I'm sorry, just don't shoot."

Greer looked down at the gun, seeming almost surprised to see it there. "Who are you?" he asked.

"What?" Fear still burned bright, but another emotion mixed with it. Hank was insulted. "Hank Swafford, I live on Greenmount. I came over with beer."

"Hank? The Halloween-decoration guy."

There it was again—*decoration*. "Why do you have to say it that way? It's my thing. I'm good at it. I used to be the best, at least around here." Anger gave Hank the strength to sit up. He still held the bat. "Then you showed up with your masks and god damned witch balls." He used the bat as a crutch and was almost upright when Greer gave him a vicious kick in the ribs. Hank toppled, gasping for breath.

Another kick sent the bat into the yard. Greer stood over Hank, and now the gun was most definitely being aimed. "You destroyed my defenses because I upstaged your paper-mâché tombstones. What is wrong with you?"

The black hole of the gun barrel filled Hank's vision. "Jesus, I'll pay for it all. Have me arrested. I deserve it."

"Stand up." Greer looked down at his wristwatch, then out into the yard. "I said stand up."

"No. Call the police. I'll just wait here." The last of Hank's beer-fueled haze had burned away. Greer was going to kill him. "This doesn't have to get any worse."

Greer rubbed a hand across his face. "Oh, I'm afraid it does. Now, stand up."

Hank didn't move.

"I'm not going to kill you, but I will wound you in some very nasty places if you don't stand up right now."

Hank stood.

Greer gestured to a rocking chair on the porch. "Sit down. There's a cup of tea on the table beside you. Drink it.

Hank lifted the cup. He recognized the foul smell from the first time he'd been here. "What's in it?"

"Burnt paper, remember? Some herbs. It gives perspective. Now, drink it, or I'll put a bullet in your crotch."

Hank put the cup to his lips and drank. It tasted better than it smelled, like smoked wine.

"That wasn't so bad, was it? Finish up."

Hank lifted the cup and drained it. He looked past Greer to the one remaining witch ball. The light it gave off took substance. Glowing geometric shapes spread out from the ball in all directions—spheres within cubes joining and releasing to form new and more complex patterns. "You drugged me," Hank said.

"No, just a little Taoist magic. Gives you yin-yang eyes. Let's you see what others can't."

There was no darkness. Hank saw the world with a clarity that came close to overwhelming him—the grain of the boards that made up the porch, the soft inner glow of the atomic processes that held it all together.

"I can see... everything."

"Yes, it's not something you'll thank me for. Now listen to me. You have no idea what you've done, so I'm going to tell you. I'm a thief Hank, but not some simple smash and grab man. I started with tombs, and I learned things. I learned you can steal secrets more valuable than gold."

"What's that noise?" Hank asked. It was far away but distinctive

—the electric whine of cicadas as interpreted by a children's choir.

"Ignore it."

"Something's coming." Hank stood despite the gun. He couldn't help himself. This must be the way prey felt when the big carnivores showed up. He had to get out of there. The side of the pistol whipped against Hank's jaw. Greer pushed him back on to the rocker.

"Don't worry, we have a little time yet."

Hank wiped blood from the corner of his mouth. He didn't try to stand again.

"I was a very successful thief," Greer said. "I plundered temples, even robbed a god or two."

"You're crazy." But Hank's voice lacked conviction. And his ears buzzed with the whine of cicadas.

"Made some enemies along the way, as you'd expect. A bad lot. But I had my secrets. Knew how to keep a few steps ahead. That's the key. Keep moving. Boats are good. They don't like running water. Flying's even better. There are rules to the game though, and one night a year I have to sit tight on solid ground. Do you see where I'm going with this, Hank? Can you guess what that night is?" Here's a hint. It's a time of year when you like to decorate, and it's not Christmas."

"Halloween?"

"I knew you could do it." Greer was shouting now, the gun pointed up at the night sky. Hank lunged past the man toward the sidewalk. Greer laughed. He kicked the back of Hank's knee, sending him sprawling. Hank tried to crawl. Glass from shattered witch balls gouged his hands and knees. A foot slammed into his crotch from behind, and he fell to his belly and retched.

"Just a few more words, Hank." Greer squatted and lifted Hank's chin until they were gazing eye to eye. "So, how do I keep my enemies at bay on that one night? Not guns, Hank. Bullets wouldn't phase them a bit, I'm afraid. But I had my defenses. I was always ready this year, too. I rented a new place in middle-of-nowhere Pennsylvania. There's a creek behind the house. Like I said, they don't like running water. I put up my defenses in front, a maze of distractions, wards, and traps. The only thing I didn't account for was you."

Greer shook his head. "You and your pathetic decorations. The good news is I can still get away. It's going to be tricky. I'll need your help. I think that you owe me at least that much."

"What do want me to do?"

"Only to be here. I have to stay a little longer. Let them feel my presence. Thanks to you, I'm forced to leave everything behind. No baggage. It's the only way I'll stay ahead of them. Even traveling light, they'd still catch me. That's where you come in, Hank. You're my diversion. Someone they can take their anger out on when they discover I'm gone. The time it takes them to rip your soul apart will be my head start. I think you'll agree that's fair."

Greer cocked the pistol. He looked at his watch, then sniffed the air. The wind bore the smell of ozone mixed with raw sewage. "It's time," said Greer. "Look at me. You told me liked things on the gory side."

Greer shoved the barrel of the gun beneath his own chin and pulled the trigger. The report was muffled, but the results were spectacular. A geyser of blood, bone, and brain erupted from the top of Greer's skull. But Hank had yin-yang eyes now, and he saw more. Amidst the viscera rose a living light, the soul of Elliot

Greer. It circled the remaining witch ball twice and then shot upward through the trees.

Greer's corpse—the baggage he had to leave behind—toppled to the ground.

Now the things hunting the man would come and take their disappointment out on Hank. He could hear the creatures advance, smell their stench on the wind.

Hank rushed to the front door. He wouldn't be anyone's diversion. Greer had said the creek behind the house offered some protection. He would go there. The door was locked. Hank slammed his shoulder into the thick wood, but it didn't budge.

An icy chill struck Hank like a blow. The electric cicada whine rose into a howling storm. Hank turned. Something dark rushed up the pathway toward him. The yin-yang eyes had revealed the inner light that filled all things. The creature approaching had no light. It was a void clawing its way through reality to get to the enemy it sought. Hank pressed himself against the door. He was going to die. No, it would be worse than that. His stupidity had brought Hank to the notice of creatures who considered death only the opening act.

The thing stopped. Hank didn't dare move. Didn't breathe. The void scudded toward the last glowing witch ball, weaving through the complex geometry of light the ball gave off. The creature circled the witch ball once, twice, then flowed inside it. There was a whistling sound. The sphere glowed white, then faded to a dull black.

The god damn balls work, Hank thought, and cursed himself for taking a bat to them. There was time now. He'd circle the house to the creek. He made it three steps before they found him. Creatures filled the yard. More of the clawing voids, but other things as well. A cloud of metallic white butterflies, each wing edge a razor that rang against its neighbor, filling the air with the sound of bells. A giant man, naked and grotesquely obese, dragged himself forward. Clawed children hung from his mountain of flesh, tearing away bloody mouthfuls and smacking their lips.

"Greer's dead," Hank yelled. The things in the yard didn't care. Elliot Greer would get his head start. As the creatures pressed forward, Hank had to admit it was a really scary effect.

LIVE FROM THE END OF THE WORLD

Highway 28 vanished and reappeared as the windshield wipers fought a losing battle against Hurricane Francis. This storm was Harriet's big chance. She only hoped she'd live through it. The news van hydroplaned for a heart sickening moment, then the tires caught asphalt again. "Maybe this wasn't my best idea."

Greg, Harriet's cameraman, sat hunkered low behind the van's steering wheel, eyes slitted, chin jutting forward in concentration. He shook his head. "You wanted to be in front of the camera. Now you will be. Though I still don't know why. *Behind* the camera is where the action is, and you're good at it."

"Everybody needs a dream, Greg." Harriet had started working for WRBC a year ago, her communications degree still warm. She rose rapidly from intern to assistant producer. Her coverage of the Hansen High Lunch Lady Strike was even up for a Murrow Award. But they never put her in front of the camera. And despite her achievements behind the scenes, in front of that camera was where she wanted to be.

When other girls were dancing around their rooms singing Katie Perry songs, Harriet had read news articles into a hairbrush-microphone in her best anchorwoman's voice. Strong and confident, speaking truth to a world hungry for answers. She'd never lost that little girl's dream, but desire and good elocution weren't enough, at least not for the management of WRBC. You had to look the part. At almost six feet tall, with thick features and hair that frizzed at the barest hint of humidity, Harriet did not.

Then came Hurricane Francis. Standing in gale-force wind and rain was the one on-air opportunity no one wanted. No one but Harriet Connors.

The wipers swished, and suddenly they were out of the rain. A battering gust of wind reminded them this was still a hurricane, but at least they could see now. Dare Cove, with its barbecue joints, bars, and beach shops stretched out before them under a dark and menacing sky. The roads, usually bumper-to-bumper with beach traffic, held only rolling garbage cans and whirling dervishes of paper and plastic.

Greg steered the van straight down the main drag, past plywood covered windows and empty parking lots. A few hundred yards from where the boardwalk gave way to sand dunes, Harriet shouted for him to stop. In the distance were half a dozen news vans.

"Shit." This wasn't going to work. Harriet refused to be just another reporter shouting over the wind. "All right, Greg, change of plans."

"We got thirty minutes before your first live feed. I don't know if there's time for plan changes."

Harriet had an idea. Why settle for being meteorological comedy relief? Give the viewers a story instead. "Turn around. I think I saw an open bar a ways back."

"We talking interview?"

"Yeah, the human spirit undaunted in the face of nature's fury."

"You mean people too stupid to get out of town? Might do. If they're characters."

"I think it was called... Castaway?"

"The Getaway." Greg was already putting the van through a three-point turn. "Yeah, I saw a couple of cars parked out front."

"And the sign was lit up," Harriet said, not really remembering.

"You sure?"

"Definitely."

A minute later, they pulled into The Getaway's small gravel lot. Harriet let out a sigh of relief at the glow of neon in the windows.

Greg grabbed his camera and equipment bag. "They'll be drunk off their asses you know."

"It'll be great." Harriet walked up on to the bar's porch, wrestled the door open against the wind, and stepped inside.

"I'm sorry, but we're closed." The woman speaking was thickly built and looked to be in her mid-forties. She wore a too-small Getaway t-shirt and clutched a smoldering cigarette.

Harriet had handled reluctant interviewees before. She approached the bar and launched into her spiel. "So, you've decided to tough out the storm? Looks like a great place to do it."

Actually, The Getaway stank of spilt beer and shrimp boil and looked abandoned. Tables and chairs were pushed against the walls, and graffiti like something off a Black Sabbath album had been scrawled all over the floor. A middle-aged couple sat at the only upright table sharing a bottle. The man was dressed in a western suit, complete with bolo tie and ten-gallon Stetson. The woman wore a sequined gown.

Well, I wanted characters.

The woman behind the bar narrowed her eyes, "You're from the TV, aren't you?"

Harriet heard Greg push his way in. No doubt his camera already on his shoulder. "Yes, we are. I'm Harriet Connors from WRBC News and I'd like to tell your story to the world." Harriet extended a hand to the bartender. "And your name is?"

The woman ignored the proffered handshake. "The name's Wanda Reed and I ain't no looter."

Harriet shook her head. "Of course not."

"I know how it looks, but Billy Simmons gave me the key. He said since I was staying, I might as well keep an eye on the place. On account I been tending bar here the better part of ten years."

"That is so interesting, Wanda. Do you mind if I have Greg here film our conversation?" Harriet gestured to the cameraman.

Wanda seemed to think it over. "Fine, go ahead. So long as you know we ain't breaking the law by being here."

The couple at the table drank and watched Greg set up. Wanda offered Harriet a cigarette, which she politely refused.

"All right, I'm going to say a few words just to set levels." With Greg ready, Harriet took her position in the shot. "This is Harriet Connors coming to you from The Getaway Lounge in Dare Cove, North Carolina, as Hurricane Francis—"

The door opened, letting in a howl of wind along with a muscular man dressed in jeans and a leather biking vest. The man shook rain from his untidy mullet and glared around the bar. "What the hell, Wanda?" In four long strides he reached Greg and landed a looping roundhouse to the side of the cameraman's head. Greg went down hard, turning instinctively to protect his camera.

The biker brought up his other hand and Harriet found herself looking into the barrel of a very large handgun.

"Roy!" Wanda shouted from behind the bar. "You goddamned idiot."

"Get on the floor," Roy yelled at Harriet.

Harriet knelt awkwardly; her hands still raised.

"Come on Wanda. The time draws nigh and all that shit. It's zero-hour, baby." Roy kept the gun pointed in Harriet's direction but didn't object as she crawled to where Greg lay. "Ain't no time for strangers to be dropping in."

Wanda shook her head. "Here's what was about to happen, Roy. I'd tell Harriet over there how my grandad survived Hurricane Hazel back in '54 alone on his shrimp boat. Give her all the god damned local color she could stand. Then she and the fella with the camera would go away. Do you know why that plan won't work now?"

Roy blushed as if in answer.

"That plan won't work because you came in all 'Captain Badass,' hitting people and pointing guns."

Greg gave Harriet a weak thumbs up. "I'm okay." He got to his knees and examined the camera. Roy's gun was still out but pointed only at the oddly decorated floor.

"So, what do we do with them?" Roy asked.

The older couple walked over, the man in the suit holding a bottle of gin. "Oh, why not let them watch. Film it even," said the man. The words dripped from his mouth in an unhurried low country brogue.

"They could interview us before the ceremony," said the woman in the sequined gown. "Kind of a keepsake video of what we were like before we became Lords of the Earth."

Harriet was ready to jump at any opportunity, even one from an obviously insane person. "We'd be honored to record your event. Wouldn't we, Greg?"

"Sure," Greg said, rubbing his jaw.

The woman in the gown ignored them. "If they act up, Roy can always shoot them."

Roy's eyes were riveted on Wanda. It was obvious who was in charge. "You think I should just shoot 'em now?"

Wanda came out from around the bar. "Put the gun away, Roy, and help that fella up." She crossed to Harriet and extended a hand. "Sorry about that."

Harriet stood with her help.

Wanda held on to Harriet's hand a moment longer, as if to make sure she was steady on her feet. "Listen, I know you think we're crazy and that's fine. But we're going to need you to stay here with us until we perform our little ceremony."

"And become Lords of the Earth?" asked Greg.

Harriet thought Roy might hit Greg again, but instead the man nodded so hard his mullet bounced. "You got it, Mister. Sorry about the punch. I get a little excited sometimes."

Wanda went on. "We have around fifteen minutes before we get started. You can interview Roy and the DeBors. I think they'd like that, after keeping things secret so long. Or you can get drunk. Just don't try to leave."

"And don't mess with the ceremony," Roy added. "'Cause I will shoot you dead."

"What about afterwards?" asked Harriet

Wanda gave her a sad little smile. "Afterwards, nothing much you do will matter."

"Me first," yelled Roy. He ran a hand through his greasy black hair. "I am ready for my closeup."

Greg hoisted his camera. "Could you step back a couple of feet, please?"

Roy shifted position.

"Yeah, that's good."

Harriet passed a wireless mic to Roy. "I don't even know what questions to ask. Better you just tell your story in your own way."

"Hell, yeah," Roy said. "Me and Wanda, we get the whole western hemis…" Roy scrunched up his face in concentration but couldn't find the rest of the word. "We get America and all them Mexican countries."

Harriet only half-listened, her mind searching for a way out. She went behind the bar and perused bottles. Maybe she could start a fire with one. Cause a diversion. She picked up a bottle of vodka marked "95 proof" in proud red letters.

"You gonna drink that?" asked Wanda. "Might as well let Roy shoot you." She reached over the counter and pulled up two tumblers. "There's OJ in the cooler behind you."

Harriet got the orange juice. A moment later two screwdrivers sat on the bar.

"Here's to the end," Wanda said, lifting her tumbler.

Before Harriet lifted her own drink, Roy's angry voice split the air. "You think I'm funny?" The gun was still tucked in Roy's waist band, but his hand was on the grip.

"Whoa." Harriet put her hands up. "Hey, he didn't mean anything."

Roy turned on Harriet. "You think I'm funny too?"

Harriet shook her head. "I didn't even hear what you said."

"I was just saying how, when Wanda and me start running things, we're gonna move to that castle in Orlando."

Harriet's mind blanked for a moment then she got it. "The Disney World castle?"

"Why not? Don't we deserve to live in the happiest place on earth?"

"No, that's a great choice. And you'll have the rides, you know, if you get bored."

Roy glared back at Greg. "See, she gets it."

Wanda picked Harriet's glass up off the bar. "Have a drink, Roy. And calm your ass down."

Roy bristled for a moment, then took the drink. "Fine."

The older couple crowded into Greg's shot, anxious to take their turn. "I think these journalists want a more holistic version of our story," said the man in the western suit.

Roy blew a raspberry. "Well tick-tock, Jerry. We ain't got all day."

Jerry pushed back his silver Stetson. "I'm aware of the timing. After all, I created the ceremony." He turned to face the camera. "My wife and I have been students of the occult for decades."

"Him and Sheryl teach English at Beaumont High," Roy said. He did not blow a second raspberry, but his tone implied one.

Greg adjusted his frame to include the conversation's back and forth.

"Of which you were a poor pupil, Roy Swafford," Sheryl said. "Our true studies are of a more esoteric nature. Are you familiar with Frazier's Golden Bough, Jung, Joseph Campbell?" Her eyes were glassy with gin and zealotry. "The convergence of humanity's mythologies, both greater and lesser, hint at a great coming. Not some banal messianic savior, but something beyond mere Godhood. An entity truly worthy of worship. So, when Wanda's gift showed her the arrival of this *dread divinity*, Jerry and I were well prepared to help fling open the gates and take our reward. Weren't we, dear?"

Jerry nodded. "Wanda was blessed above all mankind," he said with the fervor of a country minister. "Chosen by this God of Gods to be its ambassador over the earth, with the help, of course, of three trusted lieutenants." He gestured to himself and his wife. "She chose well, for the most part."

"Wanda Reed?" Harriet gave Wanda a closer look. "*Flight 109* Wanda Reed?" The plane crash had been big news two years ago, a hundred-and-twenty people lost. A smaller story had made the rounds also. This one about a North Carolina bartender who had called the airline numerous times, warning them to not let Flight 109 leave the ground.

Wanda took a sip of her screwdriver and grimaced. "Yeah, that was me. Didn't do no good. I tried to warn 'em, but they wouldn't listen. Nobody wants to hear bad news."

Roy laughed. "Well, after today, every-damn-body's gonna listen to you, Wanda."

Wanda finished off the last of her drink, then leaned forward and gave Roy a lingering kiss. "Let's get'er done."

Roy gave out a whoop. "Disney World, Baby!"

Harriet stepped over to Greg. "Did you get all that?"

"Yeah, I got it."

"Crazy, but kind of compelling too, right?" Harriet was already editing segments in her mind. Maybe she could make a documentary. Netflix would kill for something like this. That is, if she and Greg survived.

The would-be rulers of the Earth arranged themselves on the floor's strange designs. Jerry and Sheryl stood hand-in-hand in a large circle near the entrance, Wanda and Roy in their own circle near the bar.

"Y'all stand over there where I can see you," Roy said. He gestured to a spot halfway down the left wall. His other hand patted the butt of his gun.

When they reached their places, Greg adjusted the camera, panning across the floor, then from one couple to the other. Finally, he focused in on Wanda and Roy.

We have to go. Harriet's thought was almost regretful, but she didn't want to be around when the miraculous event these loons were hoping for failed to take place. She put a hand on Greg's arm.

He gave her an annoyed glance. Harriet had seen it before. The lens gave some cameramen a sense of detachment to the point of foolhardiness.

Harriet leaned in. "We have to make a run for it."

Greg nodded toward Roy. "The biker'll shoot us."

As if on cue, Roy opened his mouth and sang what sounded like Latin to the tune of *The Lion King*'s "Circle of Life." He wasn't bad.

Harriet spoke a little louder as Wanda and the DeBors added their voices to Roy's. "We run for the old couple by the door. Roy won't risk shooting them and spoiling his precious ceremony."

"I don't think he's that thoughtful."

"You want to wait around for the human sacrifice portion of the show?"

"All right. Just give me the word."

Harriet took one last look toward Wanda and Roy. The gun was still tucked in Roy's too-tight pants. She shifted her gaze and found herself eye-to-eye with Wanda.

Wanda looked to the doors, then back to Harriet.

Shit. She knows. Harriet ran anyway. "Go, go, go!"

Greg went, shifting his camera from his shoulder to use it as a club if needed.

The singing stopped and everything seemed to go into slow motion. The DeBors hunkered down like elderly defensive lineman, blocking the door. Behind Harriet, the pistol roared. Her feet tangled and she went down in a heap. She waited for the next shot, but that shot never came.

Roy, the would-be ruler of the Magic Kingdom, lay on the ground, blood pouring from what was left of his head. Wanda held the gun in a shooter's crouch aiming in Harriet's direction.

A crunching noise came from the doors as Greg slammed his camera into the side of Jerry DeBors' head. The old man's Stetson flew across the room as he toppled. The pistol rang out again, and a red flower of blood blossomed on Sheryl DeBors' chest. The English teacher looked at the wound, her eyes full of surprise and betrayal, then fell to the floor.

Greg reached the doors, but they wouldn't open. Harriet ran to his side, adding her own strength to his effort.

"Watch out!" she yelled.

Jerry DeBors had gained his feet and staggered toward them. Then the back of Jerry's head exploded in a geyser of blood and bone.

Greg and Harriet turned to face Wanda, their backs to the unyielding doors.

"Screw it," Greg said. There was an almost imperceptible electric whine as he turned the camera back on and pressed his eye to the viewfinder.

The gun was in Wanda's hand but not aimed at them. "You have to slide the deadbolt."

"What?" Harriet asked.

"The door, it's got a floor-mounted deadbolt." Wanda gestured to the bodies of her friends. "Truth is they're better off this way."

Greg lowered his camera and examined the door.

Harriet heard a bolt slide, followed by a blast of cold wind. She tore her gaze from Wanda and stepped outside. Greg was already unlocking the van. A moment later the engine started, and he leaned on the horn. Harriet didn't move.

The passenger side window slid down. "Come on! We're outta here."

Harriet shook her head. "I need to talk to Wanda."

Greg launched himself out of the idling van and ran to where Harriet stood. He looked ready to drag her back by force. "It's time to go. Now!"

Wanda stepped out of the bar. Instead of a gun she carried the bottle of gin the DeBors had been drinking.

Harriet stared at Greg. "Get your camera."

"Shit." Greg turned and went back to the van. "Fine, but I'm calling 911."

Wanda sat down on the step and took a long pull from the bottle.

Harriet approached slowly as if Wanda was a dog that might bite, but the woman didn't look dangerous any longer, only tired.

"People don't like bad news," she said. "And that's all I ever gave 'em."

"Why did you kill them, Wanda? Roy liked you. Seemed to me, he loved you."

Tears ran down Wanda's cheeks. "Roy was an idiot, but he could be sweet." She took another swig of gin. "And God, he was good in the sack. Killing him, all of them, that was a mercy."

Greg had the camera up on his shoulder again.

"I'm sorry Wanda. I don't understand."

"The whole thing was bullshit."

That, Harriet did get. "You mean your predictions, the coming of the—*what had Sheryl DeBors called it*—the dread divinity?"

"They were my only friends," Wanda went on. "I've had the sight my whole life, but I only ever see bad things. I try to warn people. You'd think folks would be grateful. But they just hate you for it. So, when I saw the end, I figured why not try to dress things up a little. Nothing to lose right?"

"The end of what?"

Wanda looked up to the sky then at Harriet. "Don't ask me to describe it. You'll find out soon enough."

"But it's all over, right? You stopped the ceremony," Harriet said.

"No, I told you, the ceremony was bullshit. I knew the DeBors were into the whole spooky magic thing. So, I told them what I'd seen, but I made it sexy."

"You told them they would be kings of the world?"

"Yeah, I said I'd been chosen to run the earth, and they were supposed to help me."

"And Roy?"

Wanda smiled a little through her tears. "My beautiful dumbass. He believed anything I told him. You should have heard him talking about bossing mankind around from our thrones in Orlando." Wanda sighed then went on. "You know, I didn't even mention a ceremony. Jerry and Sheryl just assumed we had to have one."

The three survivors from The Getaway Grill stood in silence for a moment while the wind battered them with stinging bursts of cold rain. "I should have shot you like I did them. It would have been kinder."

"All right, that's enough," Greg said.

But Harriet only leaned closer. "Wanda, the world isn't ending. This is only a storm. A bad one, but still just a storm." As the last word left her mouth, a peal of faraway thunder split the air. Instead of fading, the thunder morphed into something more resonant. Something between a choir of steeple bells and radio static turned all the way up. The strange noise grew louder. But that wasn't right. Bigger, not louder, like God's version of a stage whisper. So big Harriet felt herself bending beneath the weight of it all. Then the noise stopped without even an echo.

"Wanda, what was that?" Harriet followed the woman's gaze upward. Red fissures appeared in the slate gray sky. The fissures spiderwebbed out in crazy jagged patterns like cracks in a mirror. The cracks grew until they stretched from horizon to horizon. Through it all the world remained quiet but for the wind's low and constant moan. This was the fact Harriet couldn't get past. How could the sky shatter above her head and not make a god damned sound?

Wanda took another swig of gin. "Go ahead and blame me if you like. People always do."

"What's happening, Wanda?" Harriet asked.

Wanda shook her head. "Let's just say, nobody's going to Disney World."

"She's nuts," Greg yelled. He pulled the camera from his shoulder and pointed a finger at Wanda. "You're a psycho. Come on, Harriet. Let's go. The police can deal with her if the storm doesn't."

Harriet was about to head to the van when Wanda put a hand on her arm.

"I saw you, you know. On the beach."

"What?"

"In my vision, I watched you on TV. Everybody did. The whole world was watching you, right up to the end."

The whole world was watching. Harriet stared up at the shattered heavens. The rain falling on her face was warm now and smelled strangely metallic.

"Come on Harriet!" yelled Greg.

"I need to do a live feed," she said.

"What? No. We're leaving."

Harriet shook her head. "The freakin' sky broke, Greg. We can't outrun this."

Greg only stared at Harriet; his eyes begging her to join him in denial. "The feed won't even work. Everything will be too jammed."

Harriet shook her head. "The broadcast will go through. Wanda saw it happen."

She took out her phone. There were still two bars of service. "This is Harriet." She didn't have to shout. the wind was dying off. "Yeah I saw the sky. I know what's causing it."

She looked at Greg as she spoke. "We're heading to the beach now. We'll need to go live in…"

Greg shook his head, but said, "Ten, maybe fifteen minutes to get there and set up." He looked at Wanda. "That too long?"

Wanda's gaze got far away for a moment, then she blinked. "Should be about right."

Harriet relayed the timing to the station and pocketed the phone.

Greg tilted his head toward the bar. "You know, we don't have to go. Fifteen minutes is time enough for a few drinks, maybe a phone call to your folks?"

"Or yours," Harriet said. *But what would I say?* She saw Greg thinking the same thing. "You know I always wanted to be in front of the camera. Live, breaking the big story."

Greg nodded. "I guess it doesn't get bigger than this."

"What channel?" Wanda asked.

"News 9 out of Salem."

Wanda turned and walked back toward the bar. "I'll be watching."

On the beach, Harriet helped set up the equipment. The other news vans were gone. Either they'd been evacuated earlier or took off when the sky broke. An ABC affiliate had left a remote camera behind. Greg smashed it with a piece of driftwood. "Our shot. Nobody else's."

Harriet, mic in hand, stared out to sea. The shattered sky stretched over a black ocean as still as pond water. The wind and rain were gone. The world silent, holding its breath.

"I'm ready when you are, Harriet."

She waited, staring out at a vista that already seemed alien. Her dream of addressing the world from in front of a camera seemed small in the face of this approaching end. But the dream was still there, and Harriet was glad.

From the flat black waters rose a mountain of shifting flesh the color of rainbows that had died and gone rancid. In that flesh, vast tumorous eyes bubbled into existence, swelling huge as they gazed on the world, then bursting with a waterfall of ichor as more rose to the surface. Canyon-sized fissures—*mouths, those are mouths*—gaped wide, offering glimpses into an abyss full of shape and substance Harriet's brain refused to even try to understand.

Harriet turned away before her mind could shake loose from its moorings. Greg stood a few feet in front of her. His body trembled but the camera on his shoulder was steady. He held up a shaking hand, fingers extended, and counted down. Four, three, two—then pointed at her.

A feeling of pressure hit Harriet from behind. The weight of something arriving, something completely and terribly *other*. Greg's face went slack. Blood dripped from the eye pressed to the viewfinder, but the camera never wavered.

Harriet opened her mouth, half-expecting a scream to come pouring out, but the words were there, as strong and confident as they'd been when she was sixteen, practicing in front of her bedroom mirror. The world, after all, was watching.

"This is Harriet Connors coming to you live…"

THE SQUIRRELS LOOK ANGRY
TODAY

THE SQUIRRELS LOOK ANGRY TODAY;

One was on the light pole near my house, upside down, clinging to the wood like some furry insect ready to take flight, its tiny black eyes following me.

I'm not afraid for myself, you understand.

It's the kids heading to the elementary school at the end of my street, toting backpacks almost as big as they are, their heads high,

Wearing the kind of walking-to-school-smiles only seen on the last few days before summer vacation.

I imagine dark things under the bright morning sun:

. . .

High-pitched screams quickly muffled under writhing mounds of brown and gray fur.

I think of small yellowed teeth hard enough to crack walnuts.

It's silly, I know. Crazy even.

But... the squirrels look angry today.

THE GREAT SHOULD HAVE BEEN

A SIREN HOWLED. Freddie tracked it out of habit—maybe a quarter of a mile away, heading south. He laughed, then hissed and pressed a palm to his bandaged side. Cops weren't a worry anymore. He held up his hand and blinked at his own blood. "Just a little seepage," he told himself. Panic and pain gave him the shakes. He slowed the car until the tremors passed.

A robotic voice spoke through the speakers.

"AT THE NEXT STOP SIGN, TURN LEFT ON MONTGOMERY AVENUE,"

Freddie glanced down at his phone. Not far now. *This is crazy. I should go find that cop I heard. Or call the FBI.* But he didn't think they'd cut him a deal. You don't get immunity with a dead man in your trunk.

Pittsburgh should be all right for a day or two at least. But he wasn't sure. He hadn't changed cars, hadn't even switched plates. Things had gone to shit too fast. He had one more stop. If Allen couldn't do what Freddie thought he could… then what? Bleed out in some no-name motel. More likely a bullet behind the ear. He hadn't seen a tail. But a good tail didn't get seen.

"I'm not a bad man," he whispered, knowing it for a lie. "I wasn't always." That felt more right. A thousand wrong choices, some pride, some greed. Running into the wrong guy at a bar. "I wasn't always."

Maybe that's why I'm really going to Allen's. I need to be around someone who knew me before I screwed it all up. But it wasn't just that. Freddie believed. It was a crazy theory. And what did he have to back it up with? A recurring dream, twenty-year-old memories, desperation? But he remembered riding his skateboard through the high school cafeteria. He remembered watching the paint run down Chet Holman's football jersey. And despite the bullet in his side and the body in the trunk, Freddie felt hope.

"Arrived at destination,"

the phone announced.

The house was a small, brick, two-story with a postage-stamp front yard. No toys lay in the grass or on the porch. Good. Kids would make things harder. Freddie parked and got out of the car, pulling on his suit coat to cover the blood spots. He left the gun. He might have to beg, but Freddie didn't think force would work. He winced a little when he stood, but the pain was bearable.

Freddie knocked. Muffled words sounded inside, and then the door swung open. Allen stood in the entrance. Freddie took a minute to be sure. His mind adding pounds and redistributing hair on the high school memory of Allen he carried in his head.

Allen must have been doing the same because, at first, no

recognition appeared behind the man's wireless spectacles. Then an unsure smile began to grow. "Freddie?"

Freddie nodded. "Yeah. In the flesh."

"Jesus, what are you doing here?" Allen sounded surprised and a little annoyed. "You should have called. You obviously know where I live. You couldn't friend me on Facebook or something?"

They stood there, neither moving. Freddie suddenly felt convinced that Allen knew about the body in the trunk and the men who wanted Freddie dead.

"You got even skinnier, you lucky bastard," Allen finally said, and his smile grew more genuine.

"You didn't," said Freddie. They laughed and Freddie's suspicions melted away in the familiar sound.

"Well, come on in. Let me get you a beer."

The door opened onto a small living room. Laundry lay half-folded on a sectional sofa. An empty plate sat on the coffee table in front of the TV.

While Allen went for beer, Freddie lowered himself onto the couch with a gasp.

"It's good to see you. Surprising, but good," Allen called from the kitchen. Glass clinked and he bustled back in holding two beers. "Hope your taste in suds hasn't improved." Allen sat on the sofa's other section and took a swig from his bottle. "How's Philly? You still in the old neighborhood?"

Freddie sighed and took a pull from his own drink. He didn't know how to start. Silence filled the space between the two men. Not the comfortable kind.

Allen leaned forward, his smile uneasy again. "What? You show up out of the blue and don't talk?"

"No kids?" Freddie asked.

"No. I mean, yeah, I got two girls. Twins. They're not here is all." The smile disappeared altogether now. "They live with their mother in Tennessee. She got remarried to a guy who writes songs. An honest-to-goddamned cowboy, if you want to know. Now, why don't you tell me what's going on."

A car drove by outside. Freddie's eyes followed the sound.

"You worried about somebody else stopping by?"

Freddie waited until the car had moved on. "You remember riding skateboards through the cafeteria?"

Allen looked blank for a moment, then chuckled. "The ramps," he said. "Thank God for handicapped access. And you jumped and landed on the table. Whose lunch were you standing in?"

"Marjorie Holmes," Freddie said. "I had a giant crush on her, and there I was, standing on her tater tots."

"I think she was impressed though, right? Later, didn't you two… you know?"

"Yeah. Those two weeks of detention were so worth it."

Silence again. Even if a bit more pleasant.

"You know, in that suit, with your hair all slicked back, Freddie… you look like central casting's idea of a mobster."

"Do I?" asked Freddie. "That's funny."

Another car drove by. This time, both men stayed silent until it passed.

"What kind of trouble did you bring with you?"

"It never happened," said Freddie.

"What?"

"Skateboarding in the cafeteria. It didn't happen."

"Of course it happened," said Allen. "We were both there, along with, what, a hundred and fifty assorted students and teachers?"

"Yeah, it happened, but… you made it happen."

"I have no idea what the hell you're talking about."

"I have these dreams."

"Dreams? You're not making any sense, Fred."

"Shit. Listen, okay." Freddie sagged on the couch. His strength gone. He didn't think he could stand. "Doesn't it seem crazy? I mean, we ride skateboards through the cafeteria. I catch some big air and end up standing on a table in front of the girl I've been jonesing for since eighth grade. It was something right out of a movie."

"Okay," said Allen, "But it happened."

"How about the time we catapulted cans of paint onto the football team? Freaking bull's-eye, paint all over them. Nobody gets hurt. No cans smash into some kid and put him in the hospital. Hell, it was a miracle we hit them at all. I tried it about a year ago. Took a board and laid it over a cinder block. Put a brick on one end and stomped on the other. The brick went in the right direction exactly one time and even then, it nearly took my head off. What we did shouldn't have been possible. The paint catapult, the skateboarding, half a dozen other things. It was all too perfect."

Allen shrugged. "So what?"

"I think about those times in high school a lot."

"Maybe a little too much," said Allen.

"Everything we did worked out. But after you moved, things changed. Nothing came easy anymore. I started to wonder, why couldn't my life be more like high school?"

"Jesus, Freddie, you sound like a bad Springsteen song. Except you're crazy on top of being pathetic. Sure, we pulled off some amazing shit, but just because the rest of your life—" Allen paused. "Hell, let's be honest. Just because the rest of *both our lives* haven't measured up to those years, it doesn't mean they didn't happen." Allen's eyes strayed down to the side of Freddie's suit coat. "Are you bleeding? That's it, Freddie, I'm calling somebody. Ambulance, police, or both?" Allen stood and pulled his phone out of his jeans pocket.

"I started having these dreams," Freddie said. He wasn't worried about Allen calling the authorities. If things went south, it would happen before an ambulance or cops could arrive. Unnoticed by Allen, another car had come up the street and this one Freddie could hear idling in front of the house. "The dreams weren't about the crazy shit we did. They were about The Great Should Have Been."

Allen looked up from his phone.

Freddie went on. "In the dreams, that's what you called it. We'd sit on that old flea-bitten couch in your basement, and you'd say, 'Today should have been different. In the Great Should Have Been, we rode our skateboards right down the goddamned handicapped ramps and blasted through the cafeteria like rockets.' You told that story so good and so true that I could see it. I could feel the wind pushing back my hair; hear the other kids cheering. We both felt it. Then somehow, your story changed the world. The Great Should Have Been turned into what was."

Allen sat down. He still held the phone, but he hadn't called anyone.

"You ever have dreams like that, Allen?" From the look on Allen's face, Freddie thought he had. "The thing is, I think those dreams are my real memories. Two teenage losers wishing their lives were like the movies. Except, somehow, your stories made it happen."

Allen shook his head. "You're just remembering when we came up with the ideas. Like you said, all that crazy shit went off without a hitch. We must have spent a lot of time planning it, right?"

What Allen said made sense. So much, that Freddie flinched at the words. But he went on. "I need you to tell me how my life turned out after high school, Allen. I need you to tell me the Great Should Have Been version."

"And what?" Allen's voice bordered on a yell. "You'll live happily ever after? Do you know how many times I've fantasized about how much better my life could have turned out? But here I am —alone. If I had that kind of power, do you think my wife would have left me for Hopalong, the yodeling asshole? I'm sorry to disappoint you, but you're crazy. I can't just tell a story and make everything better."

"You have to, Allen," Freddie said. "If you don't come up with a new story then we're stuck with mine. And I'm goddamned sure you won't like it. In my story, there's a car parked in front of this house with some very serious people inside. They're looking for a guy who made a big freaking mistake back in Philly. Hell, he'd made a lot of mistakes along the way, but this was one to beat the band. The wrong people got hurt. And the wrong people lost money. Those serious men are going to figure out which house I'm in and...well, I won't spoil the ending."

"You son of a bitch. What if my kids were here?"

"I know, and I'm sorry. I got no excuses."

The engine that had been idling outside shut off.

Allen's eyes went to the door, then back to Freddie. "It won't work."

"It will now that we're together again. You just needed the right audience. I figure the two of us we're like some sort of mystic circuit connecting. Come on, man, what the hell do you have to lose?"

"I'm nuts for doing this." Allen took a deep breath. "I don't know how you screwed your life up this badly, but here's what should have happened."

"Say the words."

"Don't interrupt," said Allen. "In the Great Should Have Been, we stayed in touch after high school. You'd take a Greyhound over from Philly and spend the weekend. I was going to community college and convinced you to move to Pittsburgh and try a few classes."

Freddie heard car doors slamming outside and low voices. They wouldn't know which house. He tried to pay attention to Allen. "What classes did I take?"

"Film studies. You figured going to the movies couldn't be too hard. But you didn't like the films they showed, not enough car chases. They put you behind the camera, though, and you liked that fine. You even helped make a student film—zombies and crap. The film got a C, but the professor said your technical work showed a lot of promise."

It wasn't happening. Freddie felt the panic coming back. He was going to die on his old friend's couch.

"Then you met Brenda," said Allen.

"Brenda?"

"Yeah. You dropped out of college after a couple of semesters. No surprise, right? Started bartending. You didn't meet Brenda at the bar, though. You met her at church. My mom made us go to Mass every Sunday. You turned around in the middle of an 'also with you,' and there she was, giving you the eye. She was big, almost six feet, head full of teased out platinum blonde hair. Steeler's earrings. Not your type, but she was pretty and not a bit shy. She asked *you* out. You slept together on the first date. One and done in your mind, but Brenda had other ideas."

"Brenda," Freddie said again. The name felt familiar, as if he'd said it a thousand times. The air thickened in his lungs. *I'm probably bleeding out*, he thought, but he hoped it was something else.

"Yeah, she wouldn't leave you alone. She'd come to the bar where you worked, boss you around, make you laugh, wearing down your defenses. I liked her. She cursed like a sailor and was a hell of a lot smarter than either of us. She was the best thing that ever happened to you and deep down, you knew it. I was best man at your wedding."

Freddie heard a sound like tearing cloth inside his head. He could have sworn Allen was glowing.

"Brenda's cousin owned a plumbing company."

"I became a plumber?" Freddie mumbled.

A knock came at the door. Both Allen and Freddie's eyes shot toward the noise then locked back on each other.

"No, shut up and listen." Allen's words spilled out high and fast. "Brenda knew about your film production classes. She convinced her cousin to let you shoot a commercial for him."

"You wrote it," Freddie said. His voice proud and excited, like a kid in class who knew the answer. "The one where the little old lady keeps getting bleeped when she says 'shit'."

"People liked it," said Allen. "We did a few more commercials. Started our own little production company. Your marriage was good. Ups and downs of course, but you guys kept it together. Having you two around probably saved my own marriage. Gave me and Marcie an example of how things could be."

Another knock sounded against the front door, heavier this time. Allen sat very still and looked at Freddie. "So, did it work, or are we about to get shot?"

Freddie honestly wasn't sure. He gathered his legs beneath him and stood up. His side hurt, then it didn't, then it hurt again. He crossed the room to the door.

The words of Allen's story seemed to hang in the air all around him.

"Don't open it," Allen said.

Freddie grasped the knob. Another knock came, hard enough to rattle the door in its frame. "Hey, babe," Freddie said, as he pulled open the door and chose to believe.

A shot rang out. A man screamed.

"What the hell are you guys watching?" Brenda asked after she'd given Freddie a quick but thorough kiss.

Allen grabbed the TV remote and turned down the volume. "It's the new commercial. We're going for a bit of a mean-streets vibe." he looked dazed.

Brenda held her husband in a half embrace. Freddie leaned on her for a moment. Tasting the kiss. Inhaling the new, but somehow familiar, scent of the woman.

"You all right, babe?" Brenda asked. "How many beers did you and Allen put away?"

"I'm good," Freddie said. "In fact, I'm great." He really was. The bullet in his side was gone. So was his suit, replaced with khakis, a flannel shirt, and twenty extra pounds. Freddie looked toward Allen. But Allen was staring at a little girl in unicorn pajamas standing on the stairs. He shot a stunned look back at Freddie, tears streaming down his face.

"I can't sleep," the girl announced. "Hi, Aunt Brenda."

Allen ran up the stairs and lifted her into his arms. "Is your sister awake?" he asked.

"Nope," she said. "Mommy's asleep too. She's snoring."

"Yeah, she does that," Allen said, laughing through the tears.

"You're crying, Daddy. What's wrong?"

"I'm not sure," said Allen. He carried the girl to where Brenda and Freddie stood and let her give them quick hugs and wet kisses. "I'm going to get this sweetie tucked back into bed," he said.

"I'll do the same with this big sweetie," said Brenda.

"Thanks," said Freddie, clasping Allen's free hand.

"Hey, I'm always happy to burn the midnight oil as long as the beer holds out." The tears had stopped. Allen's expression of mingled shock and joy was gone, replaced by the satisfied look of a man lucky enough to take a certain amount of happiness for granted.

This is real to him. Freddie could feel his own mind shifting and rearranging. He remembered he lived just down the street at 485 Freemount and forgot a two-bedroom apartment in West Philly. *Soon the old me won't exist.* Freddie smiled at the thought.

He stepped out into the night, his arm around the woman he loved. He wondered if someday he would dream about a thin man in an expensive black suit with a bullet in his side. Then the mystic circuit closed and The Great Should Have Been became simply what was.

THE HAND YOU'RE DEALT

PAIN AND NAUSEA were a sea Danny believed he would drown in. Rod might be a dumb thug, but he knew how to hit a guy. Danny tried to inhale, but Rod's meaty fist was still jammed in his gut, pinning him to the alley's graffiti-covered wall.

Rod released the pressure a bit. As Danny slid down the wall, Rod turned his hand over, hoisted Danny back up by his belt, and slapped him hard across the face with his free hand. Danny would have admired the grace of it all if he hadn't been on the receiving end.

"I need all the money, Danny," Rod said, lifting him a few more inches. Danny's gut clenched as his inseam pressed into his balls. Rod had been a professional bodybuilder in the eighties. As the sport declined and his age increased, he turned to loan sharking and book making. He was jowly now and had a beer paunch, but the strength remained, and he liked showing it off. "Twelve thousand dollars. You got it?"

Danny mumbled a reply. A swift hard backhand cut off even that.

"It was a rhetorical question, asshole. You don't have it. But what does every cloud have?" When no answer seemed forthcoming, Rod pulled Danny a bit higher into the air. He leaned into his face and asked again, louder. "What does every cloud have?"

"A thilver lienin," Danny answered around his swollen tongue.

"That's right, a silver lining." Rod smiled and let Danny's feet touch the ground. "You see, I could use a card mechanic, Danny. You've done the job before. Same gig, there's still a few college boys out there looking to lose their tuition. The only difference is you'd be working for me. Come see me. We'll talk details. You know where to find me. And I know where to find you."

Rod stepped back and let Danny slide to the ground.

Danny felt a wad of papers land on his face. He knew it was the three-hundred he'd tried to give Rod a few minutes before.

"Hold on to it. Maybe, you'll find a game."

Danny watched Rod's Gucci loafers grow more distant until they left the alley altogether. After resting a few moments, he pulled himself onto his knees. He vomited carefully. This was his best suit. Then he took as deep a breath as his bruised ribs allowed and stood.

Danny stepped from darkness onto the neon-lit sidewalk of East Carson Street. A steady stream of college students barhopped their way past, too intent on their pursuit of a good time to notice what might be happening in the shadowed alleys. Two doors down was Drake's Bar and Grill. Danny walked inside and made a bee-line for the john.

"Jimmy set me up a JD on ice," he called as he passed the balding man behind the bar.

"You okay, Danny?" the bartender asked, but Danny ignored him.

In the bathroom, he did what he could with cold water and a comb then went back to the bar.

Jimmy started a tab and left Danny to his drink. Danny stared into the gold-flecked mirror behind the rows of flavored rums. He had a small cut over his left cheekbone and his lip had obviously been split. The most painful parts of the beating, the blow to the gut and biting his god-damned tongue, still hurt but weren't noticeable.

All in all, he might pass muster with Sharon. She was pulling twelve-hour shifts and would fall right into bed as soon she got home from the hospital.

"Find yourself a nurse," he remembered his mother saying as they prepared for her act. "They always have jobs, and they like to take care of people." It had been good advice, but even Sharon's patience had an end. Danny thought he had almost reached it. He borrowed the three hundred from her. Told her he was done gambling.

"Does that include poker?" she'd asked. It was a good question. Danny didn't think of poker as gambling. He'd grown up a carnie kid. Learned to cold read rubes in his mother's mentalist act. And how to make a deck of cards dance from a drunk who'd once been one of the greatest card mechanics alive, in addition to being Danny's father. Poker wasn't gambling. When you gambled, you might lose. Danny knew all about losing. He was down twelve grand to Rod Renshaw due to a series of sporting misjudgments that climaxed when the Steelers had the bad grace to win the Super Bowl but lose the point spread. That was gambling.

Danny had lost hundreds of poker hands, but only to set himself up for an even bigger win. He'd lived high for the last few years thanks to ESPN's gambling coverage. It was beautiful. There were colleges full of trust fund kids who thought they knew how to play the game. Danny would hang out on campus. He looked young enough at twenty-seven to pass for an undergraduate. He made friends and got into games. It was like printing money.

Then he met Sharon and made promises. Promises he wanted to keep. The poker craze had petered out anyway. He'd give up that life and get a job selling cars or something. *At least I would have,* he told himself but then came the Steelers and Rod Renshaw.

Danny did not want to work for Rod. The man was cunning but stupid. He'd try to get the same old college scam running, but the games weren't there anymore. So, Rod would put Danny in a room full of very dangerous people and tell him to cheat. He'd lose Sharon for breaking his promises and eventually Rod would get him killed.

Danny stared down into his drink searching for inspiration. He didn't find any. *Maybe in the next round or the one after that.*

"Are you looking for a game?"

Danny glanced up at the mirror and almost laughed. The man who spoke looked like a Warner Brother's cartoon fox. He had a long sharp nose and a matching chin. But what really did it were the mutton chops. They were a rich dark red and thrust out at least four inches from the man's thin jaw line.

Danny guessed him to be in his mid-fifties. The clothes, a tan three-piece Harris Tweed with matching hat, were eccentric but reeked of money. The last thing Danny noticed was the prosthetic hand. It seemed out of place given the rest of the picture. This guy should have had a brass hook or some high-tech thing. The fake paw looked shabby, like something you'd listed for sale in the Penny Saver along with a walker and a bedside commode.

"I was speaking to Mr. Stracony, and he tells me you are quite an accomplished card player."

Danny glanced over at Jimmy, who nodded.

"My name is Alexander Crane."

"Danny Williams, When's this game?"

"Tonight, Mr. Williams," Crane said. "In just over an hour in fact. There are usually four of us, but our Mr. Beaumont recently lost more than he could afford and has retired from playing. I must say, I've had a rather poor run myself lately. I'm hoping a bit of new blood may turn things around."

"High stakes?" Danny asked.

"Indeed."

"What's the buy-in?" Danny held his breath. He had Sharon's three hundred, but in a real game, they usually wouldn't let you take a seat without at least a grand.

"Oh, I can tell by looking at you that you're good for a debt. Shall we go then? My driver is parked across the street."

This was bullshit. Danny looked at himself in the mirror. He did not look like money. He looked like a mugging victim in a decent suit. But Jimmy vetted the guy and Danny was desperate. It was a game, and any game was a chance out of the mess he was in.

"Let's go."

A black Lincoln pulled out to meet them as the two men stepped from the bar. The enormous driver holding open the rear door wore an old-fashioned gray chauffeur uniform that made him look like a slab of granite.

As they drove, Crane filled Danny in on the game. They played five card stud and English stud, dealer's choice. No wild cards.

"Limits?" Danny asked.

"There are no limits."

Crane answered with no emotion, and Danny's face showed none as he heard the news, but his reservoir of hope rose a few feet. Wealthy players with no limit. Twelve thousand dollars might be a stretch, but Danny was more than willing to stretch tonight.

He glanced out the tinted windows and noticed the Lincoln had taken them deep into Mckees Rocks. He watched small groups of hard-faced men gazing at the Lincoln with hungry eyes.

"Where's this game at?" he asked. He'd expected one of the nicer hotels, maybe even the Duquesne Club. Any thought they were taking a shortcut to some better part of town vanished as the Lincoln turned down a narrow alley.

"We're here," Crane said with a smile. They parked in front of a battered duplex. Lights shone from the barred windows of one side. The other half was dark. A small group of teenage boys sat on the steps in front of it smoking and laughing.

"You're kidding me, right?" Danny asked.

The tallest of the youths shaped his thumb and forefinger into a gun and pointed it at the Lincoln. The chauffeur got out and opened the rear door.

"We are going to get shot," Danny said.

The older man slid out of his seat and walked briskly toward the teenagers. Danny followed him out of the car but stood close in case he needed to get back in in a hurry.

"Shiiiit," said the tallest youth as the older man approached.

Crane began to speak. Danny couldn't hear what he said but the boys' laughter and curses echoed in the alleyway. Slowly, one by one, they grew silent. One turned and walked away from the group. A moment later two more joined him at a run. Finally, only the tallest was left. Crane walked back to the Lincoln, the teenager following him. The boy was weeping.

"This young man has volunteered to watch our vehicle," Crane said. The teenager stood at the end of the Lincoln and sniffled loudly.

"Shall we," said Crane, and walked toward the lighted entrance. Danny looked back at the teen who had seemed so intimidating when the Lincoln first pulled up. The boy's wet eyes bore into Danny's trying to share something he couldn't put into words.

Danny looked away. This was why he would fail Sharon. There was something very wrong here, and he was walking right into it. He pretended he was doing it for her. So he could get out from under Rod and keep the promises he'd made. But that was just part of it. He wanted to read the marks' faces and make the cards dance. He could feel the tingle in his fingers. The location was wrong. The crying teenager was very wrong. But the tingle in his fingers was right, and that was what really mattered— more than Sharon or Rod. He had a game.

Danny popped the joints in his neck, pushed his shoulders back and walked up the steps. A wave of harshly scented air— bleach over decay—hit him as he crossed the threshold. He followed the granite back of the chauffeur down a short hall into what he guessed once passed as a living room. Ghost shapes on the wall showed where a couch had once been, and across from that a cheap entertainment center. Danny could still see the divots in the stained brown carpet. Now the only furniture in the room was a scarred yellow Formica table with matching chairs. The chauffeur pulled one of the chairs out for his boss and waited as Crane greeted the other men in the room.

"Gentlemen, may I introduce Daniel Williams. He will be taking the place of Mr. Beaumont this evening." Crane took

Danny's elbow and moved closer to the table where two men sat. "Daniel, this is my good friend Nathaniel Lodden."

Danny wasn't surprised at the crushing strength of Lodden's handshake. The man had the weathered look of someone who'd worked hard all his life and done well by it. Despite his Brooks Brothers' suit, what Lodden really looked like was a pirate. The man's hard features were set off by a bristling salt and pepper beard that came down to his chest. A large black patch covered his left eye.

"The gentleman to your left is Mr. Leo Knock." Knock looked like Colonel Sanders, if the colonel had been a hundred pounds overweight and dyed his hair. The spiky tufts of dull gray spilling from Knock's ears and nostrils ruined whatever effect the jet-black dye job was supposed to have. Danny found the man grotesque, except for his hands. Knock's hands were long and slender, more the hands of a beautiful woman than an obese old man. Danny shook one and nodded a wordless greeting.

"Last but not least is our handler of debt, Dr. Fitzhugh."

Danny hadn't noticed the man in the fifth yellow chair. He sat in the far corner of the room away from the table. As Crane named him, Fitzhugh hopped from the chair and approached Danny. He stood no more than five feet tall and was bald as a toad. Danny extended his hand, but Fitzhugh ignored it and began padding Danny down. He was both thorough and indelicate.

"Very fine player I think," Fitzhugh said once he'd finished his prodding. Without any more comment, he went back to his chair, picked up a metal box and returned to the table. Fitzhugh opened the box, and Danny's heart stuttered. Beneath two unopened decks of playing cards, lay stacks of gold coins. Dr. Fitzhugh tossed the unopened decks in the center of the table and stacked the gold coins in front of the men. His job done, he took the now empty box and returned to his seat in the corner.

Danny sat down across from Lodden. The old pirate grinned at him. The first coin he glanced at looked old and had a large American eagle stamped on it. The second was older, and he thought the face it bore was some sort of emperor. Danny took a steadying breath. He hefted the golden emperor and felt the solid weight in his palm. What was something like this even worth? For all he knew, he could palm a few of these and not worry about the debt to Rod.

The familiar sound of plastic coming off a new deck sounded to Danny's right. He looked up from the coin to see one of Mr. Knock's beautiful hands holding out the fresh deck.

"Shall we begin?" Mr. Knock asked.

Danny took the proffered deck and began to shuffle. He'd play straight at first. He needed to see what level these men were at. He also needed to read them. See who sniffed or blinked when they drew a weak card or perhaps bit their lower lip when they bluffed. He worried about The Pirate. How do you read a man with only one eye and a beard covering half his face?

As he rifled the deck, he noted a king of spades on the bottom. His mind automatically went into the routine of how to track that king and get it into his hand when he needed it.

"How do they look from below Mr. Williams?" boomed out the pirate's voice.

Danny's stomach lurched. But his hands continued innocently shuffling as he glanced blankly at the bearded man. The pirate smiled into Danny's blameless face. "I've just one eye Mr. Williams, but it's a very good one."

Danny had never been caught cheating. He'd been accused a few times, but those accusations had mostly been sour grapes, not real suspicion. He had a routine for the occasion full of righteous indignation and sarcasm. He didn't think it would work with these men. No one seemed angry or tense not even the pirate. So, Danny simply dealt the cards and played straight. That was his plan anyway, at least for now.

He dealt, he wagered, and he watched the other players. They were good, but Danny was better, even straight. And he'd been trained to read people by a professional. Danny glanced to his left where Crane studied his hand. Crane had no obvious tells, but he played like he had a lot to lose, and could be bluffed. The pirate was as hard to read as Danny had feared. Moreover, he was a mumbler. He kept up a constant half-heard monologue, most of it seemingly directed at the cards in front of him. The mumbling annoyed Danny because he was sure it was an act and the man, despite his odd behavior, was watching him like a hawk.

He tested the assumption by moving an ace he'd seen on a cut from the top to the bottom of the deck and back again. As he did, the pirate picked up a gold coin with lady liberty on it.

"Very prettily done," he said holding up the coin but looking pointedly at Danny. Danny nodded and rifled the deck a few times.

The fat Colonel Sanders was Danny's salvation. He was a great technical player, but had a tell. When he drew a card he liked, he would look from the card to Danny or Crane. When it was a card he didn't like, he'd look first to the pirate. By itself, the tell was a great advantage. What made it golden was the other two men hated the fat guy's guts. Danny saw it in their faces whenever Knock won a hand.

When he realized Crane and Lodden would rather lose to him than Mr. Knock, Danny knew he would finish the evening ahead. He hadn't been brought here by accident. He was a hired gun and Knock was the target.

The next hand, he bottom-dealt Knock a broken straight. The pirate didn't blink. Danny spent the next two hours methodically taking Knock apart. One hour into the job, Danny could smell the fat man's sweat.

By four a.m. half of Knock's coins had been redistributed to the other three men. As he lost another hand, Knock closed his eyes and groaned. "I'm finished," he said.

The pirate looked at Knock with feigned surprise. "It's early yet Leo. Are you sure you want to square up now? Your luck could turn."

"You'd like me to go all out, wouldn't you, you bastard?"

"I'd like nothing better, fat man."

Before things could get more tense, Dr. Fitzhugh approached the table. "The game is over, Gentlemen. Are we ready to resolve debts then?"

"Yes," Knock and Crane said.

"You're damned right, yes," Lodden hissed. He pushed himself out of his chair and walked toward the door in the rear of the room. The other men followed more slowly except Dr. Fitzhugh who was looking at Danny,

"Are you ready to resolve debts?"

"Sure," Danny answered. "What about the coins?"

"If you'll just follow the other gentleman, sir," Dr. Fitzhugh said gesturing to the door. "All debts will be resolved now."

Danny stood and walked toward the door. He didn't want to go through it. The elation he felt at tearing apart Knock was gone. Danny had a bad feeling. He felt it in his fingers and his fingers didn't lie. He should turn, grab what he could carry from the table and run.

"Don't worry Mr. Willaims the debts tonight are in your favor," Fitzhugh said as if reassuring a child.

Danny stepped through the door into what had once been a small kitchen. The only furniture were two large wooden chairs in the center of the room with a plastic TV tray between them.

Mr. Knock sat in one of the chairs. His black-dyed hair stood out starkly against his sickly pale skin.

The pirate sat on the other. He half turned in his seat to face the fat man, and he was laughing.

Fitzhugh pushed past Danny to the two men. He set a leather case on the tray and opened it. "You are ready Mr. Knock?"

"He's ready," laughed the pirate. "You know what I want, don't you, fat man? I think I'll have the left one."

"Decorum, Mr. Lodden." admonished Dr. Fitzhugh.

"Let him have his fun," Knock said standing from the chair. He unbuttoned his suit, tossed the jacket on the floor, and removed his shirt and pants.

Danny took a step back. Under his suit, Knock wore a white mesh step-in like something out of an old Sears and Roebuck catalog. Beneath the mesh he was writhing. Knock unbuttoned the shoulder straps of his undergarment and let it fall away. He looked at Lodden. "You're small time, Lodden. Someday I'll own you."

Danny gagged. Knock wasn't fat. The man's body was festooned with limbs. An entire third arm hung down from one armpit. Hands were sewn in a row from his sternum down to his groin —no two the same size or skin tone. There were other things, numerous ears, assorted fingers. A patch of long pink tongues hung in concentric circles from his left breast. Eyes, a dozen at least rose like pustules on his right. The man was a forest of borrowed flesh and that flesh was alive. The hands stroked the skin around them. The tongues lashed the air. The third arm bent, and its hand pointed to the rash of blinking eyes.

"Take your pick."

"I have, and it will be the left one—Beaumont's." Lodden smiled with malice as he spoke but Danny could hear envy in his voice.

Dr. Fitzhugh took a tightly rolled piece of leather and offered it to Knock.

Knock gave one more contemptuous look to Lodden. "I'll think of this as a loan," he sneered and bit down on the leather.

Nausea rolled over Danny as he watched Fitzhugh's scalpel bite into Knock's face just below his left eye. It wasn't until Fitzhugh pushed his thumb into the incision and began working the eye loose that Danny fell to the ground and retched.

When he looked up again, Crane knelt before him, blocking the grisly scene. He could still hear Knock's harsh grunts.

"I think Mr. Williams should collect next," Crane said to the room. "This is all a bit new to him." Danny noticed Crane had removed his prosthetic hand and rolled his sleeve up to expose the stump.

Danny stood as soon as his gut allowed. He kept his eyes locked on Crane and ignored the sounds from the chairs. "I think I'll take my winnings in cash," he said in a voice that attempted confidence.

"No, you won't. You will collect your debt. There are rules to this thing, and they will be kept."

"You didn't tell me the rules." Danny hissed

"No, but you're in good and proper now and you'll abide by them."

Danny closed his eyes and turned to the wall as a particularly harsh grunt coupled with a wet ripping sound issued from the chairs. But he didn't try to leave, and when Dr. Fitzhugh called his name, he shambled forward and sat in the chair Lodden now stood beside.

Lodden whispered in Danny's ear, "Just relax boy. First time's always the hardest. At least you won."

He's not so piratical now that he has two eyes, Danny thought. The new eye had a red cloud over half of it as if a blood vessel had burst. Black sutures like fly's legs bristled around the socket. "Beaumont's," Lodden had said. Danny's mind flicked back to his first conversation with Crane. Beaumont had lost more than he could afford. He shot a glance at Knock in the other chair. The top of the man's thigh bristled with fingers. Danny wondered how much of Beaumont hung from Knock's body.

Someone said his name as if from a long way off. "I'm in shock," Danny said and wasn't sure if he'd spoken aloud or not.

"I'll choose for him," said Lodden. "Give him the hand. I saw him admiring it."

Danny heard his name again and he thought he might be nodding. Peripherally he noticed Dr. Fitzhugh bent over Knock's arm. For what seemed like hours, he watched with fascination as a red flower of blood blossomed in the white gauze taped where Knock's eye had been.

"Put the leather in his mouth when he screams," Dr. Fitzhugh said.

Danny watched the doctor turn toward him in slow motion. He wanted to explain that it didn't matter. "Old Danny has left the building Doc. He's watching things from way up on Mount Washington. You can do your worst. He's not coming back." Danny looked on impassively as Dr. Fitzhugh pressed what looked like chrome pruning shears against the flesh of his armpit. *Someone took my shirt*, Danny thought. *Lousy trick, taking a man's shirt when he isn't around to argue the point.*

Pain exploded, and the scream poured out for the half second it took Lodden to jam in the leather. Danny was back in the here and now and the pain was blinding, and gigantic, and every sharp-toothed thing. Behind the leather he kept screaming. "But I won! But I won! But I won!"

———

He awoke in the Lincoln. The pain was gone. Danny savored that for a while. When he opened his eyes again, he saw Dr. Fitzhugh.

"Back with us Mr. Williams?"

Danny blinked. The pain wasn't gone after all. It was just a different sort of animal now—annoying not deadly. And something else—another feeling he didn't try to examine yet.

"Where are we?" Danny asked. The words came out cracked, so he swallowed and asked again.

"Downtown. I didn't know where you wanted to go."

Danny looked out the window and saw the mirrored walls of PPG Plaza. He felt something throb in his armpit and tried not to think about it. "What time is it?"

"Two in the afternoon."

"Just get me to the Incline. I'll take it from there."

Fitzhugh said as much to the chauffeur and the two men rode in silence as the Lincoln headed toward Station Square. Fitzhugh held out an open palm toward Danny. On it were four of the gold coins from the night before.

"What happened last night?" Danny asked not reaching for the gold.

"You won," said Fitzhugh. He leaned forward, pulled on the collar of Danny shirt, and spilled in the coins. Something caught them. "The next game is on Friday. Be at Drake's at nine. Mr. Knock says he wants a chance to win his own back."

The Lincoln stopped as Fitzhugh finished speaking. Danny didn't reply. He got out of the car and headed toward the Incline without looking back. The Incline stuttered its way up the side of Mount Washington. Danny watched the city and thought. He took a deep breath, reached beneath his shirt and touched a stranger's long delicate fingers. His mind registered sensation from the new flesh. He felt the round solidness of the coins it held. He pressed his thumbnail into the new hand and felt pain. The sensations weren't confusing. Danny had a third hand growing from his armpit, and if he had to describe how it felt the only word that came to mind was natural.

He let out a brittle chuckle. A few hours before, he'd been worried about losing his girlfriend and being owned by a murderous thug. "Those were the days," he said into the Incline's empty compartment.

He flexed the fingers on his third hand and felt the coins spill down his torso and catch where his shirt tucked into his trousers. He took the coins out and looked at them. A spasm of panic made him flinch.

The Incline reached the top. Danny pushed his way through a group of tourists eager to get on. He needed to get control, but he didn't know how. He thought of Knock's writhing torso. The memory hunched him over like a gut punch.

Life had always been like poker for Danny. The cards might go against him for a while but then he'd spot that ace on the cut and be back in control. The Rod Renshaw situation was bad, but he would have seen his chance eventually. He had no chance with Crane since the moment he agreed to the game. He'd been used as a weapon against Knock. And now that Crane and Lodden had their fun, the three of them would pick Danny apart.

Another game on Friday. Mr. Knock wanted a chance to win his own back. Danny closed his eyes and tried to rub the images away. All that flesh Knock wagered, it wasn't his own. Through closed eyes he saw the tentacle-like tongues sprouting from Knocks chest. The man was playing with other people's property. Danny's eyes opened. He still felt shaky, but he thought, just maybe, he'd caught a glimpse of that ace. Losing wasn't so bad if you were playing with other people's money.

Danny looked at himself in the gold-flecked mirror of Drake's Bar and Grill. His lip was almost healed and the mark on his cheek had disappeared altogether. The slender, lovely hand growing from his left armpit made a slight bulge beneath his jacket. The kind of bulge a thug might mistake for a gun. Rod did, the night Danny met with him.

He took one look at Danny's sports coat and opened his own to display a pearl-handled Smith and Wesson. Instead of a pistol, Danny had pulled out a thick roll of hundred-dollar bills. He had gotten fifteen thousand for the coins. It would have been more if he'd let the dealer to run a theft check on them, but it was enough.

Rod had acted happy to get his money back, but Danny saw the disappointment in the set of his jaw. He didn't want his twelve thousand. He wanted Danny. So, when Danny asked Rod to loan him the twelve thousand back plus eight more on top, the big man didn't just laugh in his face and throw him out. He listened to the angle. How there was a chance to take out some wealthy gamblers and Danny just needed the twenty thousand for sit down money. Rod wasn't smart, but he was cunning. In the end, too cunning to let Danny just walk away with twenty thousand of his hard-earned dollars.

Danny watched as Alexander Crane moved through Drake's Friday night crowd toward him. The hand Crane extended was olive skinned, manicured, and hadn't been there last week.

Danny stood, but it was Rod who shook Crane's new appendage.

"Rod Renshaw. Nice to meet you."

Crane's eyes questioned Danny.

"Danny told me there were some worries about him getting a seat in the game tonight," said Rod. "No worries, I'm backing him."

Crane looked from Danny to Rod and now a smile played on his lips. "Are you saying you will be responsible for Mr. Williams' losses?"

"Yeah, I'll bank him. I'm good for it."

"I'm sure you are Mr. Renshaw. You'll excuse me. I need to phone my associates."

"You do that," Rod said with his usual bluster, then turned back to his half-finished gimlet on the bar.

Danny downed the remnants of his own drink in one nervous gulp. He knew he just couldn't walk away from the strange games Crane had drawn him into. Danny recalled the words of Mr. Knock "You'd Like me to go all out, wouldn't you?" That was the only way. Like Beaumont, Danny had to lose more than he could afford. But losing isn't all that bad if you're playing with other people's money.

Crane approached them again. "It's unusual, but the other players have agreed." Danny thought Crane's face looked hungry as he spoke.

"Of course, I'm coming along," Rod said sliding from his bar stool. "Got to watch out for my investment. Right?"

"Most assuredly, Mr. Renshaw, in fact, we insist."

Danny followed the two men out of the bar. Crane had his hand on Rod's arm—like a farmer with his prize pig. The plan could go wrong Danny thought. In this strange not-so-according-to-Hoyle world he found himself, Rod's Smith and Wesson might still beat a scalpel no matter what dark power wielded it

But things could always go wrong. It didn't matter now. It was time to read the faces and make the cards dance. The Lincoln pulled up as they stepped to the curb. Danny could feel the tingling in his fingers—all fifteen of them. He smiled as he slid into the Lincoln. He had a game.

PHASE II

FOLKS UP on Wheeler Mountain had their fair share of weird that winter. Bo Gifford claimed his prize heifer gave birth to a calf with two asses and Milton said there were a lot more shooting stars than normal. But I think things really started going downhill when my Ford pickup ate Richard Petty.

Little Dale found the old tomcat and named him in the tradition of our family (boys after NASCAR drivers and girls after country music songs). That orange haired monster might have started life out as Fluffy, but he finished up as Richard Petty. Dale and the twins, Delia and Ruby, loved that mangy thing. Even Shelly doted on it and she wasn't one to take a shine to neither man nor beast. Maybe there's only so much love in the world to go around, because the more Shelly and the kids gave that cat the less they had for me.

It was February when it happened. I grabbed Richard Petty by the scruff of his neck and headed for the door.

"It's too cold," said Shelly. "He's gonna freeze."

"Where the hell you think the cat slept before we took it in?"

Shelly didn't have an argument for that. Truth be told, it *was* too damn cold. The kind of cold makes you slap a jock strap on your brass monkey. But I'd been getting peanut butter and jelly for lunch because the tuna I liked went into Petty's bowl. I tossed that yowling son of a bitch into the yard like I was trying for a strike at the Bowl-a-Rama.

Let the little shit freeze.

The next morning, I staggered out to the truck after a quick breakfast of Mountain Dew and cigarettes. I was thinking about my job—twelve hours on the factory floor screwing part A on to part B. Where Richard Petty spent the night didn't cross my mind.

I started up the truck. The engine made a chunking sound and then whined into life. Petty's final yowl filled the yard like a siren. Shelly and the kids poured out of the house in time to see the blood dripping off the hood as I looked down at the mess that had been their favorite pet.

"What the hell did you do, Lee?" Shelly asked.

"Me, I didn't do a thing. The damn cat crawled up under the hood. How was I supposed to know?"

"You put him out in the cold. You knew what would happen."

It wasn't true. I tried to explain. Critters were always getting under car hoods looking for a little warmth. Most times they just high tailed it out when the engine started. I didn't plan it. I hated the cat, but no animal deserved what Richard Petty got. I would've never done such a thing on purpose. Hell, cleaning the engine would take me all day.

The kids didn't say a word. They just looked at me.

I knew the family was upset, but I thought maybe, what with the cat gone, things might get better. They didn't. I had been right about there only being so much love. When the Ford's fan blade tore through all nine of Richard Petty's lives the love died with him. There wasn't anything, but anger and blame left for old Lee Swafford, Jr.

Shelly took the kids and left a few months later. She claimed it was because I was spending all my time drinking with Milton, instead of looking for a new job after the factory let me go. That was true, but I blamed the damn cat.

I had a plan though—a way to make some money and get Shelly and the kids to come home. Maybe I was fooling myself. I heard Shelly was dating Bob Gill, owner of Big Bob's Boot Barn, and that little Dale and the girls already called him daddy. But a man's got to dream. And my dreams were fueled with propane.

Milton and I pulled into the Super Wal-Mart outside of Dayton around two am. We parked right up close to the long grey cage full of propane tanks. Construction sites went through that shit like a drunk through a case of High Life. It cost them thirty dollars a tank, but I'd sell it to them for half that and it was all profit.

Milton hopped out of the passenger seat. He already had the bolt cutters, what he called the "key to the city", in his hand. The lock clanged on to the asphalt and in five minutes flat we had twenty-five tanks in the truck bed with a tarp over them.

I scanned the parking lot as I pulled out. There were only a few oldsters camping out in their R.V.s, on their way to see America one Wal-Mart at a time. I'd rubbed some mud on our license plate. The old folks couldn't see worth a shit anyway.

Milton did the math, his eyes rolling up as if the answer was tattooed on the inside of his skull. "Another few weeks and we can go to Phase II," he said.

Milton talked fancy, but I didn't mind. He was the brains of the outfit. I'd been getting in trouble with Milton since the two of us were eight years old. He always had a scheme and there was always a Phase II. This time, Phase II was getting a flatbed truck we could paint up to look official and some uniforms with names on the pockets. We could triple the propane we carried, and we'd look like delivery men, so nobody would suspect us. Problem was, we kept drinking up the profits.

Milton grabbed a beer from the cooler and handed it to me. He took a swig off his own can and stowed it between his legs.

"We're on our way, Lee."

He noticed me staring at the truck's gauges.

"What's wrong?"

I shook my head. "Not a thing." That was what worried me. I loved that Ford, but it was an ornery machine. It burned through gas and oil like a fat man goes through fried chicken. When we started our little enterprise, I figured the first thing I'd need to spend the money on was tuning up the truck. But the thing purred like a kitten: no warning lights, no overheating. Stranger still, I hadn't put gas in the beast for a couple weeks and it still read over half a tank.

The next morning—well, afternoon—I lay on the couch in the trailer, hung over and still worried. What if the gas gauge wasn't working? It would not do to run out of gas with twenty tanks of stolen propane in the truck bed.

I pulled myself up and lit a cigarette to burn away the cobwebs. I was out of Mountain Dew. Outside, the sun was high and sweat trickled down the back of my neck. I popped the hood on the Ford and looked inside.

I stood there unable to move for a good minute then I broke and ran. I was in the trailer before the hood clanged shut.

I pulled out another cigarette to replace the one that I'd dropped outside and grabbed a beer from the fridge. My hands shook so much it took three tries to light up. There was something on the truck's engine.

Critters crawl up under truck hoods all the time. I'd told Shelly and the kids that, and it was true. But I'd never seen nothing like this. I closed my eyes and tried to make sense of the thing I'd seen. The body was long and rounded. Parts of it were covered by some sort of hard shell but you could see the meat of the thing pressed up through the gaps all grey and sick looking, like month old bologna.

There wasn't a head, just the body and at least a couple dozen legs sticking out every which way. Big fleshy sacks hung off the thing's sides, more where the legs jointed up. The sacks would swell up like a bull frog about to croak and go flat again. The legs (I called them legs, but they could have been arms or antennae for all I could figure), weren't just holding on to the engine, they were poking right through the metal. Something like rubber cement sealed up the gaps. If there were ticks in Hell, they would have looked like the thing under the hood of my Ford.

Two beers and half a dozen cigarettes didn't bring me any closer to knowing what to do. I walked outside, picking up the hatchet that lay by the woodpile. I came at the Ford from the back. Squatted down and tried to see past the pair of shiny chromium "truck nuts" that little Dale had given me last Father's Day.

There it was, caked in a camouflage of mud and exhaust dirt. Thin legs, jointed every few inches, wrapped themselves around the exhaust pipe, packing the hole at the end. My brain made a connection. The car running so well, hardly using any gas—was this critter the cause?

The whole thing was bigger than I could think, so I called Milton. He said I was crazy, or still drunk. I didn't blame him. When I told him about the truck not burning any gas, he sounded a bit more interested.

He pulled up a half hour later.

"Well, let's see your monster bug."

I yanked open the hood, this time propping it. We stood and looked at the thing wrapped around my engine.

"Start her up," Milton said.

With the engine running, the thing changed. The sacks went into high gear. You could tell there was something wet inside getting pumped along. Where the legs poked into the engine, they glowed.

We shut her down and went inside for some brain fuel. I heated up a couple of pot pies in the microwave while Milton pulled the first Miller Lite from a fresh case he'd brought.

"So, what do you think?" I said pulling the plastic back from the top of my pie.

Milton smiled. "I don't know for sure yet, but this may be big. You mind if I sleep here on your couch tonight? I got some tests in mind."

"Why don't you take the bed? I don't feel comfortable in it without Shelly."

"Fuck Big Bill and his Boot Barn," Milton said lifting his beer.

"Amen."

We kept drinking. Milton got up every so often and walked out to his truck with a flashlight. Things got blurry as the night went on. I was about asleep when Milton came through the doorway and gave a rebel yell that shook the windows.

"The critter did it," he said. He dragged me out to the trucks. He had moved his right next to mine and both the hoods were open. Milton shined the flashlight down on his engine and smiled.

"Look at that, Lee."

There was another one. It was smaller. The grey hard looking limbs weren't so dirty yet and the sacks didn't swell as big. But the thing attached to Milton's truck engine sure enough did look like the critter on mine.

Milton slapped me on the back and let out another rebel yell. "You know what this means?" he asked.

Between the beer and not being the sharpest tool in God's shed, I had to admit I didn't.

"We can farm the goddamned things. People would pay a lot of money for their old clunkers to run better and use half as much gas. Hell, this thing is all-natural and organic. Them Hollywood liberals will be out here throwing bags of money at us in a week."

I had questions, fuzzy and half-formed. Milton didn't give me a chance to ask them.

"Hop in. We're taking a ride to celebrate." I ran back to the house for a few more beers and we hit the road. The truth was, we weren't anywhere near the road most of that drive. Milton had an idea to do what he called a "stress test" on the critter attached to his engine—see if it could hold on. We plowed down every back road and through every muddy field we could get to. When the beer ran out, we headed back.

Milton checked beneath the hood. The thing was still holding on and it had grown. Legs punctured the engine in a half dozen places, but nothing was leaking. There was a thick layer of greenish gunk where the bug and the engine connected. Milton touched the stuff.

"Hell," he said. "It makes its own sealant." He pinched off a bit and rolled it between his fingers. "This stuff alone will probably make us a fortune."

I liked the sound of that. We went back in the trailer, and I got out a bottle of thirty-dollar sipping whiskey I'd been saving for a special occasion.

When I came to, the house was empty. I staggered into the front yard, squinting against the sunlight. Milton's truck was gone. That was okay. Milton was a good one. I wasn't worried about him running off and making money without cutting me in. But him leaving did make me remember the question I'd wanted to ask last night. How did we keep the truck-bugs from spreading before people paid us?

I heard something above me. I turned and looked up at the trailer's roof. I heard it again—a quick series of clicks and clacks, like a squirrel wearing tap shoes. I didn't like that sound one bit. My ladder still leaned up against the side of the porch from a few weeks before, when I'd nearly got up the gumption to clean the gutters. I climbed up slow and peeked my head over the edge.

It was a bug, smaller than the ones on the engines. About as big as a small dog. As I watched, one of the sacks hanging closest to me started to swell. I waited for it to shrink again, but it just got bigger. It burst with a wet tearing sound, and out came a bundle of stick-thin antennas dripping green slime. The thing rattled its legs on the roof, and those antennae reached toward me.

The damned critter scared me so bad my legs went out from under me. My ass landed hard in the dirt. That fall saved my life. The tap-shoe shuffle echoed on the roof and the thing leapt off the side right as I fell. It sailed over me. Its sacks flattened and stretched, looking like the scariest god-damned flying squirrel you ever saw. It landed five feet out in the yard.

Despite the pain in my ass, I was up and running before the bug-critter got its spindly legs up under itself. There was a rifle in the truck and a shotgun under my bed, but the hatchet was closest. I ran for the woodpile.

I got hold of the hatchet's wooden handle just as something sharp stabbed into the back of my calf. I felt more needle jabs on my thigh and lower back. My leg went dead, and I fell again. I turned as I went down and got the bug between my back and the rough-chopped cords of wood. There was a sound like a plate breaking and my back turned warm and wet.

I rolled and some of the bug rolled with me. Most of it still lay broken on the logs. One of its legs hung from my calf. I yanked it out and screamed. It came loose but took a hunk of me with it. Blood ran down my leg.

The thing was still alive. The thick bunch of antennae snapped back and forth in the air. I brought the hatchet down into the middle of them and was rewarded with a meaty thunk and a burst of green blood. The thing wasn't done yet. It had at least a dozen legs and most were moving. I swung at it again but hit wood. The bug scrambled over the top of the woodpile and into the long grass behind.

I heard an engine coming up the drive and ran toward it.

"Milton, we got a problem," was out of my mouth before I realized that it wasn't Milton's pickup but a late-model Lincoln pulling up the drive. I recognized the car and knew it must be Sunday.

The Reverend Archibald Snapp was a big man with a big voice. The kind of fellow who could make the church rafters ring with the good word. I hadn't seen him in a few months, but he got around to everyone eventually—checking in, seeing why you hadn't been to church.

He got out of his Lincoln looking like he'd just stepped from behind the pulpit. His suit coat and tie buttoned up tight despite the heat.

"Howdy Reverend." My voice was ragged and high. I still held the hatchet—green goo smearing the blade. I moved so it was behind my leg.

"Lee," the Reverend said right back. "Didn't see you in church today."

"No. It's been a while. I can't seem to get up the gumption since Shelly and the kids left." I wanted to jump in the Lincoln and scream at the preacher to get me the hell out of there, but I didn't. The bug had scared me half to death, but I could still hear Milton's voice in my head telling me about all the money we'd make—the kind of money that would get Shelly and the kids back with me like they belonged. It might still happen. So, the bugs were dangerous. So were deer if you weren't prepared for them.

I just needed to get in the house, grab the shotgun and call Milton.

"Lee," the preacher said. He'd been talking for a while, but his words had only just now gotten through the fog in my brain. "Do you mind if I use your bathroom?"

I thought that would be a pretty bad idea and said so. "You need to go reverend. I appreciate you coming by and all, but I'm a bit busy." I looked over my shoulder, expecting to see a bug skittering over the grass any minute.

While I was looking, Reverend Snapp reached out and grabbed my collar. There was something in his other hand, something with a lot of legs.

The Reverend had played lineman for the Hope's Rest Warriors back in high school, but I had the hatchet and was still full of fear and adrenaline.

I ignored the hand on my collar and brought the axe down on the bug. It cleaved in half and the grass was littered with green slime, bug parts, and the Reverend's hacked off fingers.

The Reverend didn't make a sound. I don't know that he even felt the blade slice through his hand. He pulled me toward him by my collar and slammed his bleeding half hand into my gut. The air whistled out between my teeth, but I'd already swung the hatchet again and buried it in the side of Reverend Snapp's knee. The big man of God went down like a felled tree. I hacked at the hand on my collar until the fingers loosened.

The Reverend was talking again. Not loud, just a chat between old friends.

"Haven't seen you at church, lately. You ought to drop by for the covered dish supper this Wednesday. Haven't seen you in church lately. You ought to…" He was on his knees swaying, the words still pouring from his lips. I stepped behind him and stared at the bunch of antennae, each one as thick as my finger. They rose just to the edge of his white collar before plunging into the skin of his neck. He started to stand, his one good leg shaking with the effort.

I swung the hatchet at where the bug pierced the preacher's neck. I kept swinging, and the preacher kept moving. Each blow slowed him down a bit, like a wind-up toy coming to a stop. It took a good while. When it was done, I stood there covered in sweat and blood—both red and green. I stared at the bits and pieces of what had been Reverend Snapp and wondered what kind of hell you ended up in for hacking up a preacher. I had a sinking feeling I wasn't going to get rich.

The bug wasn't moving, but I didn't trust that it was dead. I got the lighter fluid from the grill and set fire to the mess of flesh and bug that lay on the gravel. Smoke blew over me and I swear to God, it reminded me of church barbecues when I was a kid. I dropped to my knees and vomited until I got down to the dry heaves.

I tried calling Milton, but he didn't answer. So, I called the Sheriff's office. I stood in the kids' bedroom. It didn't have any windows, so I figured it was safest. The shotgun was in one hand and the cell phone in my other.

Sheriff Nipper picked up, which was strange. I'd expected a deputy on a Sunday, but I'd take him.

"I need to report a killing."

"Do you indeed?" The Sheriff asked the question like a man who was in on a joke.

Fear rose up in my belly.

"You seen Milton Stokes today, Sheriff?"

"I did, Lee," the Sheriff said. "Picked him up this morning for drunk driving. Turned out he wasn't so drunk after all. He showed me something damned interesting."

"Did Milton visit the preacher too, or was that you, Sheriff?" My legs started feeling weak and I sat down on little Dale's race car shaped bed.

"I never miss Church, Lee. You know that."

"Reverend Snapp is dead."

"I thought he must be," said the Sheriff. "I tell you what, Lee. Why don't you just open up a window in that trailer of yours, lay down and get yourself a little shut eye. Things don't have to go hard."

"I don't think so. I'm not living out the rest of my life with bug legs shoved up my ass. I guess that's your thing."

"All right, Lee," the Sheriff said. The man's temper was a town legend, but his voice didn't rise one bit. "I'll be up there pretty soon. We all will."

I heard the click of the line dying and let my phone drop to the bed. I thought about calling Shelly, but what if her or one of the kids picked up and told me "Just lay down, daddy. It don't have to go hard."

I was trying to figure out a way to get to them—couldn't drive the Ford—when I heard the sound of an engine in the distance. I'd have company soon.

It's dark now. I boarded everything up. I didn't think I'd have time. The cars and trucks showed up hours ago, but the men inside don't seem to be in a hurry. Waiting me out, I guess.

I can see them between the wood slats—seven vehicles, lights on, engines running. Milton's truck is out there. So is the Sheriff's and some of the deputies. I'm pretty sure that's the Mayor sitting in the blue Escalade.

I can hear the click-clack of bug legs clattering over the roof. So many it sounds like a hailstorm. It would be enough to drive me to drink if there was any beer left. I keep wishing the bugs had gotten me first instead of Milton. Milton would have had a plan. All I got is propane.

I think them bugs aren't as smart as all that, even hooked up to people's brains. Because Milton knows I kept about ten tanks to heat the trailer. Those tanks are all lined up along the front wall now. I got some road flares ready to light up, then I just fire a round off from the shotgun.

I keep thinking about what the Sheriff said, "We're all coming." Wouldn't that be something, if the people parked outside were all there were? Milton's was the first brain the bugs got a hold of. Maybe they're taking it slow; the bugs taking over the important people first. It sounds like something Milton would come up with. Shelly always said he was a little too smart for his own good.

I'd like that, if I could light up this propane and save the god damned world. Shelly and the kids would be proud.

The road flare lights up the trailer like the fourth of July. Look at them scramble out of the trucks. Milton must have seen the burst of light through the wooden slats on the windows. He must have remembered the propane. Thinks they can stop me.

"We killed the bugs," Milton yells. "We were just waiting you out to see if they got you. Everything's okay. Don't do anything crazy."

Even I'm not that stupid.

They ought to run. Wouldn't matter, not with this much propane, but that would be the smarter play. Instead, they rush the trailer. I guess the bugs do make you stupid.

The door won't last long, but I don't need much time. I'm glad Shelly and the kids left. Glad there's a chance they might be safe. Maybe killing Richard Petty was a blessing after all.

They're almost through the door. The Sheriff's in front trying to kick through the boards I nailed up. I can see Milton's face looking at me from the porch and tears come to my eyes. A board gives way beneath the Sheriff's boot with a crack. Grey bugs skitter through the opening.

Time's up.

I love you, Shelly.

I lay the shotgun's barrels against the side of the closest propane tank.

"All right you sons of bitches, here comes Phase II."

SURVIVAL IS AN ACT OF SELFISHNESS

THE SHEETS on my son's freshly made bed are south sea blue, dotted with cartoon pirate ships. The green striped pillow in my hands doesn't match the theme. The matching pillowcase, with its plumed parrot perched on a treasure chest, is in the trash, stained brown from Jason's nosebleeds. Maybe the child psychologists would say keep the old pillowcase. A sense of continuity is more important than a few stains, but I didn't ask. I don't like those stains. They're a sign that something is breaking inside my son. Something I can't fix.

Shouting bursts out downstairs. A whoop, then laughter. I listen closely. Examining tone and timbre. The way the psychologists say to. The laughter climbs, but there's no brittleness to it. Not yet.

I toss the pillow on the bed and head downstairs.

In the living room. Jason stands, his linking band still covering his eyes and ears, hands gloved. "That was bad ass, Toby. Pure bad ass. I think it was a three. A freakin' three."

For a moment, I imagine Jason lying motionless on the rug. I run to him, peel the elastic band of circuitry from his face and look into dead eyes welling blood. Is imagination the right word? Is there a term for seeing a future that's inevitable? In my head, I repeat the child neuroplasticity rates the psychologists constantly quote. Fifteen through eighteen is the red zone. We've got time.

Today, Jason's okay. Talking trash with his friend, Toby. High fiving empty air. I'm pretty sure Toby lives in Missouri. If the group hasn't changed, there's also a girl in Samoa named Natia and a pair of twin brothers who live in Pennsylvania like we do, but on the western end of the state.

My own twins, Nancy and Matthew, sit on the couch, turning their link-encircled heads in quick, short jerks. Fingers flexing in their small gloves. I check my phone. They have another fifteen minutes before their patrol ends. If Jason really took out a three, he'll be off duty for a day, maybe two. I pick up empty risperi-Juice boxes and stim-bar wrappers from the coffee table and take them to the kitchen. Jason will take another few minutes to log off with his group. Then he'll want to talk.

I pour glasses of milk and slice up a few apples. The kids can't live on junk food and antipsychotics alone. The fruit goes on a tray along with some PB&J's I made this morning. I take them out to the dining room.

Jason busts in, red pressure lines from the link band still visible on his forehead. "Dad, Dad, it was a three. Can I call Mom? Can I?"

"Whoa, champ. You eat something first."

Jason nods. "Sure, yeah. Got to feed the beast." He picks up half a sandwich and bites off a mouthful. My son is twelve years old. He's been fighting monsters since he turned five.

"How you feeling, Jay?"

"Like a winner." Jason's voice comes out in thick peanut-butter-sticky syllables. "I'm sure it was a three, I could feel it. Powerful, you know. A Gazer I think. Like the one that burned out those two battle groups in May. The thing was all eyes. I mean, not like people eyes. The shapes were all wrong, but I knew they were eyes. We could feel every part of the thing staring at us when we moved on it. Looking all the way inside us." He flexes his hands as if to mold his inadequate words into something more meaningful. "And the eyes pulled at us. The way a vacuum pulls when it gets close to your skin." Jason blinks hard, once, then twice, jerking his head back and forth each time.

"Jason?" I wrap my arms around him, keeping my voice as calm as possible. "It's okay, son. You stopped the monster. You're home now." The blinking stops, at least for now.

"Toby stuck it with a stasis bomb. But we had to push all the way inside the thing to get a lock. It was like swimming through something warm and thick. Something that stings. Toby felt it the worst. He screamed the whole time, but he got the stasis bomb locked on."

I hold my son, knowing the words will keep coming. The psychologists say encourage them to talk it out. Verbalizing is good.

"Movement for it was like breathing, I think. When the stasis locked on, the Gazer tore itself apart, trying to keep going. But, but…"

"But what, son?" My hands rub Jason's back. The psychologists say ground them in this world with contact. Hugs heal. "But what?"

"After the thing was in pieces—dead, had to be dead—it was still looking at us. Definitely a Gazer."

I kiss Jason on the forehead. "Your nose is bleeding. Let me get some tissues." I can't decide which is worse, the nosebleeds or the spastic blinking. "You kicked a three's butt. Mom's going to be so proud."

My wife Donna is not someone you can just phone up. She works on the Problem. Most people can't do that. They don't have the math. Of course, people with the math caused the Problem in the first place. They're the ones who figured out we didn't need spaceships or FTL drive to get to the stars. Just enough energy to punch into a universe next door with a slightly different set of physics, then punch back into ours.

Their math didn't predict that the universe next door would be so foreign to our own that the only word to describe it is *evil*. Or that the unimaginable things inhabiting the other universe would notice us and want to come through.

A man answers the phone. He sounds old but that could just be fatigue. We're all exhausted. "I need to speak to Donna Linderman." He'll say no. Despite the fact I wouldn't even have this number if I wasn't authorized. But you follow the protocol or get hung up on.

"Dr. Linderman isn't available."

I don't say asshole out loud, but I think it. Hard. It's easy to hate the scientists and their math. But they're our only hope of closing the doors we opened. Just like our children, with their still developing minds, are the only soldiers who can pilot the fighting drones operating just inside that other universe. "This is her husband, Patrick. Our son Jason would like to debrief directly to her. His team just came offline. They terminated a level three entity. Called it a Gazer?"

There's a moment of silence before Donna's voice comes on the line. "Hey, Pat. Tell Jason I'm putting him on speakerphone. My research crew would like to hear what happened."

Jason takes the phone. He retells his story, this time with more details. No doubt, fielding questions from Donna's team.

"Yeah. The stasis bomb worked great. We didn't know you could kill a Gazer that way. We just wanted it to stop moving so we could get a bead on the thing."

I watch him. Ready to intervene if the blinking starts again.

The twins, six-year-old Nancy and Matthew, wander in looking haggard. Kids their age run routine patrols. Cleaning out low-risk targets and calling the battle teams when something large gets spotted. Their work isn't as dangerous as Jason's, not as much chance of total brain shut down, but it's grinding. They'll join their own battle group in a couple of years. Nancy certainly. Matthew is more sensitive. The boy stores all the horrors away inside himself. I can see them dancing in his eyes. Some kids just burn out early. Looking at Matthew breaks my heart.

"Have some fruit, guys. Then it's nap time."

Jason waves the phone back and forth. "Mom says we should go to the movies tonight. If it's all right with you."

I take the phone. "Hey, are we still on speaker?"

"No, all alone."

I step out of the kid's earshot. "You really want to go out tonight? The twins are dead on their feet."

"Me too," says Donna. "But I think we shouldn't put things off."

"Yeah?" Maybe I should feel a sense of dread at her words. But I spent my dread years ago. All I have left is resignation.

"Jason's kill was definitely a level three. Second one today. We have reports of a level five at the thins in Denver. The spotter is solid. An eight-year-old veteran. She described the thing as a semi-transparent mountain full of teeth. I think we should go see that movie."

We see *The Incredibles*. An old Pixar film from the early 2000s. The movie industry isn't really a thing anymore, but theaters keep the old films in rotation for the kids. Donna sits next to me. The twins flank their big brother, munching popcorn.

Halfway through the film, Donna leans into my ear. "Come outside with me."

"No phones, Mom," Matthew whispers around a mouthful of popcorn. Donna pushes the still vibrating phone back into her pocket. We get up and walk into the Lobby.

"What's going on?" Donna doesn't speak, only pulls me out into the parking lot. Above us, jagged streaks of black lightning flash across the full moon. The moon is a thin spot. Luckily, the creatures that crossed over there don't seem interested in leaving. But the black lightning they brought with them doesn't exactly help humanity's morale.

"I'm pregnant."

I pull my eyes from the sky. My mouth moves soundlessly while words form in my brain. "What? Whose?"

"A man in Montana. He used to be a high school English teacher. His kids have great mental stability scores."

"You didn't even talk to me first?"

"You know the rules. I'm years behind."

I do know the rules. Youth Conscription Act, Young Hero Production Act, Global Government Consolidation Accords. All passed in a rush during the summer of 2125 after Pvt. Margaret Wilmette traveled successfully to Moon Base Luna via multiversal transfer and was dissolved moments later by something resembling a giant acid-filled starfish.

"No. You work on the Problem. You're exempt from the fucking Young Hero Production Act."

Donna takes my hand. "I need to do this. Having this baby, it's an act of hope and I can't go on working without hope. Neither can you."

"But you won't be there. I'll be the one changing her, feeding her, holding her when she cries." Her. Jesus Christ, I'm already imagining a her. I don't care about the guy in Montana with the good mental stability scores. This child would be my little girl. She'll look just like Donna in her baby pics. I'll make her laugh, watch her learn to walk and talk. Then I'll…I'll wake her up one morning and tell her we're in a war only kids can fight. I'll strap a link band around her head, push her tiny pink fingers into reflex gloves and show her what hell is like.

But even knowing all that, I want—need—this baby as much as Donna. We could name her Margot after my mom. And for a little while at least, I'll have a child who's happy. Donna's staring at me and I realize I'm crying. "I'm glad you're pregnant."

Donna seems to think about this. She looks almost disappointed. "Do you think maybe all the good people are already dead? Only selfish assholes willing to let their children fight a war for them survived?" Before the conversation can go on, Donna's phone vibrates.

"What's happening?" War news isn't broadcast publicly, but Donna isn't part of the public.

"The five is breaching in Denver. Missiles are in the air."

I look west, as if I can see Denver from Pittsburgh. "We should go to the kids."

"No." says Donna "If a five gets through, it's an extinction level event. Let them enjoy their movie." We stand there holding hands, staring at an empty western horizon. Ten minutes later,

Donna's phone buzzes. She reads the screen, puts the phone away and kisses me. It doesn't feel like a kiss goodbye.

The missiles are a new design. No fallout on our side. We lose Denver, but the world's still here.

"Can we call the baby Margot if it's a girl?"

Donna nods.

I lie in bed that night, unable to sleep. Unwilling to take the pills that would make sleep even a remote possibility. A muffled cry comes from down the hall. Donna sits up. I'm at the bedroom door when Jason steps in front of me. His hair sticking up in tufts. Tears on his cheeks.

"I had a nightmare." Jason says and leans against my chest. The twins, their steps muffled by footie pajamas, appear behind their brother.

"Bad dreams all around, huh? Come on in."

Donna spreads out the pillows. Jason, Matthew, and Nancy climb into the big bed. Snuggling beneath the duvet. Donna and I get in after. Flanking our children like bookends, I reach across them, joining hands with my wife. In moments, everyone but me is asleep.

Tomorrow maybe the world will end. I don't have the math to solve that problem, and my brain is too old and set to fight the monsters. But I'm a good dad, at least what passes for one these days. So, I do what any good dad does. For a few hours, in this bed, I keep the nightmares away.

THE WORMS TURN

"He was completely naked. I know, he has a privacy fence, and it is his property. Still, it was a bit of a shock." After the divorce, Nell had sworn she'd never talk to Ted again. *But voicemail doesn't quite count, does it?* Except of course it did. Ted would listen eventually. Maybe play it for his new girlfriend, Kelli or Kerry, whatever she was called.

"Get a load of this. The ex has finally gone around the bend."

But no one could blame me, Nell thought. *You had to call someone when your neighbor turns out to be a monster. And he seemed so nice.*

Mr. Harrah had stood there, naked as the day he was born. Nell just knew he would glance up at the bathroom window and catch her staring. The thought made her breath catch in her chest, but she couldn't look away. Instead of turning his head, Mr. Harrah opened his mouth wide and vomited out a shower of worms.

The worms, thousands of them, not only came out of Mr. Harrah, they were Mr. Harrah. His flesh parted in long thin tendrils, crawling over each other. Nell stood there a good five minutes watching what had been her solid looking neighbor dissolve into a writhing mass. The worms roiled in a low heap under the moonlight and then disappeared into the dark soil.

"He has the most beautiful plants in his yard," Nell said into the phone. "That's why I was looking down over the fence. You know worms are quite good for—" *You're babbling, Nell,* she told herself. The voicemail cut off with a sharp little chirp. Nell hit redial and waited through three rings and Ted saying, "We can't come to the phone right now." Was that a woman giggling in the background? When the tone sounded, Nell found she had nothing left to say.

Some things she hadn't mentioned. Like how she had only just stepped from the shower when she first saw Mr. Harrah. And how their shared nudity had made her stomach feel full of warm honey, that is, until he'd changed. No, some details you did not share with your ex-husband.

"*But why call Ted at all?*" She asked herself. *Habit?* After fifteen years of marriage, it would make sense, but she suspected something darker. Ted was a bully and a tyrant. It had been his decision she shouldn't get a job, and that children for a woman as fragile as Nell were out of the question. But she'd gone along with it. Grown to depend on him making decisions, so she didn't have to.

When Ted left, Nell was terrified, believing herself to be the hothouse flower he'd wanted. But instead of withering, she'd flourished. Finding work, first as office manager at a local architecture firm, then parlaying her—'useless' according to Ted—English degree into a more lucrative position ghostwriting the firm's business proposals. She had friends now, and colleagues who valued her opinion. "You panicked, that's all. So, you ran back to the one person who would be happy to tell you what to do." For a moment a wave of self-disgust rivaled Nell's fear. She shook her head. Nothing could make her go back to living that way. Not even a monster next door.

Nell sat in her kitchen. A practical place, neat and orderly. A good place to think. What next, the police? *Hello, I need to report that my neighbor is what…a were-worm? He has a lovely garden, but the whole worm thing scares the shit out of me. Could you pop over and talk to him?* They'd have her committed.

Nell's skin prickled into gooseflesh. What if Mr. Harrah had seen her? What if he came over to shut her up? She ran to the front door and turned the deadbolt, for all the good it would do. In her imagination, a sea of worms already crashed against the house in pink fleshy waves. Long sinuous shapes pushed themselves through hidden gaps in the construction. *Do worms have teeth?*

"He never looked up," Nell said aloud. "He was too busy… coming apart."

The doorbell rang.

Nell's hand shot to her mouth, stifling a scream.

There was a pause then the sound of knuckles rapping wood.

"Ms. Phillips. It's George Harrah from next door." The knuckles rapped again.

Nell counted to five, drawing a deep silent breath with each number.

"Ms. Phillips, I can see your shadow on the curtain."

Shit. "It's late, Mr. Harrah, What can I do for you?"

"I wanted to apologize. Um, for the little show I put on earlier? I didn't think anyone could see into my yard. The night seemed so pleasant. I don't know what came over me. I'm really not in the habit of going outside stark naked."

"I didn't see anything," said Nell, hoping Harrah couldn't hear the panic in her voice. "I don't know what you're talking about."

"Oh. I could have sworn I saw you looking down at me from that little side window."

"No. Now I really must get to bed. Good night, Mr. Harrah." Nell listened for departing footsteps, but none came.

"I think you did see me, Ms. Phillips. How long were you watching?" His voice sounded more tired than threatening. But maybe that's how monsters sound right before they attack. This was all unfamiliar territory.

"Shut up, can't you just shut up and go?" This time no one could have missed the broken sob she spoke around.

"Aw hell," said Harrah. "That long. We need to talk."

"I called the police."

There was a long pause. "No. I don't think you did. They would have been here by now. I think you're still in the 'Am I nuts?' phase. Or worried anyone you call will think you are. Why don't you come out on the porch? It's weird talking through the door like this."

"Talking through a door is weird?" A bark of involuntary laughter escaped Nell's throat. "I don't think it even makes the scale tonight." She would call the police if he didn't leave soon. They could take her to whatever mental hospital was closest. Maybe she'd be safe there.

"I see your point. Listen, please. I'm not a monster. I'm just different. I'm no danger to you."

His words and the sheer stress of the situation snapped Nell's careening feelings into focused anger. "Bullshit," she said.

"What?"

Nell gritted her teeth. She attached the chain, pulled the door open a few inches and glared out at George Harrah. "I said bullshit."

He wore clothes now at least. The tan trousers and sweater vest made him seem more like an English professor than something from a horror story, but Nell knew better. "I saw what you are, or what you become. But even if you were just some guy from down the street, you're standing on my porch refusing to leave. Telling me you're not going to hurt me. I've seen this shit on the news. I know how it ends."

Then George Harrah did something unexpected. He blushed from the top of his bald head to the collar of his blue, button-down shirt. "I'm…I'm." His mouth hung open for a moment. "I'm so sorry. You're right, of course. I'm going back to my house." He paused in mid-turn, raising his hands open-palmed toward Nell. "I like it here, Ms. Phillips. I like my house, the neighborhood. I don't want to leave." There were tears in the tall man's eyes.

"Go home, Mr. Harrah."

Harrah nodded. "Goodnight, Ms. Phillips."

Nell watched him walk back to his house and go inside. Then she stuffed towels under all the doors on the first floor. After those hardly adequate protections, she made herself tea, sat in the kitchen, and thought. It was a very long night.

Nell's head snapped up, springing from sleep to panicked alertness. She yanked her stiff legs from the kitchen tiles, seeing a floor seething with worms until she'd blinked the dream visions from her eyes. "I'm alive," she said. "That's something at least." Her laptop lay open on the counter. A magnified image of *a Lumbricus Terrestris* filled the screen. She shuddered. It turned out earthworms didn't have teeth after all. Somehow the fact didn't make her feel any better.

She waited until 10:00. It was a Saturday and people were out now. Mrs. Henderson mowing her front lawn, kids riding by on their bikes. Nell walked over to Mr. Harrah's house and knocked on the door. She wore long sleeves despite the summer heat, and her twill trousers were tucked into knee-high boots. The clothes made her feel safer somehow.

Harrah answered her knock so fast she suspected he'd been waiting for her.

"Ms. Phillips," he said. "Thank you."

"For what?"

"I'm just glad it's you. Not the police or some reporter."

"It's early yet," Nell said. "Torches and pitchforks look better at night."

"I'm hoping that's a joke."

"Only a little. I'm in a tough position here, Mr. Harrah."

Harrah nodded. "Do you want some tea?"

"No, just answers. And we talk out here on the porch."

"Of course."

They sat at the glass-topped patio table and stared at each other.

"What do you want to know?" he asked.

"What are you?"

"I grew up on a farm in Iowa."

"That's not what I asked."

"No," said Harrah. "But if you want to know about me. You're going to hear how we're alike, not just the worm stuff."

"Fine."

"I'm thirty-nine years old. We probably grew up playing the same games, eating frosted flakes for breakfast."

"And watching Captain Kangaroo, I get it. You're an all-American boy. But what else are you? Are there more of you?"

"I don't have any brothers or sisters. Reproduction is difficult for people like me. I was an accident. It was only my father and me growing up."

"Are you going to kill me?"

"Jesus. I may not be human, but I'm not a werewolf. No claws or fangs. It's just, on a pretty regular basis, I need to transform into my other state."

"Worms."

"Yes, sort of. Certainly, like worms. I don't lose myself. I'm still me when I change. There's just a lot of…me."

"You don't talk about this much, do you?"

"Of course not. And no one really explained it to me either. My father was more a 'do as I do' sort of guy. He'd rather I'd never left the farm. Bottom line is that I'm a thinking, feeling person just like you. I run a lawn and garden service. I pay taxes. Watch the Super Bowl every year. I'm not a monster. I'm just different. And I don't want to be some government lab experiment. Or be burned as a witch. And if you spread around what you saw, that's going to happen. So, tell me now, so I can pack my very human Ford pick-up and start over somewhere else."

Nell stared at him for a long moment. She actually felt a little sorry for him. *How did I become the bad guy here?*

"Well?"

"You own a lawn service? Isn't that sort of cheating?" Nell chuckled. It was all too ridiculous.

Harrah sat frozen for a moment then a reluctant grin spread across his face. "Well, I like to think I'm working to my strengths."

Nell laughed in earnest. When she'd finished and wiped her eyes, she still hadn't made up her mind about George Harrah. But for the life of her, she couldn't feel afraid of the man. "This might be horribly naïve on my part, but I'm not ready to drive you out of your home." Nell stood and moved to the steps. "And, I have more questions."

"Of course," said Harrah.

Halfway to her yard, Nell remembered the frantic phone call to Ted the night before. "Uh-oh." She called again that night. Got his voice mail. "Ted, it's Nell. I wanted to apologize for my call last night. Turns out it was only a nightmare." As she spoke, Nell looked out the window at the wooden fence surrounding Harrah's backyard. Wondering if he was there and if he was himself. "I feel so silly. Sorry to have bothered you. Say hi to Kelli" She cut the connection. "Say hi to Kelli?" she repeated and shook her head. "What the hell is wrong with me?"

On Sunday afternoon there was a knock on the door. Nell thought it might be her neighbor until a key turned in the lock. She snatched open the door to reveal her ex-husband, Ted, in the doorway. "You aren't supposed to have a key," she said.

"Well, hello to you too. I kept a copy in case of emergencies. Like when my wife calls in the middle of the night about monsters."

Ted's blonde hair swept straight back now instead of parting at the side. Blue jeans replaced the business casual khakis he'd always favored. He looked fit and tan. Kelli must be the outdoorsy type.

"I want that key," Nell said.

"Fine. And I want an explanation. And maybe a thank you for driving out here to make sure you're okay." He slid the house key along the ring as he spoke until it came off in his hand.

"I called you back. It was only a nightmare."

"So, my wife is hallucinating naked neighbors who turn into worms. Oh no, nothing to worry about there."

"That's the second time you called me your wife. It's ex-wife, Ted. Or did the whole divorce thing slip your mind? How does Kelli feel about you checking up on me?"

"It's Kerri. And she can think whatever she damn well pleases. A man has responsibilities."

There was anger in Ted's voice and not toward her. Trouble in paradise maybe, not that Nell cared. She almost told him where he could stick his responsibilities. But instead began to feel guilty. Ted had that effect on her. No matter how much of an asshole he acted like, he believed he was being noble. In a twisted, selfish way he cared.

"Let's not fight." Nell walked out and sat on the porch steps. Patting a spot beside her. Ted joined her. "I'm really all right," she said.

"Not a monster then?"

Nell sighed. "George is a very nice man."

"George, is it? Are you dating?"

Nell's shoulders slumped. She bit her lip and counted to five before answering. "You don't get to ask me that, Ted. Thanks for coming out, but you should go now."

He stood. "Fine. I think about you, Nell. You know that? We had some good times."

"Leave the key. Ted."

Ted opened his hand, and the house key fell on the step.

Over the next few weeks, Nell had more conversations with George Harrah. On his porch or sometimes her own. At first, they were almost interrogations.

"What does changing feel like?"

"It hurts actually, quite a bit in fact. But after, when I'm no longer singular, it feels…amazingly freeing."

As weeks turned into months, the conversations changed. They talked less about George's condition and more about everyday life. How Nell's office politics were going. The odd customers George dealt with in his lawn business. And about Ted.

Nell told George about her calls after she'd witnessed his transformation. And about Ted's visit. "He seemed more jealous than concerned about my wellbeing. I think dreaming of a man turning into worms struck him as a bit Freudian." Texts came after. Ted "checking in." Asking about the mortgage or house repairs. Letting her know he still thought about her while at the same time telling her what to do. A bully's idea of sweet-talk. "He even called once, drunk I think, complaining about his girlfriend. I hung up on him."

On a Thursday night, while drinking tea on Nell's porch swing, George brought up his own social life. "I dated quite a bit when I was younger. Regular women. Like you. Well, you know, not able to change. I grew quite attached a few times, but I always broke things off. Didn't seem fair, them not knowing and all." He said it all in a rush, staring at the floor.

"Oh," said Nell. Surprised to find herself blushing.

Their first date was at a local Italian restaurant. They drank wine and laughed a lot. George ordered the risotto, much to Nell's relief. The idea of him sucking pasta into his mouth would have been too much like his transformation in reverse. *I'm on a date with a monster*, she thought. *And I'm having a wonderful time.* She kissed him in the driveway before they parted. A small kiss, quick and almost dainty. But the memory of it warmed her for hours. It was well past midnight when the knock on the door came.

She'd been reading on the couch. Too pleased to go to bed despite the lateness of the hour. *Don't ruin it, George*, she thought. *I'm taking this slow.* But she smiled as she approached the door and her stomach filled with a warm excitement.

Ted stood on the porch. Dark half-moons hung beneath his eyes, and his tan seemed sallow under the porch light's yellow glare. In his skinny jeans, Nell's ex-husband looked like the poster child for mid-life crisis. "I've done it. I've cast her off, Nell."

"Are you drunk?" It was a rhetorical question. Bourbon soaked his words.

"You're not listening to me. It's over. I'm coming home."

"Kelli's thrown you out?"

"Kerri," Ted said. "And we've parted ways. Differences of opinion."

"You mean she had one?"

Ted flinched as if Nell's words were a blow. "I'm not here to talk about Kerri," he said, raising his voice. "I realized the truth that night you called. You need someone to take care of you. And to be honest, I need someone to take care of." He made the words sound like an accusation and a plea at the same time.

"I don't want to be taken care of, Ted. The call was a mistake." Without thinking, she shot a quick, worried glance at George's house. "And I rang back. I told you it was only a nightmare. George is…harmless."

"George. You are seeing him, aren't you? It's understandable, of course. You're fragile, Nell. You need someone with a firm hand in your life." Ted nodded, and there was something distant in his voice, as if he spoke not to Nell, but himself. "What he doesn't understand is it's me you need. Not some nudist."

"You leave right now, Ted, or I swear you'll spend the night in jail."

Ted ignored her. "You stay here. I'm going to have a little talk with your George. He needs to understand the lay of the land." Ted walked across the yard toward George's porch.

"Leave him alone. You're not in your right mind!" Nell ran toward the back of George's house. She tried the gate entrance, but it was locked. If George was asleep in bed, fine. The police could handle Ted. But what if he was changing? She yelled and slammed her open palm against the wood. "George! My ex-husband is here! He's acting crazy!" The sound of running feet came from the front yard. Ted slammed his shoulder into the gate right beside her. Nell screamed in surprise.

She grabbed Ted's arm, and he gave her a shove that sent her reeling. He slammed into the entrance again, grunting with the impact.

"Stop it," Nell yelled.

On the third try, wood splintered, and the gate burst inward.

Inside, George Harrah knelt naked in the grass. Half his head and most of his right arm had already changed. Worms slithered down his torso to the ground.

"Jesus Christ," Ted said. He turned to Nell, a condescending smile stretching across his face. "He's done something to you, Nell. Bewitched you somehow, but I'll sort it out." Cordwood lay stacked against the fence's interior. A hatchet jutted up from a thick log. Ted snatched it up and marched toward George. Nell scrambled to her feet and ran after him.

With no hesitation, Ted crossed the yard and swung the hatchet at George's rapidly changing head. Worms showered onto the grass.

"Leave him alone," Nell shouted.

"It's all right, Nell. I'm here now," Ted reared back for another blow.

George lifted his one solid arm. The hatchet bit deep into the still human flesh, blood poured down.

He'd be screaming, she thought, *if his head were still there, he'd be screaming.*

Worms swarmed over Ted's shoes and up his pants leg, but he took no notice. He swung the hatchet again. George's arm cartwheeled through the air, a trail of blood and worms streaming out behind it.

The sight of George's sheared off arm broke Nell's paralysis. She stepped to the woodpile and picked up a log as thick as her forearm. Crossing to Ted, Nell swung the log like a baseball bat, striking him in the ribs with a thunk.

Ted grunted, but his smile didn't falter. "You need me, Nell. Everything's going to be fine now."

Nell braced herself and swung again. This time with all the rage of fifteen years of bad marriage behind the blow. The log slammed into the side of Ted's head, leaving a two-inch dent behind. Blood filled the dent, turning Ted's blonde hair a muddy red.

Ted froze; dropped the hatchet, then fell to his knees. Worms crawled up his sides.

"Jus wanted take care of you," he said. The words came out soft and dripping blood. Then wriggling shapes filled Ted's mouth, and he collapsed to the ground, disappearing under the writhing mass of George's worms. A few minutes later, both Ted and the worms were gone, leaving only dark, turned earth.

Well, not all gone, Nell thought. A few yards away, where George's arm had landed, a smaller pile of worms still crawled on the surface. *Why didn't they go with the rest?* The worms' movements slowed, and they began to knit back together. What they formed was not an arm.

"Oh my God," said Nell.

The tiny shape took a hitching breath and began to cry. The baby that had been George's arm looked only a few weeks old. Nell remembered George's words on the day she'd first confronted him. *Reproduction is hard on my kind. I was an accident.*

When George emerged from the earth again, Nell sat on the deck, holding the tiny red-haired newborn. George walked past the two of them to the clothes he'd left folded neatly on an Adirondack chair and dressed. He had two arms again, but Nell thought he stood a few inches shorter.

"There are things you didn't tell me."

George didn't speak.

"It's a girl," Nell said and shifted the child on to her shoulder. "For a while, things were sort of undecided down there. Then she changed." She stared down into the baby's huge blue eyes and couldn't help but smile a little. "The red hair is new too."

George knelt in front of the chair and patted the child on the leg. "We imprint on the first person we see. Sex, the hair, the eyes, she's going to look like you. Not exactly, but close. I'm glad. Can you watch her a little while longer? I need to pack."

"What?"

"I killed your husband, Nell."

"Ted was deranged and attacked you with a hatchet. Besides, I killed him." Nell again saw the deep bloody dent in her husband's temple. "I killed him." She shook her head in disbelief. "You just disposed of the body. What—where exactly did you?" Did you bury him?

"I didn't eat him if that's what you're thinking. He's someplace far away and very deep. I can move fast when I need to. No one's going to find him. But the police don't always need a body." His hand went from the child to Nell's hand. "I can't stay, Nell. There's bound to be inquiries. We, the baby and I, can disappear. You'll be safe."

"Don't make decisions for me," Nell said. "I hate when people who do that." She didn't feel guilty. Maybe that would come, along with grief for a man she'd once loved, but right now she only felt determined. "You grew your arm back. How?"

"It's only a matter of shifting things about."

"Could you look like someone else if you shifted enough? Ted for example. Even the hair?"

George considered it. "I probably couldn't fool his wife, but in general, yes."

Later that night, Ted was caught on tape buying coffee at a gas station near his home. Authorities discovered his sporty hybrid a week later, parked on the shore of Lake Erie. Ted's clothes lay folded on a large stone at the water's edge.

"His girlfriend left him," a kindly police officer told Nell. "His coworkers said he'd been acting erratically ever since. We followed his footsteps to the water's edge. There was no note. Sometimes they just don't leave notes."

A year later, George pulled Nell's Honda on to highway 86 west. "You sure about this?" he asked." He'd seemed leery of the trip when Nell suggested it, but she thought he'd also been pleased.

Nell looked back at Lilly, asleep in her car seat. "Yes. I'm sure. Your dad should meet his granddaughter and me for that matter. Maybe, I can even get him to tell me the story of how you were born?"

"I told you he doesn't like to talk about it. It's considered impolite to ask about our accidents of birth."

Nell groaned.

"Okay fine. But only so you don't spend the whole trip interrogating Dad. I am the son of a loving if slightly clumsy father and the hay baler he bumped into. That's the whole story. Happy?"

Nell leaned over and kissed George on the neck. "I am," she said. "I really am. Although…"

"What?"

"Wouldn't it be nice if Lilly had a little brother?" Nell squeezed George's arm. "Does your dad still own that hay baler?"

AMPLE FREE PARKING

"ONE MORE GO on the Ferris wheel?"

Tori and Zach seem tired but not grumpy, despite a long day of admiring blue ribbon vegetables, eating all things deep fried, and risking their lives on shady-looking carnival rides.

"No, Mom, the Scrambler," says Zach. "I think I saw a screw fall off the last time."

"Ferris wheel it is then." I take my teenage children by the hands, and they actually let me. The sun is low as the Ferris wheel crests the top. This is when young lovers kiss. I think of Daniel, then cut the thought off. *Nope. You don't get even one moment of my day at the fair.* I concentrate on the view, watching a rising balloon some unlucky child is no doubt crying over. *We all lose things, kid.*

"Can you see our car?" Tori asks.

"Sure, right there." I point randomly into the sea of matchbox-sized vehicles, their windshields glittering in the setting sun. "Don't you see it?"

Zach leans forward as if getting a closer look. "Nah, that's the 2018 model. Ours has wider mudflaps."

Ten minutes later, we wade into that sea of cars.

"My feet hurt," Tori says. In one arm she holds an enormous purple-and-green panda, in the other a miniature Denver Rockies souvenir baseball bat. Tori has always had a knack for carnival games, landing rings firmly around bottle necks and knocking plastic milk jugs from their perch with ease. "Carry my bear, Zach."

Zach ignores his sister's pained cries. "You win it, you carry it. Them's the rules,"

I gaze out over the cars and squeeze my key fob. No cheerful horn chirp answers. Too soon. We'd walked a good bit after we parked.

"You know where we're going, Mom?" Zach asks.

"Just a little farther." My feet hurt too. But I don't mind. It really has been a good day. The kind we'll remind each other of years from now sitting around the dining room table reminiscing. We walk for another ten minutes. The key fob still gets no answer.

"Maybe someone stole it," says Tori.

"No one stole it. It's just a big parking lot. Everybody keep looking. What did you like best, the fried Oreos or the turkey legs?"

"I liked the Elvis butter sculpture," says Zach.

"Dad always got a turkey leg." Tori's voice is small but slightly defiant too.

"Your father is at his new apartment with his new *friend*. So, no Fair for him. And no turkey legs."

We walk on in silence; me wishing I'd not tried to make conversation. Every subject seems to lead to Daniel, eventually.

Tori stumbles and lets out a surprised squeal. She drops the panda and barely catches herself on the corner of a Ford pickup. "Schnooky!"

"Schnooky?" Zach repeats. "Really?"

I look down to see what Tori fell over. There are cracks in the asphalt where it's buckled. I kneel and pick up the world's most garish stuffed animal. "Here, Sweetheart. The ground's rough. Let's watch where we're going."

Tori isn't paying any attention to the stuffed animal I'm holding out.

"Mom?" The word is high and quavery. Tori turns in a small circle. Her hands are squeezed into fists. She pistons them up and down with anxious jerks. "Mom?"

"What the fuck?" says Zach, and I don't correct him.

Only a tiny crescent of sun is visible. The sky above it is a painter's dream of pinks and purples. But that isn't what we're all staring at. The sun is setting over a horizon of cars. There's no Ferris wheel in the distance, no bright midway lights. No mountains. Where the hell are the mountains?

Something gives way inside my chest. The bottom falling out of the place where I keep my ideas of how the world works. I reenact Tori's slow pirouette, my eyes tracing the darkening horizon. A horizon of Buick's and Lincolns. Escalades and Fords.

Keep it together, Janet. *You keep it together for the kids.* But I don't. My panicked mind picks a direction. I think I see some Prius-shaped cars that way. We drive a Prius. So, our car must be over there too. I'm running now. The car has to be there. It's where they keep the Priuses.

At least I don't go far. Not exactly mother of the year, I know, but I stop. Footsteps slap the asphalt behind me, then come to a scuffling halt. The kids are there, holding hands, eyes dancing with panic. It's going to be okay. We're together.

I wrap them in my arms and close my eyes, willing the world to be a normal, sensible place. But the world doesn't cooperate. The world is neat lines of cars as far as the eye can see.

Zach has his phone out, holding it up high in the air. He moves it to the left, then the right. "There's no service."

I take mine out and dial Daniel without thinking. Nothing happens. "Save your battery," I tell him.

Zach looks up at the phone a moment longer, then stows it in a pocket.

"It's a depression." I try the words out. Seeing if they make sense out loud. "We walked down into a natural depression. But the angle was so slight we didn't notice." I take a deep breath. Letting the words sink in. Watching for the kids' reactions.

"That's why it looks like the cars go on forever." The sky is darker. It helps that the horizon isn't so far now. I can almost believe. "We just need to pick a direction and walk until we're out of the… depression or whatever. It's probably the same reason the phone won't work."

The idea of getting back online shoves past Zach's doubt. Tori has her eyes on the ground. She's lost Schnooky the Panda somewhere in their panicked run, but still holds the miniature bat.

I point to my right. "Due North," I say. As if I have a clue what direction I'm heading. But fake it till you make it, right? Zach and Tori follow along.

We walk an hour before the sound of Tori crying brings me to a stop. It's dark now. Stars shine down from the black velvet sky. No halogen floodlights buzz into life to illuminate the sea of cars.

"What's wrong, Tori?" The question is so ridiculous I flinch as it comes out of my mouth. But Tori answers.

"I have blisters and I have to pee."

Zach sighs as if he's annoyed by this, and I want to smack him.

"Shut up, Zach."

"I didn't say—"

"You stay here. We're going to go to the other side of this car and take care of some business."

Zach leans back against the dusty SUV. "Okay."

We're back in under three minutes, but Zach is gone. I call his name into the night. Tori lets out a cracked sob and her breath comes in rapid wet bursts.

"Zachary Daniel Young. You get back here this instant!"

He steps out from between two cars and a stone rolls off my chest.

"I'm sorry, Mom. I had to go too."

"You have to say something." My voice is high with fear and anger. Zach goes to his weeping sister, hugging her tight, and my anger flows away on a wave of love and relief. "I think we should stop for a while. The fair will close sometime soon. People are going to come for their cars. We just wait, right? Easy-peasy." But shouldn't there be people here already? Someone else who left when we did. Or just arrived to see the tractor pulls and whatever has-been band was rocking the midway that night.

I bury those thoughts and try the door on the SUV next to me. It's locked, of course. "Come on, just a little further." A few vehicles down, there's yet another pickup truck. This one has oversized wheels and black foam plastic molded over the metal of the truck bed.

Truck *bed*. There's a word for you. My legs feel like dead weights and Tori isn't the only one with blisters. *Time for a nap in the truck bed*. I almost giggle, but I'm able to stop the sound. Mom isn't cracking up. Nope, solid as a rock.

I let the tailgate down. "Everybody in the truck bed." No one laughs. They just climb up with a few assorted grunts and groans.

"I'm cold." Zach says. He's leaning against the back of the cab, rubbing his thin arms. Tori and I both have on jeans, and we'd brought just-in-case hoodies. I had told Zach shorts and his beloved Green Day t-shirt weren't enough. But he ignored me, and I didn't have the patience to argue. Mother of the year.

I don't say I told you so, at least. "This calls for a Zach sandwich." Tori and I scoot up on either side of my shivering son. I put an arm over both their shoulders. "Better?"

He nods and lays his head against my chest. Tori lays her head on her brother's shoulder. The stars are out in force now. It would be a sweet moment if we weren't lost in Hell's parking lot. The panic wells up. When we were walking, it wasn't too bad. Movement meant we were doing something about the problem. Now only my mind is moving, and I don't like the directions it takes. Asking questions like *what happens when you get hungry?* I'm already thirsty. The kids must be too. But no one has mentioned it.

Because no one wants to think about food and water. Like you don't want your mind going there now. Why worry about those things?

We're just in a parking lot, not the desert. *But why haven't you seen anyone else?*

My heart races. I need to get up and move despite the blisters. I take out my phone instead. No service. But I read old texts. Notes from the kids asking to be picked up, even old arguments with Daniel that I didn't have the strength to erase. The utter normalcy of it all calms me enough to sit still.

The kids drift into sleep. I join them, off and on. My head falling then jerking up into startled consciousness.

A sleepy voice cuts through my semi-doze.

"I don't see the dippers." Tori squints up at the night sky. My little scientist. She and Daniel draw star charts and carry a telescope into the backyard on clear Colorado nights. Tori closes her eyes again, drifting back into sleep. I'm left looking at the sky. I don't draw star charts, but Orion's belt is hard to miss, and I know how to find Venus. Except I don't find either. The sky above us is full of strangers. I never fall back to sleep.

The sun rises over a landscape of only cars.

"Nobody came." says Tori.

I just shake my head. I have no words.

Zach slides off the tailgate and stretches toward the sky. "I'm thirsty."

More silence is my only answer. I'm thirsty too. One night, and my swollen tongue sticks to my teeth when I try to swallow. Finally, I stand in the truck bed. *Start small Janet. Water.* "Come on."

We're all on the asphalt now. I walk down the line of cars peeking into side windows. In the console of a white minivan, I see what I'm looking for. An oversized cup, complete with lid and a plastic straw sticking out at a jaunty angle. Maybe it's empty, but maybe it's still full of lukewarm Coca Cola. I'm almost dizzy with the thought of it.

I take off my hoodie and wrap it around my fist. When Tori was seven, we took two years of Tae Kwan Do together. I've broken boards. Six years ago, but I broke them.

Deep breaths. Hoodie wrapped around my fist. Just have to focus.

My fist connects with a muffled thunk. Even with the jacket padding, a bolt of pain shoots all the way to my elbow. The window doesn't even shake. I elbow it next. Less pain, but the window still doesn't give. I pull my butt up on the hood of the car parked closest. Kicking at the van's driver side window again and again. Why is this so hard?

Zach and Tori stand nearby, staring.

"Find a rock."

"Did you try the door?"

"Shit." I run around the van, trying the handles. I always had to remind Daniel to lock the car. The kids aren't looking for rocks. They're trying the doors on nearby cars, so far with no luck. We try twenty cars in what seems like under a minute, without a single open door.

Tori leans against a rusting LeSabre and slides down the side until she's sitting on the asphalt. "I want Dad."

Zach stands beside his sister. "We shouldn't even be here. This is Dad's weekend."

"Don't you dare."

"It's true." Zach's face is red now.

I tell myself he's just a kid. That he's scared to death.

"But you had to come to *the Fair*. Because it's a *family tradition*. But we're not a family anymore. No matter how many fairs we go to."

"Your father…." I stop myself. I'm scared too, and angry, but if I start talking, I won't be able to stop. Daniel *should* be here. He should have been sitting up front with me on the drive here, singing Beatles songs in his off-key baritone. He should have been there to kiss me at the top of the goddamned Ferris Wheel. And when bullshit impossible things like eternal parking lots happened, he should definitely be here holding his kids and telling us everything will be all right.

"You folks lost?"

I spin so fast I almost trip. I can hear the kids jumping to their feet.

The man who calls to us is about fifty yards off. The rising sun behind him takes away any details other than that he's tall and thin, like Daniel. He waves a hand at us.

He's walking faster now. The hand not waving holds something long and thin.

Zach blows past me at a run. He's laughing. "Are we glad to see you!"

"Zach, wait!" Maybe Zach is thinking what I thought. That the approaching man looks like Daniel. Is Daniel. That we needed him so badly he just appeared, and now he'll make everything okay. Tori comes to my side, still holding her tiny souvenir bat. She's laughing too.

Relief replaces my anger. The man isn't Daniel, of course, but he'll be someone who can help. Things are going to be all right.

As my son reaches him, the tall, thin stranger swings the tire iron like he's going for a home run. Zach's head flies backward, his body following along. His feet pump in midair, as if he can escape into the sky. Then he hits the ground and lies very still.

The man runs toward me. His hands are empty now. Maybe he thinks the tire iron isn't necessary to deal with me and Tori. Maybe he's right. As he closes the gap, I can see the long lank hair flying back from beneath his cowboy hat and the dark beard that hangs to his chest.

I push Tori away from me. "Run! Hide!" I turn back to the crazed stranger who may have just killed my son. He hits me in a full body tackle. I slam on to the asphalt under his weight. All my air rushes out of me and I can't get it back.

The man pins me with his hips. Large hands circle my throat. "Water? You got water? You got food?"

Through dimming eyes, I see Tori standing above the man. She brings the toy bat down with both hands, splintering it against his head. The cowboy hat tumbles off, but that's all the paltry weapon accomplishes. The man's red-rimmed eyes never leave mine as he grins and squeezes.

My world fades to black, and then something hot and viscous sprays my face. The choking hands loosen, then fall away. Air fills my starved lungs, and the world comes back into focus. The hands that choked me now flutter like red birds at the bearded man's throat, slapping at the splintered end of Tori's bat where it pokes through the side of his neck. His blood comes out in rhythmic but slowing spurts.

I buck my hips, and the dying monster falls sideways onto the asphalt. He makes a high keening sound like a balloon losing air through a tiny hole. I'm on my feet, coughing and kicking the man's shaking body. I don't want to ever stop. Then I remember Zach flying back through the air. A corona of blood around his head.

Tori is already there, kneeling beside her brother, hands on his face. There's a dent in my son's forehead. So very deep and seeping blood. The world goes black again and I feel myself falling and falling, but somehow never reaching the ground.

I come to, leaning against a truck tire. There's water dribbling into my mouth, and I've never tasted anything so sweet. Tori squats in front of me, holding an Evian bottle to my lips. I can only focus on the sensation of the water running down my throat, then my mind explodes into thought, as if it was one of those dried sponges that expand to ten times its size as soon as water is added.

I spring up. Zach lies in the same spot. A pink backpack pillows his head. Blood stains the straps.

"It's the creep's." Tori says from behind me. "His backpack. His blood. Not Zach's. The water was in the backpack. Zach swallowed some. But he won't wake up and his eyes are…his eyes are…they're not right, Mom."

I look back at Tori. Her long hair hangs down over her face. Arms crossed tight across her chest. In one hand, she holds the creep's tire iron. Her eyes aren't right either. But Zach comes first.

I pull up one eyelid and let out a choked sob. Zach's eye is a solid sheet of bloody red. Brain bleed, cranial pressure. Half-remembered phrases from *House* and *Gray's Anatomy* pop into my head. But what can I do about it? I'm in a goddamn parking lot, not an operating room.

Zach's eyes fly open. His arms and legs go rigid, then relax in rapid succession. I hold him as well as I can. "I'm here. Mommy's here and I love you so much. So, so much, my baby boy." I say the words, looking into those red eyes that probably can't see me.

I see him, though. I see him, minutes old, mottled pink head pressed to my breast. I watch two-year-old Zach run down our cracked sidewalk, arms wide for balance. I see him at seven, fighting over eating anything green on his plate. "I love you so, so much."

His whole body jerks and bloody tears run down his cheeks. More rivulets of red stream from his ears. Then he's still, so still. And I don't know if it's me or Tori whose scream fill the air.

We find a nice car, a Jaguar. It's parked at an angle to take up two parking spaces. The tire iron takes out the window a lot better than my elbow. We spend some of our precious water cleaning the blood from Zach's sweet face. I sit him behind the wheel—seat belt in place, foot on the gas. He'd been so excited about getting his license next year. Used to ask me to let him carry my keys in the grocery store, because people who carried keys drove. I never let him. Afraid he'd somehow lose them. Mother of the year.

The creep I leave where he died. I haven't seen any birds here. Nothing alive at all but the creep and us. But I hope there are buzzards and fat black flies, and I hope they enjoy him.

The backpack has Slim Jims along with another liter jug of water and a greasy white paper bag half full of stale popcorn. We pick a direction that's not the one the creep came from and walk.

Tori's hair is longer now, and I no longer think of Daniel at all. We search cars as we walk. Smash a window, pop the trunk. The tire iron is the perfect tool for this place.

We eat car snacks. And drink cold coffee from half-full Starbucks cups. Once we found a Pontiac hatchback with the keys in the ignition. I drove for hours until the endless lines of cars made me cry. We ran the air conditioning all day and listened to *The Best of Queen* until the gas ran out and the battery died.

Tori and I both wear caps now. I carry the creep's pink backpack. Tori's backpack is gray and has pouches on the side for water bottles. Her pack came from an elderly couple.

Hey, you lost?

They spoke German in loud, frightened voices, and carried water bottles. "*Nein, bitte hör auf!*"

The tire iron is the perfect tool.

We find our Prius parked between a Ford pickup and a green Toyota with a bumper sticker proclaiming, *My kid beat up your honor student*. I remember this bumper sticker. Zach read it out loud when we parked here. He thought it was hilarious.

I dig the key fob out of my pocket and point it toward the Prius. Tori is beside me now, One hand holding mine. The other hand is clutching the creep's spotless tire iron. We don't wash our hair, but we always clean the creep's tire iron.

I press the fob. Headlights blink. The high-pitched chirp of the horn fills the world. I've forgotten how my legs work. I'm not in my body, I'm in a line of slow-moving traffic with two happy, well-fed children, talking about what the weirdest-shaped vegetable will be at the fair. My vote is a turnip shaped like Mother Teresa. Zach says religious vegetables are so last fair. He's hoping for a David-Bowie-shaped zucchini. For a moment, I almost believe I can hear a Calliope in the distance. Then Tori tugs at my hand and we walk away from the Prius, toward the car-strewn horizon.

AGNES MULVANEY'S BEST CHRISTMAS EVER

ROY STOOD in front of the Hope's Rest Senior Living Center and waited for the world to end. His coworkers ran past him toward their hatchbacks and pickup trucks in the parking lot, but Roy wasn't bothered. This was his seventy-ninth Armageddon. He checked his phone as always and still found no texts from his ex-wife Gina or their son, Rudy. No heart-felt goodbyes. No, I love you.

Metal crunched as a dozen drivers tried to pull out at once. Roy felt embarrassed for them. You couldn't outrun a nuclear war. The residents had the right idea, calmly watching from the warmth of the Christmas decorated lobby. At their age, imminent death just wasn't something to get worked up over.

There was a theory why everyone relived the memories of their last moments before the loop started up again. Something about the need for a mental reset. Roy suspected this theory was bullshit. The senior center was lousy with bullshit theories these days. Even Roy had a few. Theories about the people in the Santa hats. About what lay beyond the darkness at the edge of the parking lot, and most importantly, how Mrs. Mulvaney might be able to bring his family back to him.

Not much longer now. Roy counted down. Three… two…—timing was everything—one. He flicked his cigarette out over the parking lot, red tip tumbling end over end. Then God cleared his throat, and the horizon ignited in a sheet of flame.

For the eightieth time, Roy opened his eyes, standing alone in the supply closet on Christmas morning. He dropped the cleaning supplies he held and made for the door. Dr. Sorenson would be heading to Mrs. Mulvaney's room. Roy had to get there first.

In the hall, a woman in blue scrubs and a Santa hat pushed a cart loaded with the day's prescriptions.

"Did Dr. Sorenson take Mrs. Mulvaney her meds?"

The nurse nodded.

Roy pushed past the woman and jogged down the hall.

"Merry Christmas," she called.

"Yeah, Merry Christmas." Roy ran down identical tan carpeted, green wallpapered corridors, using the knickknacks residents personalized their doors with as signposts. Turn left after Ms. Hankins' print of The Last Supper. If you see Mr. Phelps's mounted big-mouthed bass, you've gone too far. He stopped at the ceramic cat next to Mrs. Mulvaney's door, letting his breath slow. She'd still be asleep, and he didn't want to wake her.

He slowly turned the knob and went inside. The rooms were smaller in the memory care ward. No kitchenette, just a wall mounted TV, reclining chair, and a bed with rails. Agnes Mulvaney lay tucked beneath a brightly colored patchwork quilt. A smile played on her lips.

Everyone knew Mrs. Mulvaney was responsible for the never-ending stream of Christmas Days they found themselves trapped in. Knew it the first time her visitors arrived for Christmas dinner. They just didn't know how she did it. Some believed Agnes's powers came from the new dementia drugs she had started on that fall. Others thought she must be some kind of brain-addled god. One thing everyone agreed on was you don't mess with the lady who keeps you from burning up in a nuclear firestorm.

Or so Roy had thought until yesterday—could he call it yesterday?—when he'd overheard Doctor Sorenson talking to some of the other medical staff.

"She's got to be stopped. We can't hide in this sugarplum daydream forever." Most doctors were okay, maybe a little full of themselves, but Sorenson had a god complex. Roy guessed running into an actual god was a little too much for the man.

Footsteps in the hall announced Sorenson's arrival. Roy stepped to the bathroom, pulling the door almost closed. He waited for the doctor to lay out Mrs. Mulvaney's medication, then stepped out and clamped a lanky forearm around Sorenson's neck. He looked over the doctor's shoulder at the pills.

"Those aren't the right meds," he hissed. Agnes took the same pills every morning. Roy had memorized their colors and shapes. "Put her real pills back on the tray. Three purple octagons and two yellow gel tabs."

The doctor spasmed like a dog drying itself. Roy was so surprised he lost his grip.

Sorenson made a noise like an angry duck, then found his voice. "Agnes. Roy's gone crazy."

Agnes shifted slightly, but nothing more.

"Agnes!" Sorenson yelled this time, but to no greater effect.

Roy's fist caught the doctor right below the left ear. Sorenson fell to the ground. Roy had learned something. "She's not going to wake up, Doc. Not until 8:15. Not if you fire a cannon off in here. Now, where are the goddamned pills?"

Sorenson crawled for the door. Roy stopped him by burying a knee in the small of the doctor's back. Sorenson screamed. The pills were in his pocket. Roy took them and laid them on the nightstand.

"We can't keep going like this," the doctor said, his voice echoing off the tiles.

"You don't get to make that choice, Doc." Roy was crying as he lifted Sorenson's head. "I don't want to do this, but you're too damned smart. You'll try again and I won't be able to stop you. This is self-defense."

Roy slammed the doctor's face down onto the tiles, repeating the motion until blood spattered the floor and the doctor no longer struggled. Roy rolled him over, flinching at the caved in face and the red bubbles that appeared with each of the doctor's wheezing breaths, but 8:15 was coming fast. He wrapped his fingers around the doctor's fat neck and squeezed. "It's self-defense."

Agnes Mulvaney grunted in her sleep. Roy checked the time. *Shit.* He dragged the corpse into the hallway and was toweling up the last traces of blood when Mrs. Mulvaney sat up.

"Merry Christmas, Roy."

"Merry Christmas, Mrs. Mulvaney." Roy held the towel behind his leg and hoped his shirt wasn't bloodstained.

"Oh, Roy, call me Agnes." She didn't seem to notice anything amiss.

"All right, Agnes." Roy filled a cup with water. "You go ahead and take your meds."

Agnes looked down at the yellow and purple pills. "Where's Dr. Sorenson? He usually brings my medication."

"He's running behind. I just saw him in the hall." *With his nose and mouth so pounded out of shape, his own mother wouldn't know him.*

Agnes swallowed the pills under Roy's careful eye. When the last gel tab disappeared, he let out a sigh of relief.

"Do you need any help this morning?" Part of Roy's job was helping his charges out of bed or getting them to the bathroom. He knew Agnes's answer before she said it.

"No. I feel pretty good. Christmas miracle, right?" She swung her legs on to the floor and rose to her feet, her movements those of a spry seventy-year-old, not an octogenarian who had spent the last year in a wheelchair. "I bet everyone's going to be feeling better today."

"I bet you're right," said Roy. "I'll leave you to it." But he didn't go.

Agnes gave him a questioning glance.

"Uh, I was hoping I could introduce you to my wife and son today."

"Oh, that would be nice."

"Yeah. They're definitely coming to spend Christmas with me here. Since I have to work."

Agnes nodded.

"Rudy, my boy? He's a good kid. Taller than me. Black wavy hair, like his mom, Gina. She's not as tall though. Only five six." *Not too much detail. Keep it simple.*

"Family is so important."

"Yeah. So, it would be great if you could meet them."

"I'm looking forward to it," said Agnes.

"Great. I'll see you soon then, Mrs. Mul—Agnes." He opened the door as he spoke, but only wide enough to slip through.

Strong hands grabbed him as soon as he stepped into the hallway. Gertie Simpson stood in front of Roy, one hand pinning him to the wall, the other pointing at the dead doctor. "What the fuck, Roy?"

"It's not what it looks like."

Gertie was a big woman, as tall as Roy and outweighing him by fifty pounds. "What it looks like is you killed Doc Sorenson. The only reason I'm not screaming murder is folks here are hanging on by a thread and I don't want to be the one who cuts it." She shot a glance at the room Roy just left. "Mulvaney?" her face drained of color. "She okay?"

Roy had his hands up, placating. "She's fine. It was Sorenson. He changed the pills. Maybe to kill her, maybe just to stop whatever it is she's doing."

"How do I know you're not lying?" The sound of doors opening came from a few corridors away. "Shit. Grab his legs."

"What are we—?"

"Grab his fucking legs." Gertie already gripped the corpse beneath the shoulders. "We'll take him to the parking lot. Everybody comes awake inside the building. No one will be out there."

"Thanks."

"Shut up, Roy."

But Roy did not shut up. He told Gertie about Sorenson bitching in the dining room and the wrong-colored pills.

"It does sound like something the son of a bitch would try."

Roy froze, almost making Gertie drop her cargo.

Gertie started. "What?" Then Doctor Sorenson, face intact, walked past them. He was dressed the same as the corpse they carried: blue oxford, tan slacks, and tasseled loafers. The only difference was the red Santa hat perched on his head.

Seeing him, Gertie *did* drop her cargo. The dead Sorenson's head struck the carpet with a thump. The live version nodded at them. First Gertie, then the corpse, and finally Roy. "Merry Christmas, guys," he said, voice hearty with good cheer. As he turned the corner, he began to sing an off-key rendition of "Jingle Bells".

Gertie let out a long breath. "Guess I should have expected that." She picked up dead Sorenson again. "Come on, before we run into somebody real." They made it outside through a service entrance to the parking lot.

Roy scanned the cars. "His keys are in his pants, but I don't know which one is his."

"I do. I keyed the bastard's car once." Gertie pulled them toward a black Mercedes. They laid the corpse down near the trunk. "You take it from here. I've touched him as much as I want to."

Roy popped the trunk and managed to get the dead doctor inside on his own. Gertie lit two cigarettes. After Roy slammed the trunk down, she handed one to him.

"What now?" asked Roy.

"Well, I can't exactly call the police." She blew smoke through her nose. "You don't seem psychotic."

"Except there's a body in that trunk."

"Was he really going to kill her?"

Roy nodded.

"Okay then."

"That's it?"

"You looking to get punished? I'm a cook, not a jailer. Besides, I think I'm leaving."

"What? *No*, Gert. You saw the news. The bastards started WWIII. I see the explosion every night before Christmas Day starts up again."

"Yeah?" Gertie seemed genuinely interested. "You see it? I'm always in the kitchen cutting onions. All the cell phones start screaming and then, *bam*. It's Christmas morning again and I'm still in the kitchen."

"I'm in the parking lot. They set the sky on fire, Gertie. You're not going to roll out of here on to the set of the *Road Warrior*. You'll die."

Gertie shrugged. "Doc Sorenson didn't leave, and he's dead as shit. And he's not the only body in a trunk. You know that."

Roy knew about the suicides. A nurse in bed with an empty bottle of pills. Improvised nooses in the bathroom. Bodies they disposed of quickly for fear of upsetting Mrs. Mulvaney. All of them replaced minutes after death by still-living, but more Christmassy, versions of themselves. All wearing vacant smiles and Santa hats.

"I'm not trying to be the Road Warrior," said Gertie. "But things might not be so bad. It's been a few months. Maybe I ride out of here right into a Red Cross camp."

"Or maybe your teeth fall out and you die shitting blood. People have left. No one's come back, Gertie."

"You are a ray of sunshine, Roy."

"Because I don't want you to leave." Roy meant it. He had shared the occasional beer with Gertie and her kitchen crew out at El Capitan's on Route Eighty, but he would not have called her a friend. This was their longest conversation by far, but he wanted her to stay. "I think we might be able to change things. Maybe. A little. I got this theory." He asked permission to go on with his eyes.

She nodded.

"I think if you talk to Mrs. Mulvaney—suggest things enough times that she gets those suggestions stuck in her head—then they'll happen."

Gertie laughed. "What? I tell her I want Zendaya to show up and get freaky with me in the walk-in and it's just wham, bam, thank you Mrs. Mulvaney?"

"Maybe. Zendaya might be wearing a Santa hat and a blank look, but that's the idea. Maybe other things to. Maybe she brings the world back, you know, like it was before."

"If Mulvaney has that kind of juice, why isn't there a world out there already? Not just a parking lot, then nothing?"

"I don't know," said Roy. "Jeez, maybe Agnes just isn't thinking big enough. That's why we suggest things. Start small, work up to the larger stuff."

Gertie turned suddenly and kicked the Mercedes. Kept kicking until her breath came in short, sharp gasps. "Fuck, fuck, fuck!" Her anger spent, she lit another cigarette and leaned against the dented car. "Where are we, Roy, where are we really? Has it actually been two months or five minutes? I don't know if I'm any more real than that Santa-hat-wearing freak who passed us in the hall. And I need to be real, Roy. I need to know I'm not just a figment of some old lady's imagination."

Roy stood silent. No answers to give.

Gertie surprised him with a quick, rough embrace. "Good talk," she said, then walked back to the door.

"Thanks again for the help."

Gertie didn't even turn around. "Sure. Don't kill anybody else." Then she was gone. Roy finished his cigarette and followed her.

He did his rounds, helping patients when needed. Everyone *was* feeling better, just like Mrs. Mulvaney said. They exchanged wheelchairs for walkers. Walkers for canes. Of all those stuck in Agnes Mulvaney's eternal Christmas, the residents seemed the most unphased.

Roy understood. Their days had been essentially repeating for years. At least now they weren't shitting themselves. At noon everyone made their way to the dining lounge. Roy was positive the Christmas tree in the corner had grown a few inches.

He spotted Gertie and gave her a wave. She did not wave back. Roy made his way to the front entrance. The automatic doors were open, letting in cold air and a stream of visitors. Agnes Mulvaney's children and grandchildren. Distant cousins and childhood friends. All smiling. All wearing Santa hats.

A chorus of Merry Christmases buffeted Roy as he pushed through the throng to the doors. Outside, luxury cars and minivans were popping into existence in empty parking spaces. Parents unstrapped ever more happy grandchildren and great grandchildren.

Roy looked for the rusting Escort Gina had gotten in the divorce, along with full custody of their son. Had he mentioned the car to Agnes?

"Roy!" Gina emerged from between a Volvo and a Lexus.

"Hey," was all Roy could get out at first. He waved until his voice came back. "Is Rudy with—?" A tall young man stepped up behind Gina. Dark hair like his mother's peeked from beneath his Santa hat. Roy ran to them. Gina wore heavy red blush and sparkly eye makeup she'd never be caught dead in. And instead of jeans and a Star Wars tee, Rudy wore a sport coat and a striped tie. Their images blurred as tears filled Roy's eyes.

Roy's wife and son returned his embraces in a shoulder-patting, perfunctory way. "Merry Christmas," they said.

"I'm so sorry." Roy pulled his son closer. "About the drinking. The divorce. That I wasn't there when things ended."

Neither Gina nor Rudy replied.

"Come on, I need to introduce you to someone."

Mrs. Mulvaney stood near the enormous Christmas tree surrounded by her well-dressed relations. It took Roy five minutes to excuse his way through the crowd.

"Agnes," he called when he finally got close enough. Agnes handed off the infant she'd been cooing at and turned to face him. "I wanted you to meet my wife and son."

Gina and Rudy both immediately said, "Merry Christmas."

Roy spoke over them. "Gina never wears makeup. Maybe just some lipstick and eyeliner. She's an office manager at a law firm. Real smart."

"Oh, a professional woman," said Agnes. "I was an executive secretary until I met my Elliot. God rest his soul."

"Okay," said Roy, nodding. "Rudy plays baseball. Loves it. Good looking kid, huh? Takes after his mom, like I said."

Agnes smiled politely and looked past Roy to the sea of relatives.

"Well, I guess we'll go have dinner," Roy told her.

"All right, Roy." Agnes put a hand on Gina's arm. "You're as lovely as Roy said, dear. And such a nice-looking boy. You all seem very happy together."

"Yeah," said Roy. "We are happy." He took Gina's hand in his. She didn't let go. Roy led them to a table away from Agnes's family. They sat down to plates full of turkey and stuffing. Roy wanted to find Gertie. Show her his wife, his son. *See, they're here and they love me because Agnes Mulvaney believes they do. And is it real, Gertie?* How could that question even matter? Roy took a bite of the best stuffing he had ever tasted. His wife and son sitting beside him. He hoped Christmas would never end.

GOD IS A WHEEL

RANDY'S PHONE pinged from its mount on the van's console. He dropped his eyes just long enough to see the word eBay. Another sale. At this rate, half the new stock would be sold before he got back to Nashville. Long live the god damned entrepreneurial spirit.

He pulled over onto the road's shoulder and picked up the phone. Twelve sales in the last thirty minutes. Toilet paper, more toilet paper, and ten hand sanitizers. Randy liked the sanitizers the best. The little bottles took up less space, and the shipping was cheaper. Best of all, he could cut the shit with glycerin and double his money.

With a few keystrokes, he confirmed the sales, then took down his account. SouthernManSales was no more. Randy's stock listings would now show up under LuckyCharmTraders. He had fifteen more dummy accounts waiting when LuckyCharm got too hot. *I even wear a mask and glasses when I mail the stuff out. Best pandemic ever!*

His eBay account sorted, Randy pulled up the map. He wanted to get back to Nashville before it got too late. There was a ton of

TP to pack for shipping. *Let's see, I'm a couple hours out… maybe one more pissant town. Ignore the Piggly Wiggly, hit the Dollar stores and gas stations.* He looked back at the boxes in the rear of the van. He had done well today. A bunch of toilet paper twelve packs at a dollar store in Monteagle. Six boxes of sanitizer from the gas stations he'd hit.

Randy eyed the map. There wasn't much out this way he hadn't already emptied. Hope's Rest was twenty miles too far, and he had cleaned out Oglethorpe the week before. "Wait, we have a winner." Olwynsville, Tennessee, lay only five more miles down Hwy 32. Maybe they would cuss him out for a carpetbagger, but nothing ventured and all that.

Randy pulled the van back on the highway and practiced his spiel. "My grandma's nursing home is all out of supplies. I'm just trying to help out." All those poor wrinkled asses with nothing to wipe them. It was enough to bring a tear to a grown man's eye. The truth was, most shop owners were more than happy to sell all they had for the right price. Randy's lies just added a little moral lubricant to the transaction.

The Olwynsville town-welcome sign had two enormous wagon wheels mounted at each end. *Maybe wagon production was the town's last big industry.* The sign boasted a population of 1800 souls and proclaimed the slogan, "A Town That Fears God Need Fear Nothing Else."

Well, good. Maybe they didn't need hand sanitizer if God kept the COVID away. Randy drove down the main street. A single lonely traffic light already blinked yellow, though it was barely past three in the afternoon. People lined the streets, pushing baby carriages and chatting in small groups. There was not a mask to be seen, and the conversations were being held a good deal closer than six feet. Maybe the citizens of Olwynsville really did believe God protected them.

A woman in a yellow sun dress sat on a wooden bench in front of the town courthouse. Her blonde hair cascaded down in soft curls around her face, and she bounced a laughing infant on one knee. Randy pulled the van over and rolled down the window. "Excuse me, Ma'am."

She looked up, her smile so beautiful for a moment Randy lost himself in it. "May I help you?" she asked.

Randy could only stare for a long, silent moment. *They grew'em right in Olwynsville, evidently.*

"Well?" The woman's smile grew a little wider.

Randy had the feeling she knew the effect she had on men and was enjoying his reaction. "Uh, hi, I was wondering if there was a gas station nearby."

"Why yes." The infant in her arms gave an angry yawp, and the woman bounced her knee some more. "If you go past the church on the corner and turn right on Beaumont Street, you'll see Elmer's about a mile down the road."

"Do they have a shop, or is it just a gas-and-go sort of place?"

"Oh, Elmer's has a little bit of just about everything."

A gaggle of children tumbled past, laughing and arguing over who was 'it' in the game they played. Randy followed them with his eyes, then looked back to the woman and child. "You don't wear masks, huh?"

"Oh, no. We don't need them." She paused for a beat as if something had just occurred to her. "I'm sorry, is that what you're looking for, masks? Like the folks are wearing on the TV?"

"Sure," said Randy. "Masks would be great."

"Well, I imagine they'll have them at Elmer's. He's got all that kind of stuff."

"Well, okay then, I appreciate the help." Randy could not believe his luck. A town full of fanatics who didn't believe they could get sick. He'd clean them out before the first case got diagnosed.

"We're thankful for you."

"What's that, ma'am?" Randy's window was already halfway back up and he had only partially heard her words.

"I said thank you."

Randy nearly laughed, thinking of the money he would make from these people. He almost felt bad, but not bad enough to pass up a golden opportunity. He put the van in drive. "You are very welcome."

A mile later, an old-fashioned neon sign, unlit and leaning slightly, announced Randy had found his destination. "Elmer's Gas and Gulp" had all of two pumps, both bearing hand-written signs proclaiming them "Out of Order." The shop, a clapboard facade with a large dusty picture window, was open though, and pretty good sized.

A boy, tall and gangly, his bowl haircut trimmed high over his jug-handle ears, affixed plastic letters to a sign out front. He turned and stared blank-faced at Randy's van, then gave a half-hearted wave.

Randy returned the wave a bit more enthusiastically. The words on the sign read, "Hand Sanitizer Here."

Randy parked between a late model Ford pickup and another van and walked to the shop. The first thing he heard, other than the bell above the door, was someone letting loose a rasping cough. Randy almost turned around right there. He had enough supplies in the van already. The irony of him picking up the COVID on this trip was not lost on him. He'd rather not give karma the opportunity. *What the hell, five minutes in and out and I'm gone.*

The interior of Elmer's was murky with tobacco smoke. Maybe that's all Randy had heard. A smoker's cough. He eyed the group of men sitting on rockers and stools in a semi-circle around the shop's high counter. They were old for the most part and heavy-set. Nearly all of them wore overalls and flannel shirts. Baseball caps and a few cowboy hats pulled low over their brows. The youngest of the men, past sixty at a guess, but not by much, was the cougher. Unfortunately, he wasn't smoking.

The man behind the counter looked oldest of all, but the years had not bent him. He stood tall and straight, his broad flannel-clad shoulders making the space behind the counter seem cramped. He did not look like a bumpkin. He looked like someone you didn't mess with. "May I help you, son?"

"Yes." Randy pulled up the story that had served him well so far. "My name is Randall Tucker. My grandmother lives at the Holy Rock Senior Home." As Randy spoke, his eyes flicked over the shelves running the length of the store. There were six double siders, two of them stacked full with pump bottles of Purrell. And was that box on the bottom shelf full of N9 hospital masks? *Jesus, I'm gonna be rich.* "The home was expecting a government shipment of basic supplies. You know, the stuff that's hard to get right now. Sanitizer, masks that sort of thing. But the supplies never came. So, I've been driving around checking for places that might have extra they're willing to part with."

The man in the rocker let loose another explosive cough and nodded. "You can't trust the government for nothing," he said, then gasped a bit with the effort of speaking.

The big man behind the counter—Elmer, Randy decided—pointed toward the shelves. "Well, as you can see, we're pretty well stocked."

"Yeah, I noticed. Would you be willing to part with all of it? They could really use that stuff at the home, and I'll pay a good price. I'm not looking for charity."

Elmer held up a big hand. "Let's not worry about money."

Randy blinked. This was too good to be true. Was he about to get a fortune in sanitizer donated to him?

"You know it's when need is greatest that God provides." Elmer said.

"Amen," Randy said, nodding, though Elmer's words seemed directed to the man with the persistent cough. "I have some empty boxes in my van. I'll just go and get them."

Elmer stepped out from behind the counter.

Randy stopped, facing him. He thought of the man with the cough and hoped Elmer didn't want to shake hands.

Elmer only stood, a solemn look on his lined face. "We're awful thankful for you, son."

The bell above the door rang. Randy turned in time to see the jug-eared boy from outside rushing toward him, a heavy pipe wrench held high. Elmer's large leathery hands clamped on to Randy's shoulders, pinning him in place.

As a child, Randy had taken a summer of karate at the local YMCA. The one thing he remembered from those few weeks of awkward kicks and punches was the instructor saying to never pull away from someone grabbing you, just drop. Gravity always trumps brute strength.

Randy fell to his knees, striking the tiles with a crack. He felt the breeze from the wrench passing over his head. The hands on his shoulders were gone. He scrambled forward on all fours, past the jug-eared boy to the door. Outside, he climbed to his feet and sprinted for the van. Gravel slid out from under his sneakers. *I'm gonna fall. I'm gonna fall. I'm gonna fall on my face and they'll catch me.* The thought repeated itself even as he pulled open the van door and threw himself behind the wheel.

The engine turned over and Randy jammed the car into reverse, half-hoping one of the old men or the kid with the wrench would be behind him trying to block his way. There were no screams or sounds of breaking bones as he pulled backward. The men stood on the porch glaring at the van, but not daring to get too close. Randy yanked the wheel and shifted into drive, showering gravel at Elmer and the rest of the lunatics.

He peeled out of the parking lot and turned up Beaumont Street, only to jam on the brakes. "What the hell!"

The street was filled with people.

"Shit!" Randy was close to tears. He laid on the horn. "Get out of the god-damned way!"

As Randy screamed, the townsfolk spread out, filling the sidewalks and neatly mown lawns that flanked the road. He recognized some of them from his drive through town. The beautiful blonde was there, and the children who'd played tag.

"I'll do it," Randy yelled. "I will run your asses right over. I mean it!" They couldn't hear him, or maybe chose not to. It didn't matter. The words were for Randy. Convincing himself to step on the gas pedal. He imagined the thumps of bodies striking the fender. The way the van would lurch as it ran over fallen children. In the rearview mirror, the jug-eared boy loped toward him, the wrench still clutched in his hand.

"Your fault!" Randy screamed as he lifted his foot off the brake. "This is you people's fault!" He jammed his foot down on the gas as the horn howled. The van lurched as if about to take flight, then the engine coughed and gasped like the sick man back at Elmer's, before dying all together.

Randy heard the crunch of broken bones, the screams of children, as his van barreled through the crowd. But that wasn't reality, only his mind giving him what he had expected. In the real world, the smiling crowd only strolled closer to the stalled vehicle. Some of them waved.

The driver's side window shattered inward, bringing Randy back to his senses. *I should have buckled my seatbelt*, he thought as grasping hands shoved their way inside. Randy's vision whirled as he was lifted and pulled from the van. He saw the smiling faces of the townspeople, snatches of bright blue sky, the blank eyes of the jug-eared boy. Then his breath left him with a woosh as his back struck the pavement. The sole of a heavy-looking work boot eclipsed the rest of the world. Then came pain and darkness.

———

Randy awoke to the feeling of soft lips pressing against his own. A mix of talcum powder and light flowery perfume tickled his nose. The face of the lovely blonde woman from town hovered before him. He tried to reach for her, but his hands wouldn't move. He was on his back laying on the ground, his arms stretched out tight. A wave of pain washed over him, dredging up dim memories. "The son of a bitch kicked me in the head," he said.

The woman stepped back. She still held her child, now pressed against her shoulder. "I'm Bonnie Pruitt and I'm thankful for you."

A man stepped up to the spot where she'd been. Thirtyish and balding, he wore a bright yellow polo shirt with a name tag Randy couldn't focus on. "My name is Bill Simmons. I manage the Burger Barn next to the bank." He bent and pressed his lips to Randy's for a brief moment, then pulled away. "And I sure am thankful for you."

"What the hell is going on?" Randy cried, but Bill had stepped away to be replaced by a gray-haired woman named Mildred who wore horn-rimmed glasses and announced she taught eighth-grade English at Olwynsville Elementary school. She kissed Randy and thanked him as the others had.

Randy tried to lash out at them, but his hands and legs were held fast by ropes. Between the kisses and introductions, his clearing head tried to make sense of his surroundings. The ropes holding his hands and feet were staked to the earth. His arms stretched back over his head as if he were reaching for a high shelf. He could barely brush something hard with his fingertips. Craning his neck back, he could see what his fingers were touching, a wheel, standing upright on its rim. From his vantage point, the thing seemed enormous, but it probably stood around five feet high, wooden spokes radiating out from a metal reinforced center. Randy remembered the welcome sign at the city limits. Wheels like this had flanked the sign. *The Town that fears God need fear nothing else.*

A little girl of no more than four bent and gave him a peck on the cheek. "I'm Jennie, thankful fo' you." Randy heard people awwing. He bit at the next man's lips. Terry Swafford, owner of Terry's Used Cars, pulled back with a curse. Randy tasted blood.

The unseen crowed roared with laughter. "He's a feisty one," a voice called out.

"People know where I'm at," Randy yelled. "They'll come looking for me. You assholes are going to rot in jail." Now Elmer's lined face hung above Randy. There was pity in that face and an aching sadness, but the features were set in stone. The face of a man who had made a lifetime's worth of hard decisions.

Elmer squatted down and took hold of Randy's chin. He wiped away the bit of blood with a thick thumb. "Randall Tucker, God is a wheel." He spoke in a loud, carrying voice, as much for the crowd as for Randy. "The Wheel of God turns. Some are broken beneath it, so others may be carried on to glory." Elmer bent and pressed his lips to Randy's. He stayed there longer than the others. Randy could taste tobacco and coffee on the man's breath. "We are all so thankful for you, son." Elmer stood. "Larry Dumont. Come forward."

Randy heard the rasping cough of the sick man. He seemed to have gotten worse. His breath a resonant wheeze.

"All right. I lied," Randy yelled, his voice high with fear. "I didn't need that stuff for an old folk's home. I was selling it online. I sinned, okay. But"—a sob broke unbidden from Randy before he could go on—"but, the Bible says God forgives you if you ask and I'm asking. So that means you got to let me go. Right? 'Cause God would want you to. I'll go away and not say anything." Frustration briefly overtook terror, and his words turned harsh. "Come on, you freaks. If you're all about God, you have to let me go. That's the rules."

Elmer stood at one side of the wheel, Larry Dumont on the other. They hefted it upward with mutual grunts. A moment later, the wheel hung over Randy's face. A rough-worked iron band circled its perimeter.

"No, Jesus Christ no," Randy closed his eyes, waiting for the sickening thunk, but the two moved on, struggling beneath their burden.

God is a wheel, Elmer had said. Randy never really thought about such things. If God existed at all, Randy imagined him as a white-bearded giant on a throne somewhere, his holy eye hopefully on that biblical sparrow instead of whatever trouble Randy Tucker was stirring up.

A town that fears god, need fear nothing else.

The wheel, now held over his shins, was all Randy feared. Maybe God was just that, the thing that scared you the most. Then Larry and Elmer let go of their God.

The sound of the wheel's metal band shattering his shin bones filled Randy's ears, along with applause from the crowd. Then Randy's screams drowned out every other noise. The two men lifted the wheel again, moving back up Randy's body. They stopped above his knees and the God of Olwynsville came down again. Dark red stains spread over Randy's jeans. Something sharp and white poked through the denim covering his left leg. Randy passed out when God shattered his femurs, only to awake moments later with a scream as the wheel came down on his forearms.

Pain, Randy discovered, has a limit, a point where the mind refuses to acknowledge the agony, at least for a while. He felt nothing as the crowd surged forward, untied his bonds, and lifted him up. No scream escaped his lips as they threaded his broken arms and legs through the wheel's rough wooden spokes. His stomach lurched a bit as they mounted the wheel atop a thick wooden pole. He began slowly spinning, then the world, blessedly, went away.

When Randy came to, the wheel had ceased its turning, and the pain was back. He hung at an angle. His head lolled off the wheel's lower edge, the world upside down. He did not know how much time had passed. The crowd of townspeople were gone. Only one man stood before Randy—Larry Dunmore, the coughing man, the man who, with Elmer's help, had shattered Randy's bones.

"I am thankful for you, I am thankful for you, I am thankful for you," Larry repeated.

Randy thought the man might have been standing there a very long time. Larry wasn't coughing anymore, and his breath flowed easily. He put a hand on Randy's cheek and kissed him. "Thank you." Then he took a hold of the wheel, and with an effort, started it turning again. As Randy slowly spun, he gazed out on the field behind him. A dozen posts stood upright in the grass, a wheel atop each one. Men, or what were once men— now, only bones and shreds of rotted black flesh—hung from the wheels' spokes. His own wheel kept turning, and Randy found the strength to scream.

Elmer sat on the stoop in front of his gas station and watched his nephew add letters to the sign. The sound of Randall's dying cries gave the old man no pleasure. "The Wheel turns," he muttered.

"How's that look?" the jug-eared boy asked. The sign now read, "TOYLET PAPER, BIG SALE!" Elmer gave him a thumbs up. The boy wasn't very bright, but he was a good kid.

"Come on," Elmer said. "I'll help you unload Randall's van, then we can have some Cokes and a couple of Moon Pies." By the time Elmer and his nephew finished their moon pies, the wheel had turned, and the night was quiet.

A SONG FROM THE DARK

THE BUICK LURCHED along the pitted road, Samantha's stomach lurching with it. "I'll never eat pie again."

When her supervisor at the Census Bureau agreed to give her Farragut County, Samantha had been both pleased and a little worried. Farragut had only one proper town. The rest of the populace lived on tiny farms scattered through dense stretches of pinewoods. It was a far cry from the row houses of Pittsburgh where she had grown up, but that was why she'd wanted to canvas there. In the fall, Samantha planned to declare her major in anthropology with a concentration in folklore. Interviewing people well outside of her city-girl comfort zone seemed like good preparation.

Friends in the city made Deliverance jokes and her overprotective father even offered to come with her. Driving home after her first day of canvassing, Samantha had to laugh. "No deranged killers, after all," she said to herself, releasing a tremendous cherry-scented belch. "The real danger turns out to be indigestion."

The farm families not only happily answered Samantha's questions, they wouldn't let her leave without a taste of cherry or blueberry pie. Samantha rubbed her distended belly. "Such good pie."

Coming around a looping curve, she spotted a dark shape blocking the road. Samantha stood on the brake, and the car skidded to a halt a yard from the trunk of a fallen pine. Needle-covered branches hung down over her hood.

"Jesus Christ." Samantha had Triple-A. Did they drag trees off roads? "No," she said to herself. "You call the police, dummy." She pulled her phone from her pocket, expecting no signal, but three of the four bars glowed. Before she could dial, the low rumble of an engine sounded in the distance.

"Oh, shit." Samantha lay on the car's horn. Headlights appeared. Samantha tapped on the horn some more. A minute later, an enormous pickup slowed to a stop on the opposite side of the fallen pine tree.

The door opened, and a tall, thin man in bib overalls stepped down from the cab.

"Damn," he said in a high, reedy voice. "This your tree?"

Samantha felt herself blush, as if the tree really was her fault. She got out of the car and stood to face the man. "No," she said. "I just found it here."

The man nodded. "Mighty inconsiderate place to leave a tree." He grinned, showing teeth so straight they had to be dentures.

"Yeah. I was just about to call the police."

"Maybe they'll arrest it," he said and chuckled. "I'm just joshing you." He tugged on a branch and let go. "I can handle it," he said, looking up at her. "I'll have to go back to the house and get my son and a tow chain, but it won't be much of a problem to pull off the road."

"That's great."

"I'm Randolph Burke, by the way." He extended a hand over the pine and Samantha shook it.

"Samantha Collier. You sure we don't need the fire department or something?"

"Nah, I got the equipment." He patted the truck's hood. "No point owning a beast like this if you don't haul something now and then." Burke looked back along the curving road, then at Samantha.

"You want to ride up to the house with me? I hate to leave you here all alone. It's going to be dark in a few minutes."

"Maybe I ought to call the police and wait for them," Samantha said. She didn't know this guy from Adam.

Burke nodded. "Go ahead and call 'em. Truth is, though, it's going to take about an hour for them to get out here. Me and my boy will have this tree cleared in half that time. I really would feel better if you were safe with me instead of standing on the side of a dark road. You could use the facilities if you need them and meet my Martha. There's still peach pie left from supper, I think."

Samantha couldn't help but smile at the mention of pie. Moreover, she could use a bathroom. She imagined herself, pants down, squatting in the dark woods. That decided it. She slipped her phone back into her pocket. "You know, that sounds pretty good, Mr. Burke."

"Well, all right then," he said. "Let's get going."

Samantha pulled the car onto the narrow shoulder. She took her census file folder along. If someone did plow into the Dodge, no point losing a day's work.

She climbed over the tree and into the truck's cab. Burke backed the big truck up about a hundred feet and turned up a dirt road. "What are you doing out in the pines anyway?" he asked.

"I'm a census taker."

"And they sent you out here? Kind of cruel and unusual, don't you think?"

"I volunteered. I just started a degree in anthropology. Thought this would be good practice for being out in the field. I'm only asking how many people live in your house now, but later I'll be collecting folklore, maybe even music like Alan Lomax."

"I'm afraid we're not all that interesting around here. We mostly sit around and watch TV like everybody else." Silence followed, as if Burke had decided to prove just how dull he was. Samantha stared out at the unending line of trees.

"I got something that might be up your alley though," Burke finally said. "I mean, anthro-po-logically." He pronounced the word slowly, as if he feared getting it wrong.

"Yeah?"

"I don't know that it's folklore. But it's sort of unique to the area. I could tell you about it."

After a day of recording household incomes, Samantha was ready for something interesting. "That would be great."

Burke nodded. "Well, right now we're on Burke property. The wife and I bought the land as a foreclosure 'bout twenty years ago. The previous owner, Tommy Beane, was in prison at Frackville and that can get you behind on your mortgage.

"Back then the place was all scrub grass and pine except for a good-sized house—filthy, but solid. Tommy hadn't done any farming. So, Martha figured we'd find a still or a pot field in some hidden spot. But we never did.

"After a couple of years, we whipped the place into shape, even started making a profit on lumber and pumpkins. Then one day, I got a call from the state police. Tommy Beane had broken out of Frackville in an ambulance. The authorities thought he'd probably get out of Pennsylvania fast, but they wanted to warn us in case he planned a homecoming."

The truck slowed down as if storytelling had drained the lead from Burke's foot. "You ever read anything by Steven Hawking?" he asked out of the blue.

Samantha blinked. "The scientist? I tried to read—what was it— A *Brief History of Time*? I didn't get very far."

"Hmm," Burke seemed to chew on that for a minute, then launched back into his story. "Well, sure enough, one night around a month after he busted out, Tommy Beane came home. I was over on the northeast corner of the property. The land ain't much good for farming over there, but I'd been thinking of logging it. The sun was setting, and I'd started back to the house when I heard voices. It was a man and a woman. The woman sounded in trouble. I don't claim to be brave, but I was a good bit younger then and I had my hickory walking stick with me.

"I took off at a run toward the voices. The man was yelling, and I could hear an engine rev. Then, all of a sudden, everything stopped. And I mean stopped. One minute, screams and roaring engines, then nothing. Like someone pressed the mute button. It froze me in my tracks."

The truck slowed to a halt. Samantha looked out the side window at the pine trees towering into the night. A tingle of genuine fear started in the pit of her stomach.

"Right here. This is where it is—the black hole."

"What?"

"The black hole. When I walked in from the edge of the pines, the car and the woman were gone. There was only Tommy Beane, standing by what looked like a pit. But it wasn't a pit. It was a black hole like on the science shows. And it's still there."

Samantha looked out the windshield. The hill continued down another dozen feet before flattening out. She didn't see a pit, just browned pine needles. She chose her words carefully. "Mr. Burke, I don't think that's possible. I mean, wouldn't something like that…well, destroy the earth?"

"I suppose you learned that from Professor Hawking," Mr. Burke said, his voice thick with contempt. "Scientists say a lot of things about black holes, but they don't have one on their farm, now do they?"

Samantha had no answer for that. She tried changing the subject. "Mr. Burke, do you think we could go get the tow-chain for the tree? My roommate will worry if I'm not home soon."

Burke ignored her, slowly edging down the hill until the truck sat flat. The headlights cut through the blackness, revealing what looked like a big hole in the ground, or maybe a pond, about fifteen feet across. Burke reached under the dash and flipped a switch. The truck's fog lights came on along with a row of halogen deer-spotters mounted on top of the cab. They lit the hill bottom like a night game at PNC Park.

"You see," Burke said.

Samantha opened her door as far as she could and squeezed past a pine trunk, more to get some distance from Burke than to look at the so-called black hole. She heard him opening his own door as she brought out her phone and thumbed in her passcode. She'd call home before Burke could object. Once people knew where she was and whom she was with, maybe everything would be all right. She just needed to keep the man distracted. Examine his black hole for a minute. At first, she thought it might be a pool of oil. But that couldn't be right. There wasn't any smell other than pine resin. And the light acted funny. There was no reflection. The light just stopped. It was kind of bizarre.

"I must have dropped just about everything you could think of in there," Burke said, sounding nostalgic. "Roman candles stripped down cars. Don't know where it all goes. Just in and gone. You can't fill the thing up. It looks solid, but it's not. Go ahead and touch it. It's just like air."

Samantha squatted down near the hole's edge, looking into the inky nothing of the pit. She didn't want to touch it, didn't want to be near it. "This is amazing, Mr. Burke. I'm glad you showed it to me." She thumbed her roommate's number and pressed the phone to her ear as she spoke. "But it's getting late. I better call in and let people know where I'm at."

"Hell," Burke said, his voice right behind her. "Nothing ever comes easy." Something flashed and crackled.

Samantha found herself on the ground in a fetal position. The taste of iron filled her mouth, and her eyes wouldn't focus. She spat blood and scrambled on her hands and knees, away from Burke's voice. Blind luck took her from the pit toward the trees. She stopped, looking back as her sight cleared. Burke stood by his black hole, not moving. The plastic stun gun he'd used on her held loosely at his side. He pressed her phone to his hear.

"Voice mail," he said, and tossed the phone to the ground. The screen glowed from beneath the pine needles near his feet, then blinked out. "I need you to touch the dark, Samantha. Just dip your foot in." Burke sounded calm, even reasonable, but he also sounded hungry. "It'll be an experiment."

Samantha took hold of a pine trunk to pull herself up. Sharp metal bit her flesh. Looking closer, she could see barbed wire stretched from tree to tree like a metallic spider web.

"What the hell is going on?" she screamed.

Burke didn't look up. He only had eyes for the darkness of his black hole.

"You're going in there, Samantha," he said. "You can't get away through the trees. People have tried. But I must have strung a mile of barbed wire through those pines. You'll just tangle up."

"What people?"

"My experiments," Burke said. "This black hole is a mystery now, isn't it? Something like it needs studying. Tommy Beane got me started. The first time I saw the hole, there he was, rocking his head back and forth like that blind singer. What's his name?"

Samantha was circling the pit, her eyes scanning the pines for a break in the barbed wire. "What?" she asked. The question came out high-pitched and cracked.

"Oh, come on, it's right on the tip of my tongue."

To Samantha's surprise, the name popped out, "Stevie Wonder?"

"That's him," said Burke, sounding pleased. "Tommy was doing his Stevie Wonder impression. Even sounded like he was singing to himself. So, I walked up and poked him in the back with the hickory. He was a little thing. Maybe five feet five in his boots. But you know what they say about small guys. He came at me like a cornered rat. I got my hickory in between us and brought it across the side of his head. It wasn't that hard a lick, but it stunned him, and he stepped into the black hole.

"Tommy just stood there for a second, staring down at his boot, then he sat back on the pine needles. His foot was getting drawn in—not fast, but steady—pulling the rest of him along with it.

"I tried to help him. But he wouldn't even take my hand. I yelled, 'Just take off your boot, you damn fool!' Tommy only laughed at me. He said once you touch the black, it took you. The truth was, he seemed fascinated by the whole process. Finally, when it got to about waist high on him, he looked over at me and said, 'It's gonna sing for you now.' Then he pitched forward and disappeared into the darkness."

Samantha had kept circling the pit as Burke spoke. Now, she stood only a few feet from the truck again. "Well, did it sing?"

"Not really singing per se," Burke said. "But it made sounds. Something way beyond music. And once it ended, I needed to hear those sounds again. So, I started experimenting. I worked things out after a while. You can shovel rocks in all day and not hear a sound. Toss in a cat, and all you get is the hell scratched out of you. But if you experiment with a living, breathing person, it's Casey strike up the band." Burke seemed to be trying to smile as he spoke, but his lips only quivered. He wiped tears from his eyes with his empty hand.

What was it she heard in his voice, guilt, grief? Samantha wondered what could make this psycho feel anything near those emotions. Then it came to her as spontaneously as Stevie Wonder's name had. "Where's your wife, Martha, Mr. Burke, and your son?"

"You don't understand. I need to hear the song from the dark." Burke made a noise in his throat, a sort of keening whine. "I loved my boy." His empty hand went to his face again. This time, his nails dug bloody furrows down his cheek. "You've never heard the sounds. You got no goddamn right to judge!" He shook his head hard and finally got a weak smile going. "So, you gonna make a break for it, or are you going in?"

"I'm thinking about it," Samantha said as she estimated her chances.

Burke shrugged. "I don't mind waiting. I don't get much company. Eventually, I'll get my pistol out the glove box and shoot you in the leg. After you bleed a while, I can roll you in. I'd rather not. You seem like a smart woman. Most of my experiments go in screaming. It wouldn't have to be like that for you. You could go like Tommy. Just dip your foot in. It didn't seem to hurt him none. You could tell me what the process feels like—contribute to the advancement of science."

"You make things seem pretty reasonable," Samantha said, and then darted for the side of the truck. If she could squeeze between the trees and the door, maybe she could get that pistol. If there even was one.

But Burke was quick for an old man. The bite of the stun gun burned into her side. Samantha tried to aim her momentum toward the truck's door as her legs gave way, but slammed into a pine bough instead. She fell to her hands and knees and waited for the pain to pass. *Maybe I can roll under the truck. Crawl out that way.* But she didn't believe it. Then her hand felt something hard and cylindrical buried beneath the pine needles. She shoved deeper, gripping what she'd found.

"Well, come on, girl," said Burke. "You don't want to make this hard." The crackle of the stun gun sounded behind her.

"All right," she said, gathering her legs beneath her. "I'm coming."

Samantha surged up, clutching the wrist-thick pine branch she'd found. The white arc of Burke's stun gun filled her vision, and Samantha swung at the weapon with all her strength.

She missed.

The branch passed harmlessly over Burke's weapon before connecting with a wet crunch against the side of the old man's head. Samantha's second swing struck the stun gun, reducing it to a shower of black plastic.

Burke staggered back from Samantha—the left side of his head a swollen purple mass. Blood poured down his face and over the bib of his overalls. Samantha stepped forward, and with all her strength, slammed her the branch into the center of the old man's chest. Burke fell backward, sliding a good three feet. He clawed at the loose pine needles, trying to slow himself, but it was no use. His head entered the blackness.

Arms and legs flailing, Burke disappeared slowly into his black hole.

"How does it feel, Mr. Burke?" Samantha shouted between ragged breaths. "Don't you want to contribute to the advancement of science?" Then Samantha's shouts turned to sobs. She was still sobbing when the black hole began to sing.

Burke had been right. It was beyond music, maybe beyond sound. Vibrations swept over her, filling her mind and body. Not an assault. The tones were soft—insinuating. It was sex, love, and a thousand stronger emotions she had no name for. Samantha knew there was much more to it than she was experiencing, like the sonic equivalent of an iceberg's tip. A crescendo would come if she could just listen long enough. Something that would bring her understanding and a sense of completion beyond anything she'd ever felt before.

Then the song ceased, leaving only a fading memory of something glorious and the need for more. Samantha stared at the spot where Burke went in. She didn't know how long the song had lasted, but her eyes stung as if she hadn't blinked in a long time.

I need to get home. Samantha kicked through drifts of needles until she found her phone. *Call the police. Hell, the FBI, maybe NASA.* She looked down into the black hole. Now even the memory of the song was fading, like a beautiful dream you can't cling to. Only the need remained.

Samantha shook her head. There was nothing beautiful here. She walked back to the truck. Her file folder lay on the floorboard. She opened the glove box. Sure enough, a revolver was inside. Samantha realized she was humming to herself. "Stop that," she said and bit her lip hard. *Call the police.* But her fingers didn't move. She looked at the census records full of the farm families' names and phone numbers. *They'd all been so nice. They'd probably want to help if I called. But probably wasn't enough. Daddy was in Pittsburgh. He'd come. Nothing would keep him from helping his little girl.*

"No." Samantha threw the phone down and walked away. "You get your head together. Breathe. You go back and get the phone. You call the police and tell them exactly what happened. They won't believe you, and that's good. They'll show up expecting something's wrong."

Samantha looked at the trees. Everything was going to be okay.

The phone was against her ear again—ringing. In her other hand, she held Burke's revolver. Samantha didn't remember going back to the truck. She was humming again. She tried to stop, and her throat made the same keening whimper she'd heard from Burke.

"Hello, sweetheart," her father's voice said from the phone.

Samantha fell to her knees, her keening growing louder. She needed to hear the song. She had to. "Daddy, I need you—"

"Where are you, Sam? What's wrong?" His voice was full of

concern and the beginnings of fear. He would come. He'd always been there when she needed him.

Samantha imagined her father, arms and legs flailing like Burke's, as the darkness drew him in. She screamed and flung the phone toward the black hole. "I love you, I love you, I love you," she called in rapid-fire gasps until the phone disappeared into the darkness.

Samantha dropped the gun. She sat down at the black hole's edge; her knees pulled up to her chest. She tried to look past the pine branches and see the stars, but above was as dark as below. *Maybe no one would find the black hole. Or if they did, they wouldn't hear the song right away and could really study the thing.* Samantha was humming again. This time, she didn't try to stop. *I should leave a note, a warning.* But she didn't trust herself. If she got up now, she'd go for help. Bring people here. She'd do whatever she had to if she only could hear the song again.

Maybe the next person will be stronger. Samantha thought. *I was stronger than you, Randolph Burke. Just not strong enough.* She cried for a little while. Then wiped away her tears. *It will be an experiment.*

Then Samantha closed her eyes, stretched out her leg, and touched the darkness.

.

THE MEANING OF HALLOWEEN

"Trick or Treat," Sidney said. He repeated the words, then pointed to Meikare. Teaching the Amawaka boy bits of English helped pass the time. Even the beauty of the Brazilian rainforest got tedious after a month of daylong marches.

Meikare grinned but said nothing.

"Come on, kid. You're going to like this." Sidney pulled a fun-sized Snickers bar from the pocket of his cargo shorts.

Meikare reached for the candy, but Sidney closed his hand.

"Trick or treat," he repeated.

The ten-year-old's grin froze, then straightened into a hard line. His hand blurred, drawing the machete that hung at his waist.

"Whoa," Sidney said. He stepped back dropping the candy into the grass.

The boy shoved against him. Sidney, already unbalanced, fell to the ground. Meikare brought the machete around in a vicious arc, neatly beheading a long, striped snake. The snake's fangs bit convulsively at the empty air.

Meikare knelt and picked up the fallen Snickers bar, handing it back to Sidney. "Trickertreat?" he asked.

"Yeah, I think you earned it."

Oket, Sidney's guide, squatted nearby rearranging supplies.

"I'm going to give your grandson a Snickers bar," Sidney said. "It has nuts in it." *Were nut allergies even a thing down here?*

Oket regarded Sidney with disinterest.

"And he killed a snake."

The guide nodded and turned his attention back to the supplies.

"Okay then." Sidney handed over the treat, smiling as Meikare shoved the chocolate into his mouth. "Happy Halloween, kid." He stood and stretched. Sweat rolling down his skin. *October 31st should not be this damned hot.* Sidney wished he were back in Pittsburgh.

Truth be told, he wished he'd never come. This was supposed to be an adventure.

"You go in under the radar. You and one guide," the company rep had said. "You verify the mineral deposits, do some sightseeing, and there's a big fat paycheck waiting when you get back. A lot more than you make teaching Geology."

Sure, the whole thing was a bit hinky. The indigenous zone was off limits to mining. But Sidney wasn't mining. Just scouting and taking samples where Nav-Corp was already sure the rare earth deposits would be. Besides, weren't adventures supposed to be a bit hinky?

It turned out Sidney didn't much like adventure. The rainforest was mostly mosquitoes and humidity. And the mineral deposits were not such sure things after all. To top it off, they were a week and a half behind schedule, and he was missing his favorite holiday, Halloween.

Oket drew his own machete "We go," he said. The guide spoke English but was so taciturn it hardly mattered. The strong-silent act had been why Sidney hired the man. The other guides had bragged. Oket simply said, "This is my world. You listen. I keep you alive."

They had a system. Oket walked ahead to scout the best route and get rid of any immediate dangers. A few minutes later, Meikare would follow, babysitting the soft American. Sidney had to admit he liked the arrangement. Despite his early misgivings about Oket's grandson coming along, he soon realized he preferred the boy's company to the old man's.

Meikare spoke almost no English but had the decency to smile and nod a lot. "Trickertreat?" the boy asked.

"Maybe later, kid"

"Okay." It was the first word Meikare had learned, and he used it often.

Sidney figured they would hike a few hours before Oket doubled back and called out "We sleep" or "We eat." So, to pass the time, he talked about home. "Back in my world, it's cold in October. The leaves turn colors, and you rake them up into piles and jump in them."

Meikare nodded and smiled.

"On Halloween, people give out candy by the pound. As long as you're dressed up and know the magic words."

They reached the top of a rise and paused for breath. A narrow valley spread out below them. Within the green expanse, Sidney spotted a burst of red and gold. He blinked waiting for the colors to resolve into some flowering tree or maybe a flock of exotic birds.

"That's an oak tree," he finally said. "And the leaves are changing." Sidney really couldn't be sure. The tree was pretty far away. But the shape and color seemed right. "That's impossible." Or maybe not. Sidney was no botany expert. He only knew it looked like home.

He tapped Meikare on the shoulder and pointed toward the colored leaves.

"Okay," the boy said.

"We go," said Sidney pointing again.

Meikare frowned.

Sidney could see the boy wanted to run ahead and ask his grandfather. Oket would scowl and turn back to his chosen route. If Sidney argued, Oket would simply answer, "I keep you alive."

This is ridiculous, Sidney thought. *I paid good money for a guide; shouldn't he take me where I want to go?* Then inspiration struck. "Trick or treat?" he asked and patted his pocket.

"Trickertreat okay," said Meikare.

Sidney pointed toward the tree again. "We go there, then trick or treat." Suddenly going to that tree was all Sidney wanted. To stand under branches full of fall leaves and perform the ancient ritual of Trick-or-Treat with his last two snickers. A little taste of home.

Meikare hesitated but the lure of chocolate proved too much.

The forest thickened as they moved downhill swinging their machetes. Sidney expected Oket's harsh voice at any moment. Abruptly there was nothing left to cut. They stepped into a clearing. It wasn't large, only twenty yards or so. In the center stood Sidney's tree. It was perfect. Pure Norman Rockwell. Red-gold leaves hung from the tree limbs practically glowing in the afternoon sunlight. More formed a circular carpet beneath the spreading branches.

Sidney stared, a dopey grin on his face.

Meikare pulled on his sleeve hard enough to make Sidney take a step back. The boy pointed up the hill and tugged again. He looked unhappy. "We go."

"Don't worry, I'll tell Oket I made you come. I wanted you to see this. It's what I was talking about. Halloween. He said the word again pointing at the tree. "Halloween."

"Trick or Treat?" asked Meikare.

Sidney nodded.

They ate the last candy bars while looking at the tree that shouldn't be there. Meikare licked chocolate from his fingers and turned back to the path.

Sidney knew he should follow, but he was not quite finished with his little miracle. With a whoop, he ran to the carpet of leaves kicking them high in the air. Surrounding himself in a shower of red and gold. Leaves swooped and twirled. But they did not fall.

More leaves rose from the ground arching themselves through the air. Beneath them lay a second carpet. This one of bones. A leaf landed on top of Sidney's hand. He felt a pinch, like a doctor's needle. He grabbed the leaf crushing it. The thing was leathery. Its body cracked as Sidney squeezed. He tossed it to the ground. The top of his hand welled blood. Two more of the leathery things dove onto the wound. Another landed on his cheek, biting.

Sidney flailed, scraping the creatures off as fast as he could. More bites stung his arms and legs.

Meikare stood frozen at the forest's edge, his eyes wide, mouth still rimmed with chocolate. Sidney moved toward the boy. He had made a mistake, that's all. He had forgotten this wasn't his world. This was Oket's world and Meikare's. If he could get back to them, they would know what to do. They would save him.

He stumbled forward one step, two. Shrill cries rent the air like a children's choir gone mad. Sidney looked up at the thousands of reddish-gold shapes hanging from the branches above him. *No. Not hanging*, Sidney realized. The things above him crouched, waiting for prey. *Waiting for me.* They burst from the branches then, filling the air. Shrieking as they came. Red and gold shapes poured over Sidney. Tiny needle-sharp teeth tearing flesh, draining away his life sip by sip.

Meikare ran, tears half-blinding him as he stumbled through the forest. He found his grandfather, grim-faced with anger at the top of the hill. The boy dragged the old man down to the clearing, but they were too late. All was quiet now. The leaf things once again hung unmoving in the branches. Where Sidney had last stood lay a mound of leaves, more red than gold, rising from the forest floor as if raked up and ready to be jumped in.

Meikare knew his forest home could kill. His grandfather had taught him to avoid a thousand dangers. And more importantly, that there were always more to learn. Now, it was Meikare's turn to teach his grandfather about this new threat. He even had a name for it. The one his American friend had taught him. He pointed to the beautiful tree whose leaves bit and killed and pronounced the word with slow precision.

"Halloween."

A DANCE OF HOOF AND HORN

"JUST HEAR ME OUT, Luther. The commandment says, 'Thou shalt have no other gods before me.' *Before me.* No one's asking you to stop going to church on Sunday. With these small ones, it's less idolatry and more a business transaction. Think of the community. Think of your daughter's future. You know the rewards."

"I do know the rewards. I want you to tell me about the risks."

Cyndi, thirteen at the time, stared out through the window. Maggie Hayes stood in their overgrown front yard beside a snow-white lamb. Maggie, dressed in her name-brand clothes, the sun glinting off her salon-perfect hair. *She was like me once, a nobody girl from a nobody family.* Now she was *everything* in their small town, at least to people in the know. The girl who'd been chosen.

Cyndi made up her mind. In the end, her decision was the one that mattered. The men's voices faltered as she walked outside and knelt in the summer warm grass. The lamb's wet muzzle pressed against her lowered forehead.

Three years later, Cyndi gazed at that same animal. It stood unmoving in the small paddock. Head high. Legs squared. Cyndi tried to only see what the state fair judges would notice. The pristine white wool. Hooves shining like black glass. The clear sharp eyes.

Duttur was as perfect as Cyndi could make her. She needn't have gone to the trouble, not for the judges or for the few fair-goers who wandered from the crowded midway to the livestock tents. Cyndi wasn't here for blue ribbons.

The Ultra-Cruz whitening shampoo and ProPink finishing oil. The hours with a fluffer brush. All that wasn't for the judges, it was a sign of respect. An attempt to make others see what Cyndi did when she looked at the animal. For a moment, the ewe's dark eyes locked on to Cyndi's soft green ones. Cyndi felt a rush of love and something stronger. Something like fear and joy so tangled she could never separate them.

"She's a pretty one."

Cyndi turned around so quickly she almost tripped over her boots. The ewe didn't move at all.

A boy leaned against the metal rungs of the paddock fencing. He was seventeen years old, but if Cyndi hadn't known better, she would have guessed his age as early twenties.

Broad was the term that summed him up best. Thighs that strained against the denim of his Wrangler jeans. Shoulders befitting the linebacker position he played on the Grundy High Warriors. A wide face so open and honest you couldn't imagine a lie coming out of those full lips.

"Hello, Jim, I'm Cyndi Kelley."

Jim pushed his sweat stained cowboy hat up with a thumb and squinted at Cyndi, a question formed on his face.

"Maggie Hayes told me about you."

Jim's grin flatlined, and he gave a slow nod. "Were you friends?"

Cyndi thought about that. Maggie had taught her the things she had to know. How to harvest the sweetest grass. The right words and how to say them, like a song—a hymn—as she pulled the brush through Duttur's wool.

"Not exactly friends. She taught me to show," Cyndi said. "And told me about Bart Mears, Lettie McCloud, and Big Jim Swafford and his bull Butch."

Jim rose up off the gate, straightening to his full six-foot-five as if to justify the name. "Lettie don't show anymore," he said. "She got a full ride to Sewanee. I didn't really like her, to be honest. You know, chickens and all. But Maggie was a good one."

They stood silent for a moment, out of respect for Maggie, or maybe just from a lack of words. A stray wind brought calliope music and the smell of fried pastry into their shared quiet.

"It's early yet," said Jim. They both looked up as if they could see the noon high sun through the tent's red and white fabric. "You want a fried Oreo? I'm buying."

Cyndi looked back at the ewe. Duttur bleated out a low baaa and munched at the already short grass. "Make it a funnel cake," said Cyndi. "I'm an old-fashioned girl."

The funnel cake glistened with oil beneath its snow hill of confectioner's sugar. The first two bites were heavenly, the third a cloying mess, like every funnel cake she'd ever eaten. Cyndi handed the paper plate to Jim. "You have the rest."

Jim took an enormous bite that left a white-powder goatee around his mouth. He tossed the rest of the fried batter in a nearby trash barrel, raising a small cloud of yellow jackets.

"You're right. Can't ride the Scrambler with a belly full of funnel cake." He stood and pulled out a thick pad of ride tickets.

Cyndi sat for a moment. She wondered what Jim was up to. Did he feel bad, maybe wanted to show her a good time in case things didn't go well for her tonight? Was he looking for an advantage? Did someone like him think they needed one? Cyndi took his extended hand and let him help her up. God, he was strong.

The Scrambler felt like the end of days. Jim put an arm around her shoulder. "I don't want to squash you on the turn."

It was a lame line, but Cyndi allowed it, and when the g-forces shoved her against him, she didn't mind all that much. Next, they got in line for The Dragon, a pretty tame looking roller coaster. A short, heavy-set boy stopped beside them.

"Hey, Jim. Did Butch win any ribbons?"

"Nah. But maybe he'll do better this evening."

"Who's your girl?" He paired the question with a crude smile.

Before Cyndi could get in that she wasn't anyone's girl, Jim spoke up.

"She shows Duttur now. Cyndi Kelly, this here is Bart Mears."

Bart nodded. As he did so, he gave Cyndi a long, appraising look. All lechery had evaporated. "What you two doing together? You making plans out of school?"

"Wouldn't think of it, Bart," said Jim. "We're just enjoying this fine day."

"You want to cut line?" Cyndi added. "Ride the Dragon?"

Bart shook his head. "I got shit to do. But I'll see you two later." He turned and walked away.

"So that's the pig boy, huh?"

"He's no joke, Cyndi. You'll see."

They tried the games next. Neither was any count at tossing rings or knocking over milk bottles. But Cyndi hit every target in the shooting gallery. She picked out a giant purple panda and proudly handed it to Jim.

He took the stuffed animal and held it to him like a baby. "This is my last year."

"Aren't you just a junior?" Most who showed, did so at least through high school. Maggie had been in her second year of college. It wasn't unheard of to stop earlier. But it wasn't usually by choice.

"I got early acceptance at Tennessee Tech. I'm going to be an engineer. You don't have to keep showing. You get to move on."

"But people count on us."

Jim nodded. "Yeah, soft rains, fertile fields, and all that good shit. I got someone just about trained up enough to take over. His folks are eager for him to get started. They think it's his big opportunity."

What would it be like to just stop? She'd been tending to Duttur for three years under Maggie's supervision. This was Cyndi's first fair. But already she could not imagine being anywhere else.

The sun hung low in the sky now. She would need to go soon. There were preparations to be made.

"One more ride? Please?" Jim took her by the hand and tugged her toward the Ferris wheel. "I might not be able to use these tickets tomorrow."

His words made Cyndi's arm break out in gooseflesh. "That's not funny. Someone doesn't always have to…" She couldn't finish the sentence.

"You're right. Bad joke. I'm sorry."

Cyndi accepted the apology and let herself be pulled along. One more ride wouldn't hurt, and the line was short. A man with bad teeth and wide hips pushed the safety bar snug against their laps and gave Jim a wink. A moment later, they rose from the earth in a smooth arc, despite the whine and clank of the ancient gears. Above them, the first sprinkle of stars appeared in the darkening sky.

As if in answer, the lights of the midway buzzed into glorious rainbow life.

The swaying car paused at the top. The first breath of fall blew across Cyndi. Despite her fear of what might happen later, she felt an enormous joy.

Jim wasn't taking in the glittering view. He stared at Cyndi instead. She knew he wanted to kiss her. It was a cliché. A kiss at the top of the Ferris wheel. A story your grandparents might tell you about how they first met. Cliché or not, Cyndi was tempted. Would his lips taste of powdered sugar?

When he leaned in, Cyndi turned her head.

Jim let out a sigh. "Can't we just be regular people for a few seconds?"

Cyndi shook her head. The top of the Ferris wheel wasn't nearly far enough to escape the choices she'd made and the obligations those choices saddled her with. Jim had those same obligations. Was this a trick? Had he and Maggie kissed on this same ride a year ago? Did Maggie let her guard down for a few bites of funnel cake and the promise of romance?

Cyndi didn't look at Jim. Instead, her eyes searched for the tents where the animals were. Her sheep, Jim's bull. She moved her hand on top of his and squeezed. No. They couldn't be like regular people. Not even for a few seconds, and he knew it.

The Ferris wheel spun through its last slow rotation and the man with the rotting smile released the safety bar. Cyndi stood and walked away without looking back. For the first few feet, she could still feel the heat of Jim's body where they'd pressed together.

The smell of cooking grease and the screams of happy children faded, replaced by the warm scent of livestock and lowing from the cattle enclosures. Duttur stood waiting near the entrance to her stall. The Ewe was larger than before, her wool as white as forgiven sin. If the judges could see her now, they'd give her every blue ribbon in the joint.

Cyndi's skin tingled as she drew closer. The tingle spread into her skull. She felt like singing and crying all at once. Felt like dropping onto the dung-spotted ground and prostrating herself. Instead, Cyndi took the metal box from among the neatly arranged brushes and bottles of Hoof-Shine and Wool-Brite. The box was heavy. The contents clanked as Cyndi hefted it.

She opened the gate, and Duttur stepped out of the enclosure. Cyndi followed a few respectful feet behind.

Cyndi and her family had enjoyed the rewards of what she did. The swiftly approved bank loans. Crops that glowed with health and were not touched by insects. Status. Popularity.

"Tell me about the risks," her father had said at the beginning, three years before.

But the risks had still been Maggie's then. Cyndi had only learned. Learned the high-lilting song that made her stomach flutter as if she were leaping from crag to crag along some rocky mountain top rather than kneeling bare legged in the dew-soaked grass. Learned how to harvest the new-grown hay beneath a crescent moon, her own crescent of sharpened silver slicing through the pale green stalks. Learned the dance of hoof and horn. But then she'd only danced with Maggie, and it was almost like a game. It would not be a game tonight.

Cyndi did not know how long she had walked before spotting the outline of the tent, black as the night sky but lacking any twinkle of stars.

Behind her, Cyndi heard a rough snort. She looked around. The sow stood five feet high at the shoulder, her skin scrubbed a glowing pink. Rows of swollen teats hung off her massive belly. Bart Mears sat astride her broad back, holding a metal suitcase like something from a spy movie in his lap.

Bart's sly smile was gone. Tonight, he was the boar. All rage and hunger. Just as Cyndi was agility and surefootedness. Bart held Cyndi in his red-rimmed eyes as he slid off his patron.

Cyndi felt the girl and her rooster before she saw them—a hot madness like wings beating inside her head. The rooster was red, with thick clumps of feathers at its ankles from which long white spurs curved up. The girl following behind was tall and thin and walked with an odd, jerky gait. Lifting her knees high before stepping forward, toes first as if testing the ground. This girl scared Cyndi in a way the boy and the giant sow could not.

Cyndi stared out into the night, looking for Jim. Maybe he was already in the tent. Already girded for the dance. Cyndi knelt and opened her black metal box. The curling horns of the helmet shone silver against the black velvet interior. She stripped off her flannel shirt and denim jeans, down to a white sports bra and matching shorts.

Bart wore only dingy white briefs now, along with gloves and boots ending in cloven iron. His headgear was rough leather and anchored the short white tusks at his jawline. Each sharpened tusk ended in a barbed point. Gutting blades. The boy whipped his head from side to side and gave out a rough, throat-grinding snort.

Cyndi positioned her horns and slid the thick metal forehead plate into the woolen sheath that held it in place. She worked slowly, filling her diaphragm with the cool night air and singing out the words Maggie had taught her. Words that were supposed to center and strengthen her. But Maggie lay cold and still in Hope's Rest Cemetery, and Cyndi didn't feel centered.

The sow and Bart walked past her and into the black tent. A spray of red pimples lay across Bart's shoulder and his ass was flat beneath his sagging Fruit of the Looms.

The Rooster and the tall thin girl entered next. A curved brass beak covered most of her face, and a coxcomb of knives rose above her head. The long rapier-sharp spurs at her ankles seemed like overkill.

Cyndi tightened the last straps of her iron-hooved gauntlets with her teeth, like Maggie taught her. Then followed the others through the flaps of the tent.

There were no flickering torches or electric lights inside. The animals themselves gave off a golden effulgence the moment they crossed the threshold.

Jim was there. He wore snug fitting athletic shorts. Light reflected off his pale skin, highlighting the knots of red scar tissue earned at previous dances. The horns Jim wore were enormous, and the bull that stood behind him dwarfed Jim's wide frame. Strength radiated from the beast like thunder from a stormy sky.

The gods took their places at the points of the compass. The Bull to the north, the Cock to the south. The Sow to the west and Cyndi and her Ewe in the east.

Cyndi stood in front of Duttur, the horned helm secure on her head, her hands heavy with the iron of her gauntlets. She looked at Jim, at Bart in his tusks and underwear. The thin girl with her beak. *We should look ridiculous.* But there was nothing ridiculous here. Solemnity and terrible purpose hung thick in the air.

Only a small god. A trifle, Maggie's father had said. Cyndi wondered how he'd feel about these trifles if he had to stand where she did. *You'd crap your L.L. Bean twill pants.* But not your children. Not Maggie, or Jim. Not even me.

Jim stepped forward and to the left. He moved his thick neck in a figure eight, slicing the air with his horns. Cyndi followed the sharpened tips with her eyes as she also stepped to her left.

They were all in motion now. Bart launched himself towards the center of the rough circle they made. He hit the ground in a shoulder roll and came up within inches of Cyndi. The tusks rose, angled to disembowel. Cyndi threw herself to the side, kicking out as she went. She felt the boot connect, but it was only a retreating blow.

Bart didn't press his attack. Just stood there, one arm covering his ribs.

Maybe I did more damage than I thought.

The dance continued. Feints and counter feints.

Behind them, still as stone idols, their gods conversed. Some of it, Cyndi heard. Grunts and growls. But the greater part of the conversation took place somewhere beyond her understanding. She imagined threats made, alliances proposed.

We're part of that conversation, though. Maggie had said. *Just kids, but we affect the decisions of gods. Our pain. The pain we inflict. It changes the math.*

Bart still held his one arm to his side. His breath came in hitching gasps. *Cracked a rib, did I?* Maybe just a bad bruise, but the boy wouldn't be performing anymore acrobatics tonight.

The tall girl shrieked and leapt a good five feet, one leg held high. The target was Jim. Cyndi wondered where she got the nerve. The spur arced down toward Jim's chest. He reared back. The spur grazed him, drawing blood. Jim bellowed as he brought his hooved gloves together on the girl's knee. The shriek she let out this time was not a cry of battle, just pain. She scampered back on her hands and one good leg.

Could it be ending so quickly?

Too close, she's too close. The realization came to Cyndi seconds too late. The leg that seemed so damaged arced toward her like a scythe. Cyndi tried to dodge, but the spur caught her shoulder, piercing it through. The pain was like a scream trapped in her flesh. A hot tearing pressure that blotted out thought. Bart let out a victory bellow as he raced towards her. Jim came behind him.

Tell me about the risks.

Cyndi's senses slowed as death approached. She could hear them now. The gods. Their voices were wind howling and the drum of heavy rain. The wail of newborns and the screams of the dying. They were not small gods at all.

Cyndi felt Duttur's sadness like a warm breath. And it was enough. Enough to be grieved for by a god.

The spur withdrew. Fresh agony ripped through Cyndi's shoulder, but the hope was greater than the pain. The tall girl must not trust the others. She should have left the spur in until Boar and Bull ripped Cyndi's life away. But what if they turned on her? The spur trapped the tall girl as much as it did Cyndi. She wasn't willing to take that chance. She disengaged, and Cyndi was free.

Cyndi leapt away, crouching before Duttur to face her attackers. She could barely move her injured arm, and a teen-age boy wearing metal tusks was about to spill her guts on the hard-packed earth.

Bart suddenly flew sideways, swatted aside by a swing of Jim's massive arm. Jim stood before Cyndi now, even larger somehow. Heat came off him in waves and the full lips that had wanted to kiss her on top of the Ferris wheel were set in a determined frown.

Jim crouched, dipping his long horns toward her. There would be no happy ending here. Jim wouldn't sweep her into his arms and make a mad escape to somewhere gods didn't hold sway. This dance would end in sacrifice. *But why did Jim want to do it himself?* Pity? Did he think his horns were more kind than Bart's tusks or the mad girl's curved beak?

With a groan, Cyndi swung her near useless arm at the horn closest to it. Metal clanged against metal. The blow barely rocked Jim's head. But it was enough.

Cyndi jumped, turning sideways as she rose, sailing between the glinting horns and over Jim's lowered head. He saw the danger and tried to rise from his crouch. But his upward momentum only added to the force of Cyndi's iron hooves as she drove her coiled legs into the base of his neck.

Bone snapped, and for a moment even the gods were silent. Cyndi stepped away and kneeled before Duttur. She sang the hymn of praise and made a request. *Let it be enough. No one has to die. The blood we spilled, the pain we've suffered in your names. Let it be enough.*

Bart and the tall girl rushed in, tusks and beak bent to the sacrifice.

The answer to Cyndi's prayer was no.

Cyndi pretended not to hear the choked screams of the dying boy, free from service to his god at last. She sat before Duttur and gazed into the ewe's deep, peaceful eyes.

Jim's parents would come later. They'd smuggle home the bull and their dead child under the cover of darkness. A few days afterward, there would be an article in their local paper about the terrible accident that ended such a young and promising life. Farming had always been a dangerous profession. The friendly coroner would fail to notice the corpse was a few days longer dead than it should have been.

Cyndi felt no guilt. They'd all known the costs they might pay. But she wished she had kissed Jim at the top of the Ferris wheel that afternoon, when his lips were still warm and sweet with powdered sugar. Cyndi wished that very much.

THE ONCE AND FUTURE KING

You couldn't see the Bellagio fountains or the looming triangle of the Luxor from The King's 24-Hour Love Me Tender Wedding Chapel, but if you needed to tie that eternal knot of love at an obscene hour but not an obscene price, the King was there for you.

The voice of Lou Anne Hogan, full-time card counter and part time wedding videographer, came through the dressing room PA. "We got our first couple in 10 minutes, boss man."

Harry Sullivan pulled a blending sponge along a jawline softened by twenty years of four-dollar prime beef buffets and all-you-can-eat breakfasts.

From speakers in the wedding hall, the silky baritone of The King complained about being caught in a trap. Harry kept the door closed, and a towel shoved in the crack underneath, but he couldn't escape that voice.

And why would you want to? asked the spirit of the late Elvis Aaron Presley

The sponge veered in Harry's hand. He took a steadying breath. *I've got ten more minutes. Let me have them.*

The voice didn't respond. Harry thought about the bookcase he'd finished building today in his tiny garage/wood shop. Understated design, soft rounded edges and a tiger grain mahogany so warm it glowed. He could still smell the sawdust and Tung oil.

Work of beauty, said the King. *You're an artist with a hand plane, Harry. But it's time to take care of business.*

Harry's hips shot to the left. He took back control before they went through a whole gyration. "Not yet," he said aloud. Harry cast his mind back in a futile attempt to block out The King. Back twenty years, when he'd been married and teaching high-schoolers wood shop in Pittsburgh.

Harry rarely dwelt on his fate these days. There was no point in looking backwards. But building the bookcase had brought his old life back.

Do you really miss it? asked the King. *You're in Vegas, baby.*

Harry could admit his old life hadn't been all that exciting, but he'd had his students and Samantha. "I was happy," he said, pulling the jet-black pompadour wig over his graying comb-over. But all that was before the spirit of Elvis Presley had come into his life.

Harry's hips gyrated once, twice, then a third time. Elvis the Pelvis, indeed. His voice dropped two octaves and dripped warm Memphis honey. "Dearly Beloved, thank you for coming here tonight. Thank you very much." The corner of his mouth twisted into the half smile, half snarl a million teenage girls had dreamed of.

It's time, Harry, said the King.

Harry felt that strange combination of joy and violation that always came when he gave himself over to The King's possession. He popped the white satin collar up to full mast and pulled the rhinestone jumpsuit's zipper down a few inches.

In the wedding hall, the opening strains of "Thus Spake Zarathustra" built to its inevitable climax. Harry slipped on his gold TCB Shades and stepped out of the dressing room.

He took his position on the hydraulic lift behind the podium. Head lowered; arms extended as he rose. "Thus Spake Zarathustra" struck its final triumphant chord as a blue spotlight outlined Harry. He gave a hip gyration and smiled down at the eager couple. Then the voice of Elvis Presley let out a scream like an air horn in Harry's head and he collapsed in a heap.

"You okay, boss?" called Lou Ann from behind her control panel at the back of the chapel.

The bride-to-be, a woman with an impressive amount of makeup and even more teased out blonde hair, stared down at Harry. The groom stood beside her, a thin-faced man with bright red hair, acne scars, and wide eyes that glanced nervously from Harry to the Wedding Chapel doors. The couple's mouths moved, but Harry couldn't understand a word. The spirit of Elvis whooped and hollered, drowning the external world out.

Harry! It's her. Mary Leigh Swafford, The Holy Mama. She who's gonna bring forth the new King.

"Shut Up!" Harry shouted, clutching at his aching head.

The concern went out of the would-be bride's eyes. "Excuse me?"

Her tone got through to Harry, even if her words didn't. "Not you, The King." The ginger-haired man pulled Harry to his feet.

"Are you okay?" asked the woman a second time. "These nuptials are a rush job and if you aren't up to it, padre, I need to find a wedding chapel that can do the job before…" She put a hand on a belly enormous with child.

Harry took a deep breath. For a moment Elvis was silent. Not just silent, Harry could feel The King's mood as well as hear his voice. The spirit inside Harry's head was reverent,

This is it, Harry. Why I brought you here all those years ago. For her and for the baby. The King born again.

Her baby is going to be you? Harry had been a good catholic before running away to Sin City. Things started to make a strange sort of sense. "She's your Virgin Mary?"

He'd asked the last question aloud.

"Hardly," answered the woman, and let loose a hearty stream of laughter that made her hand go back to her belly. "But I intend this kid to have a daddy all legal and proper before it gets here."

So let me get this straight. This woman's baby is going to be the new Elvis?

You got it, Harry. The King will sing again, baby!

And you needed me to leave my home in Pittsburgh and the woman I loved and run a 24 hour wedding chapel for twenty god damned years, so I'd be here now to marry her to this red-haired Joseph.

Prophecy doesn't have a timetable, Harry. The King's voice was impatient. *And I couldn't be born out of wedlock. Wouldn't be proper.*

Harry shook his head. *Twenty god damned years. Well, maybe I just won't do it.*

But you got to, Harry. You marry this sweet mama, here to Joseph. Can you believe his name really is Joseph? I kid you not. Then she gives birth to the new vessel for my spirit to enter.

Harry had just about made up his mind. If The King wanted him to do this, he would have to pull his strings like a puppet. He was about to take off his wig when Elvis's last few words sunk in. *Your spirit goes in the baby? As in, you won't be in my head anymore?*

Sorry Harry, I'll miss you too.

Not a whisper? You'll just be a normal baby?

Baby King, said Elvis.

Not one note of one song jangling through my head?

I know we had some good times, but that's the way this works.

Harry ran to the podium and turned to face the slightly confused couple. "Thank you for coming to The King's 24 Hour Love Me Tender Wedding Chapel. Thank you very much." He reached beneath the podium and pressed a memorized series of buttons, then gave a thumbs up to Lou Ann.

The soft blue spot again shone down on the podium. Pink and lavender footlights joined in, glimmering along the edges of the dais. Just as the first soft strains of "Love Me Tender" flowed from the speakers, the wooden doors of the Wedding Chapel burst in with a crash and a shower of splintered wood.

A stooped woman holding an aluminum cane the same silver-gray as her hair stood in the doorway. She was wide and heavy and wore a hot pink sweatshirt that said *Slot Slut* in foot high black letters. Beside her was a biker type right out of central casting. Long greasy hair, goatee, lots of leather and oversized engineer boots. The sawed-off pump shotgun the man cradled in his arms seemed so part of the outfit that it took Harry a few seconds to notice it.

The last member of the trio was Las Vegas PD. She had her side arm out but wasn't pointing it anywhere yet.

Harry blinked hard. There was something else. A black aura surrounded each of the strange threesome. A black that jittered and spiked like bad reception on an old console TV.

Lou Ann stepped from behind the camera, walking toward the cop. "What's going on, officer?" was all she got out before the first of the officer's bullets threw her backwards. The smell of blood and cordite filled the hall. Harry stood frozen as the biker brought up the pump and fired.

Buckshot peppered the dais. Mary and Joseph shoved themselves behind Harry's podium.

Harry still didn't move. He couldn't take his eyes off of Lou Anne's collapsed body. A bullet slammed into the wall a few feet above his head. The cop stood in a shooter's stance, her pistol leveled in Harry's direction. The old lady in the Slot Slut sweatshirt was sprinting down the aisle, cane held high, the biker hot on her heels. Their black auras spiked and jitterbugged around them.

Harry finally ducked. "What the hell is happening?"

The groom looked at Harry. "We didn't exactly invite them."

Then the King's voice broke in. *You got to get out of here, Harry.*

"No shit." Harry jammed a green button, and the dais began its steady and much too slow descent.

It's the forces of Chaos, Harry. They're trying to stop my return.

The lift was only halfway down. But it was enough. Harry jumped the last four feet onto the basement floor. "Come on Red. We can help down your bride." The fiancée jumped, and the two men did their best to ease the pregnant Mary down beside them.

Harry sent the lift back up just as the shotgun roared again.

"We have a limo." Harry motioned for the frightened couple to follow him and jogged toward the garage. The Limo, a '75 Fleetwood, gleamed under the flickering fluorescent lights. Lou Ann had convinced Harry to buy it. She said more folks would be willing to get married off the Strip if we could pick them up in a sweet Caddy. As usual, Lou Ann was right and now she was dead.

I'm sorry, Harry. I liked her too. She was a fan, said Elvis as Harry opened the door for the bride and groom.

Lou Ann didn't die for you. She died because of you. Fuck you King and fuck you being reborn. I'm taking these people to the police. He shot a glance at Mary's belly. *Or maybe a hospital.*

Harry did his best to help Mary into the back seat. As he started the car and pulled out of the garage, he half expected to hear gunfire and fully expected to hear The King arguing with him. Harry heard neither. The nearest hospital was only a mile or so away. He would see Mary got her baby safely delivered. *If the King wants more than that, he can take me over and drive himself.*

Harry? It was The King. But not how Harry had ever heard him before. *They'll die, Harry. Those folks in the chapel weren't bad people. The Chaos got inside them, took them over.*

Like you got inside me?

But I'm the good guy, Harry. You got to admit I never made you shoot anybody.

Harry turned on to Allaveda.

The Chaos will be at the hospital. It can't let Mary live. The new King will do what I couldn't. Bring harmony to the world.

Harry looked into the rearview. Mary leaned back against the leather seats, doing some sort of Lamaze breathing. Joseph held her hand.

Why aren't you just taking over? The King had done it before. Harry hadn't wanted to leave Pittsburgh. He'd been a hostage in his own body as The King drove the family station wagon west.

I can't. Not now.

What, you suddenly grew a conscience?

No. it's part of the whole prophecy thing. Someone has to help me. They have to perform the wedding. They have to protect Mary and make sure the new King enters this world. And they have to do it because they choose to.

Harry pulled over and threw the car into park. *Are you saying you can't control me anymore?* The question was almost rhetorical. If The King could still take Harry over, wouldn't he be doing it?

"Why the heck are we stopping?" The groom asked. He had a high voice with long southern vowels.

"Shut up Joseph." Harry closed his eyes and did his best to concentrate on the spirit of Elvis inside him. *King. What would happen if I just got out and walked away right now? Hopped a bus east for Pittsburgh?* Tears filled Harry's eyes and he wiped them away. *Or maybe just called my wife to let her know I'm alive and I never stopped loving her. Could I do that now?*

There was no answer.

Harry put his hand on the door handle.

Okay. The King's voice was quiet and tinged with desperation. *Nothing, all right. Nothing would happen to you. And yes, I'd be gone, out of your head. But there was a reason I chose you all those years ago. Hell, you weren't even a fan. But you were good. A good, decent man. I needed someone who'd do the right thing when the chips were down. Even though I took advantage and ruined their life. Someone who would save the world from the forces of Chaos.*

Harry pushed open his door. He thought about his wife.

Or at least would save a woman and her unborn kid. It's up to you, Harry.

Harry stepped out of the limo. The lights from the strip blotted out every star. He spat on the asphalt. God, he hated Las Vegas. Then Harry got back in the limo and started the engine. "Okay then, King. If I can't go to the police or a hospital, where do I go?"

"The Westgate," said Mary, her words ending with a hiss of pain. The King echoed the same phrase in Harry's head. Harry knew the Westgate Casino. Knew Elvis Presley had played two shows a night there back in his Vegas heyday.

"Why there?" asked Harry. Before anyone could answer, the rear windshield exploded in a shower of pebbled glass. Harry slammed his foot on the gas and the big Caddy heaved forward. A police car rammed the back of the Caddy. Grandma Slot Slut hung out the passenger window, holding the biker's shotgun. The gun roared again. Harry ducked close to the steering wheel, jerking the Caddy from side to side.

Get to the Westgate, said Elvis. *I'm strongest there. I'll send as much help as I can.*

What help? The answer came in the form of a heavy-set man, in a sequined jumpsuit that matched the one Harry wore. The man dove from the curb, arms wrapping around the shotgun toting granny. Overbalanced, the murderous mee-maw popped out of the window like a cork from a bottle as the police car swerved into a light pole.

This is my town, said Elvis. *My people are everywhere.*

The Caddy roared and surged forward. The Westview was only about ten minutes away if Harry kept to the back streets and there were no more surprises.

"Jesus!"

A woman's torso slammed across the windshield. She wore a white skin tight dress. A sash emblazoned with the word "Bridezilla" ran from her shoulder to her hip. Harry stood on the brakes. The woman on the Caddy's windshield slammed her head against the glass, leaving a smear of blood.

Harry could see the pedal-bar the bride-to-be had leaped from, blocking the street in front of the Caddy. Bottles of Gray Goose and Goldschläger, thrown by the rest of the bachelorette party, burst against the limo. The bottles exploded against the windshield glass, mixing with Bridezilla's blood.

Harry blew the horn and turned on the wipers. Neither of which made a bit of difference to the situation. He looked over his shoulder and jammed the Caddy into reverse. Bridezilla slid off the booze slicked hood. She got to her feet and let out a scream.

Harry paid no attention to the scream, but the blare of airhorns made him turn. A city bus plowed through the intersection at full speed. The Pedi bar burst apart like a child's toy. Blood-streaming bachelorettes went airborne. For a moment, Harry locked eyes with the bus driver. A woman with jet black hair and gold taking-care-of-business sunglasses.

The bus sped off into the night as a blood-stained satin Bridezilla banner floated down on to the asphalt.

All three of the limo's passengers whispered "damn" in solemn unison. Then Harry shifted into drive and hit the gas. Sirens sung out in the night. Gunshots came in quick angry bursts lending a tempo to shouts, screams and the twisting metal sound of cars striking cars.

The forces of Chaos and the forces of The King were locked in battle all around them. Harry kept his eyes on the road but couldn't help glimpsing the men and women in Rhinestone jumpsuits or jail house rock leathers giving their lives to keep the way clear for the new King.

He pulled on to Joe Brown Drive. The Westgate rose in white, glowing splendor only a half mile away. Harry didn't see anyone chasing them. No cop cruisers or pedal bars.

"I think we're going to make it." As the words left Harry's mouth, the Caddy's passenger door flew open and a big man in a tiny car pointed a pistol at Harry through the opening. His black aura sputtered around the fez he wore.

"God damned Shriners!" Harry yelled and swerved hard. He felt the bullet whiz past his head and out the driver's side window. The door of the limo swung wide as the Caddy turned. The mini car careened away before the Shriner could get off another shot. More bullets pinged off the limo. Shriners and their mini cars filled the road.

"Get down," shouted Harry. "We're taking a shortcut." He angled the limo toward the Westgate and stomped the gas. The limo rocked as a trio of mini Rolls Royces went down beneath its wheels. For a moment the Caddy took flight as Harry bounced over the cement median and jumped a curb. Then the wheels grabbed asphalt, and they blasted through two parking lots before jerking to a halt.

Ahead was the entrance to the Westgate. Harry could see figures outlined in jagged shadow around the doors. The crowd grew as he watched.

What am I doing? I don't owe the ghost of Elvis Presley a damn thing. Certainly not my life. Harry didn't look in the rearview mirror. But he knew the skinny red-headed groom and his pregnant bride were there in the back seat. Holding on to each other for dear life.

Well, Harry, what's it going to be? It was his own voice that asked not The King's smooth southern baritone. He thought about the hundreds of couples married under his watch. Late nights playing blackjack with Lou Ann, the growl of Freemont Street on a Saturday night. Well, twenty years ought to count for something.

"Hold on kids."

The Caddy burst through the Westgate's glass doors, doing better than twenty-five miles per hour. Harry laid on the horn and jammed the brake. The limo did a full sliding 360 before coming to a screeching halt with its nose inches from the lobby's life-size bronze statue of The King. And almost no one noticed.

Harry spotted a few hotel staff and security guards who sprung out of the way of the sliding Caddy. The rest of the people in the lobby were too busy doing their best to kill each other. At least sixty Elvis impersonators faced off against nearly twice as many black auraed agents of Chaos.

A young jail house rock Elvis jumped from a marble fountain, clotheslining a bottle wielding waiter. Three women with matching blonde haircuts and dark auras swarmed an elderly Asian Elvis sporting a fifteen-inch pompadour. He was dragged to the ground in a heap of spandex and high heels. Harry's door yanked open. He squinted, expecting a broken bottle or some other weapon. Instead, a woman in a bell-bottomed black jumpsuit (with cape) extended her hand.

"Come on, man, we got to get you three to the auditorium."

In the back seat, Mary let out a scream. "Contractions," Joseph shouted. Harry and Joseph did their best to help Mary out of the back seat as Elvis impersonators surrounded the car.

"Let's take care of business!" shouted the lady Elvis in black. The phalanx of Elvi pushed their way through the lobby as Harry, Joseph, and Mary hunched in their center. The forces of Chaos threw themselves at the protecting impersonators. A six-foot tall showgirl buried a carving knife in a *Blue Hawaii* Elvis's shoulder.

A second later she went down from a vicious spinning kick thrown by an Elvis dressed in a red silk trimmed karate gi.

But there were only so many Elvi and more of the Chaos-controlled men and women were pouring in through the shattered entrance.

Lady Elvis held up a hand, bringing the other Elvis's to a halt. "You get down this hall to those double doors. That's the auditorium. You can lock it from inside. We'll hold 'em off as long as we can. You worry about bringing back The King." She pulled a 45 caliber Colt 1911 from beneath her cape and offered it to Harry. Harry just stared at it until Joseph reached out and took the gun.

Harry and Joseph flanked Mary, each holding an arm as they made their way down the hall. Behind them, the dozen Elvis impersonators left, burst into "Jailhouse Rock" as the Chaos possessed mob attacked.

The double doors of the auditorium closed behind the three-person wedding party, cutting off the sounds of singing and battle. Harry turned the deadbolt. The room was all red velvet with life-sized framed posters of The King in all his signature-looks lining the walls. They marched down the center aisle to the stage.

You did it Harry. I knew you would. The voice of The King was back.

Mary stifled a scream and slid down to the floor, her back against the stage. Joseph kneeled beside his bride to be and looked expectantly at Harry.

I didn't do it for you. Harry said.

Well, you sort of did. Okay, fine. You did it because you're a good man, Harry. Just like I knew you were.

Harry took a deep breath and looked down at the bedraggled couple. "Joseph…" He paused, realizing he didn't know their last names.

Brody, Elvis said. *Joseph Brody and Mary Lee Swafford.* Behind Harry, something heavy slammed into the auditorium doors.

"Joseph Brody, do you take this woman to be your lawfully wedded wife?"

"I do," said Joseph.

Mary gasped out a muffled shriek. "And I take him!"

Harry nodded. "Then, by the power invested in me by the state of Nevada, I now pronounce you man and wife. You may kiss the bride."

As the bride and groom's lips touched, the doors of the auditorium burst inwards. The old woman in the Slots Slut sweatshirt stood at the head of the crowd. One side of her face was blood raw with road rash and she'd replaced her silver cane with a fireman's axe. Behind her, men and women brandishing everything from guns to broken off chair legs stood ready to attack.

Joseph put a hand on his wife's swollen belly. "Tell the kid I would have loved 'em like my own." He stood, pulling the Colt from the waistband of his cheap tux, and walked back up the aisle.

Harry kneeled before Mary. As she screamed her way through another contraction. "It's gonna be okay," he said. Very much doubting the words.

Shots rang out behind Harry. Marry screamed again, but from a different sort of pain. Harry turned to see a mist of blood puff from Joseph's left shoulder, but the groom did not fall.

Granny Slot Slut raced down the aisle, a gun wielding Shriner to either side of her. Joseph's left arm hung loosely at his side. He raised the Colt with his right and fired.

One of the Shriners went down in a heap.

The second Shriner fired, but his shot went wide.

Joseph's return shot took off the remaining Shriner's fez, along with the top of the man's skull.

Granny Slot Slut jumped the last few feet. The axe arced down toward the redheaded bride groom. Joseph's bullet took her just above her right eye. She seemed to hang in the air for a moment as her jagged black aura tried to push her onward, then flickered and died along with her. Joseph emptied the Colt into the crowd as a dozen more bullets ripped into him.

"King," said Harry, not knowing if the spirit of Elvis was still there. "I think this may not work out after all."

Mary screamed one last time. Bullets slammed into the surrounding stage.

"I see it," shouted Harry as The King's voice repeated the self-same words. "It's coming."

A head appeared, already crowned with black wavy hair.

Thank you Harry, said the King.

Harry lifted up the blood streaked newborn. "It's a girl."

One last word echoed before the old King's voice faded from Harry's mind forever. *What!?*

Another bullet struck the stage, then the new King—Queen?—opened her eyes, hitched a breath and wailed.

The sound of that cry, bold, pure, and perfect, flowed through Harry, bringing a rush of joy so intense he almost dropped the child he held. That first cry expanded out, taking a part of his soul along with it. Harry felt the voice of the new King flowing over the casino through the Chaos possessed men and women who'd attacked them. Then further still, washing Sin City clean as new snow.

When Harry could finally take a breath, he laid the baby in Mary's arms. Behind him, the once murderous mob lay scattered on the floor of the auditorium, blinking and shaking their heads; their dark auras swept away by the voice of the new King. Harry walked up the aisle and kneeled for a moment by Joseph's still body. Reverently, he closed the dead man's eyes.

"You would have made a great dad."

A man in a valet's uniform sat on the carpet a few feet away.

"Hey," said Harry. He said it a few more times and finally had to shake the man before the valet looked at him.

"I need a wheelchair," said Harry in slow, measured tones.

"What?"

"You're going to get me a wheelchair and bring it back here." Harry rubbed his thumb and forefinger together. "Big tip." The familiarity of those last two words finally got through.

"Yes, sir."

The dented, bullet riddled Caddy ate up the miles from Las Vegas to Pittsburgh. They'd gotten pulled over twice since leaving the strip. Each time, the officer took one look at the child in Mary's arms, bowed their head for a moment, and went back to their cruisers.

Now Mary and Harriet were asleep. Harry drove and wondered if his wife had remarried. Whether she would believe the story of where he'd been all these years, and finally what she'd think of being an honorary grandparent to the Messiah.

Whatever her reaction, Harry couldn't wait to see her. What happened after that, Harry wasn't sure. He'd learned the world was too strange a place for him to make long-term plans.

ABOUT THE AUTHOR

Frank Oreto lives in the wilds of Pittsburgh, Pennsylvania, where he has kept the love of a good woman for twenty-three years, raised three wonderful children, and once wrestled in ramen noodles for charity.

He has also written innumerable stories of the weird and creepy variety, some of which you hold in your hands.

And Frank is tickled pink that you took the time to read them.

DRAGON'S ROOST PRESS

Dragon's Roost Press is the fever dream brainchild of dark speculative fiction author Michael Cieslak. Since 2014, their goal has been to find the best speculative fiction authors and share their work with the public. For more information about Dragon's Roost Press and their publications, please visit:

http://www.thedragonsroost.biz